Courting Cate

Courting Cate

LESLIE GOULD

BETHANYHOUSE
a division of Baker Publishing Group
Minneapolis, Minnesota

© 2012 by Leslie Gould

Published by Bethany House Publishers
11400 Hampshire Avenue South
Bloomington, Minnesota 55438
www.bethanyhouse.com

Bethany House Publishers is a division of
Baker Publishing Group, Grand Rapids, Michigan

Printed in the United States of America

Library of Congress Cataloging-in-Publication Data
Gould, Leslie.
    Courting Cate / Leslie Gould.
        p.   cm. (The courtships of Lancaster County, 1)
    ISBN 978-0-7642-1031-0 (pbk.)
    1. Amish—Fiction. 2. Lancaster County (Pa.)—Fiction. 3. Single women—
Fiction. 4. Farmers—Fiction. 5. Man-woman relationships—Fiction. I. Title.
PS3607.O89 C78 2012
813'.6—dc23   2012028889

The Scripture passage in chapter 13 is from the Holy Bible, New International Version®. NIV®. Copyright © 1973, 1978, 1984, 2011 by Biblica, Inc.™ Used by permission of Zondervan. All rights reserved worldwide. www.zondervan.com

All other Scripture quotations are from the King James Version of the Bible.

This is a work of fiction. Names, characters, incidents, and dialogues are products of the author's imagination and are not to be construed as real. Any resemblance to actual events or persons, living or dead, is entirely coincidental.

Cover design by Jennifer Parker
Cover photography by Mike Habermann Photography, LLC

Author represented by MacGregor Literary, Inc.

12   13   14   15   16   17   18   7   6   5   4   3   2   1

For Hana,

oldest daughter of mine,
full of strength and style, hope and humor.

My grace is sufficient for thee: for my strength is made perfect in weakness.

2 Corinthians 12:9, KJV

But now I see our lances are but straws,
Our strength as weak, our weakness past
  compare,
That seeming to be most which we indeed
  least are.

Taming of the Shrew, V.11.173–75,
William Shakespeare

C H A P T E R

1

When I was seven, *Dat* caught me under the covers reading by candlelight.

I knew it could be dangerous, so I sat straight and tall, using my head as the center pole, being extra careful in my quilt-made tent. My left hand steadied the candle holder as my right clutched the book—*Anne of Green Gables*—checked out that afternoon from the Lancaster County bookmobile parked near Paradise, the closest village to our home.

Perhaps Dat came to check on Betsy, my little *Schwester*, asleep in her crib across the room. Or perhaps, in his ongoing state of grief, he wandered the house. He must have, by the light of the moon, seen the odd shape on my bed and stepped closer to investigate.

At the sound of his footsteps, I blew out the flame and remained statue-still, even as he pulled the heavy quilt from my head. Aghast, he held his hand out toward me. I extended the book. He thrust it back. I handed him the candle. He clasped it tightly.

"Don't you ever, ever do that again," he said.

The next evening a flashlight sat beside my bed.

That was what I thought about as Dat, who was also now

my boss, stood in the doorway of my office in our shop just down the hill from our house. I was twenty-three, not seven. I sat at my desk, not on my bed. But I did have a book in my hand.

"Just taking my break," I said, slipping it onto my lap and then wrapping both hands around my mug of coffee as the scent of maple sawdust from our cabinet shop tickled my nose.

I sneezed. The clean-up crew hadn't done a proper job.

"I need those accounts." Dat's deep voice reverberated through the tiny room.

"They're on your desk." I thought that would get him moving, but he didn't budge. He filled the doorway with his height and broad shoulders. Others, both Amish and *Englisch*, knew him as Bob Miller, were awed by his business acumen, and considered him handsome, but of course I didn't have an opinion on any of that. He was just my Dat.

"*Jah?*" I met his eyes. "Is there something else you need?"

He shook his head slowly, but then said, "Are you going to the singing? On Sunday?"

It was only Thursday. "Oh, I don't know," I answered and then sneezed again.

"I think you should." He pushed up the sleeves of his white shirt.

"Dat, I'm too old for—"

"You need to stop reading your life away and start living it." His face reddened up to his full head of dark hair as he spoke, and his blue eyes grew serious.

It was so like him to think it had to be one or the other. I could do both . . . if I wanted to. But the truth was, I preferred reading over everything else.

He continued, "I don't know what I'll do without you,

but I can't wait to find out." He forced a smile and, placing his varnish-stained hands flat on my desk, leaned forward.

"*Ach,* you'll probably just start another business." I opened the manila file on my desk. "Your latest is taking off like a bee in a bonnet." I hoped to distract him from his favorite topic—getting me married.

Instead he leaned closer. "What are you reading?"

"Oh, just something I picked up from the bookmobile."

He put out his hand.

My face warmed, but he was my Dat. I slid my chair back a little, raising the book, and then handed it to him.

He read the title out loud. "*Rural Country Medicine.*" A puzzled look crossed his face. He held the book up. "Why this?"

"I'm interested. That's all." I wasn't going to tell him I hoped to write an article, or maybe even a book someday, on first aid for people who lived in rural areas.

He put the book on the edge of my desk. "Cate . . ." His voice sounded desperate. "My businesses are *gut,* jah? They support our family, employ our people, and allow us to give to God's work. But they mean nothing. . . ." He stopped, took his handkerchief out of his back pocket, and wiped his forehead, even though it was a cool spring day. "What I want most is a houseful of grandchildren."

I nodded. "Betsy will give you that, I'm sure." Betsy, at age seventeen, had already joined the church, saying she had no desire to go on a *Rumschpringe*—a running-around time. "She's eager to settle down."

He shook his head and leaned against my desk.

"Oh, no, she is," I said. Every Amish boy who had met her dreamed of courting her. No Amish boy had ever wanted to—genuinely—court me.

"She may be wanting to have a home of her own," he said. "But that's not what I'm referring to. I want *you* to stop living your life through these books. I want *you* to marry and have children. Jah?"

I tried to make a joke of it. "You're that ready to get rid of me?" But my voice fell flat. I knew he had wanted me to marry for the last four years.

"Your mother and I were parents by the time we were your age." His voice wavered. "I want you to be happy."

"I am happy to be keeping your accounts"—for both his cabinet and his consulting businesses—"and seeing that Betsy's raised." Which wouldn't be accomplished until her wedding day.

"And after she marries, I'll take over running the house." Which I kept failing at, miserably. I much preferred reading and writing to cooking and cleaning.

"Speaking of . . ." He stood up straight. "Isn't it your turn to cook supper?" He'd implemented a new edict to re-domesticate me.

"Ach, is it?" I'd totally forgotten.

He nodded.

We usually ate by five, only a half hour away. I had no idea what I would fix. I used to handle the household chores, although never with aplomb, but once Betsy was old enough, she eagerly took over. Over the years I'd forgotten everything I used to know.

"Maybe you should start reading recipe books," he said.

"Maybe . . ." I stood and picked up *Rural Country Medicine*. I'd finish it when I went to bed.

Dat stepped back to the doorway. "Could you at least go to the singing and"—he coughed a little—"try to be kind."

I raised my eyebrows.

"Betsy tells me you're not very—"

"None of those boys are nice to me, if you recall." I stared up into his face. "None of them want to court me. The sooner you get used to it the better."

"Ach, Cate. Stop being dramatic. There's a man out there who's meant to be your husband. You'll be a mother yet."

I'd given up all hope, but it seemed to be beyond my Dat's comprehension, regardless of how many times I'd tried to explain it. Besides, it wasn't as if I hadn't already raised a child. I'd cared for Betsy since her second day of life. Sure, I'd only been six, but I'd been tall enough to be nine and responsible enough to be twelve. I'd had my grandmother's assistance until Betsy was five, but after that it had been just me.

"I'd better get the potatoes on to boil." I slipped past him and into the hallway.

Dat's office, not any bigger than mine, sat to the left. The front of the building held the showroom and the back the shop, where the crew constructed the custom cabinets. They'd all gone home at four, or so I thought.

As I stepped out the side door into the cloudy afternoon, twins Mervin and Martin Mosier tipped their straw hats toward me. Their older brother, Seth, had treated me badly while we were growing up—until two years ago, when I put an end to it. But M&M, as I called the twins, had continued his example.

"Why haven't you two gone home?" I smirked, knowing full well the reason. I asked it anyway. "Waiting for Betsy, jah?"

"No. We just finished cleaning up." Mervin had his thumbs hooked in his suspenders. The two were almost identical, with sandy hair and hazel eyes, although Martin carried a little more weight than his brother and had just lately taken to wearing a pair of ridiculous aviator sunglasses.

"Well, you didn't do a very good job. The dust is spreading all the way to my office." I motioned for them to follow me and marched back into the building, down the hall, noting the clicks of their steel-toed boots on the concrete behind me.

I flung open the shop door, expecting to see sawdust all over the floor. There wasn't any. However, in the far corner sat a huge pile. "Why isn't that in the Dumpster?" I spun around to face them.

"Your Dat said to leave it." Martin twirled his sunglasses between his thumb and index finger.

I crossed my arms and scowled.

"Honest, Cate," Mervin said. "He said a landscaper is going to haul it off."

Dat hadn't said a word to me. "Well, tidy it up a bit more." My face warmed.

They didn't move.

"Now!"

Mervin grabbed the push broom from the corner, while his twin stared at me, saying something.

"Pardon?" I took a step toward Martin.

"Having a bad day?" He met my gaze.

"How about a bad life," Mervin muttered, his eyes on the floor as he pushed the broom toward the pile, stirring up more dust.

I crossed my arms. "I have no idea what you're talking about."

"I'll be blunt," Martin said. "You're acting like a shrew again."

My eyes narrowed. "How rude!" I spun around again, stumbling as I did. They both chuckled as I bolted toward the doorway.

And Dat wondered why I didn't bother going to the singings.

Regaining my composure, I called out, "Go straight home after you're done."

The last thing I wanted was to have them hanging around, looking for Betsy to make an appearance and readying themselves for another attack at me.

"I have an announcement to make tonight, at supper," Dat said at six thirty, as he washed in the utility basin just inside the back door.

I stifled a groan.

After Dat dried his hands and headed for the living room, Betsy said, "I don't know how you can balance all those accounts, but not be able to get dinner done on time." Her muscles flexed as she whipped the potatoes, but everything else about her exuded femininity. Her newly sewn lavender dress. Her starched *Kapp* and apron. Her blond hair perfectly wound into a bun at the nape of her neck. Her big doelike brown eyes.

Nearly everything about us was opposite. I had Dat's dark hair. She was fair like our mother. I was tall. Betsy was petite. I was serious. She was happy.

She was the epitome of an Amish young woman. I clearly wasn't.

Fifteen minutes later, after Dat led us in a silent prayer and the food had been passed around, we were finally eating.

"Delicious," Dat said as he swallowed his first bite of potatoes. "These are your best yet, Cate."

I glanced at Betsy, sure she'd let him know I didn't make them. She just smiled sweetly.

I couldn't stand to be deceitful, though. "Actually, Betsy made those," I said. "She helped me out, a little."

Dat's face fell. "Well, then," he said and kept eating in silence.

I'd made a casserole from the leftover chicken Betsy had roasted the night before, adding broccoli and cheddar cheese, but I'd overcooked it and it had hardened to the bottom of the pan.

I'd also made baking powder biscuits, but keeping with the theme of the supper, I'd burned those too. I watched Betsy take a bite of hers and then follow it with a long gulp of milk.

We sat at the oak table, made by Dat when he and *Mamm* first married. It was large enough for five times the size of our small family. A few years ago, he'd remodeled the kitchen. Surrounding us were high-quality cabinets made of cherry. The countertops were Formica, though, not the granite or other top-of-the-line material we sold from the shop. Dat said that was far too pretentious for our simple life.

We did have a propane refrigerator and stove, although both were smaller than what the Englisch put in their houses. A woodstove, located in the corner of the kitchen, heated the house's main floor during the long winter months and on cold spring days too.

The coziness of our home usually comforted me, but at that moment I was flustered by my failed supper. I usually avoided doing what I wasn't good at, but it seemed with his cooking edict that Dat was catching on to me. I couldn't help but dread his next announcement.

The clock chimed seven o'clock. On a normal evening, we'd have been finished with the dishes by then.

"Dat," Betsy said extra sweetly, reminding me of just how sour I was feeling. "Are you hiring? Either in the showroom or the shop."

"Who do you have in mind?"

"Levi Rupp," she said. "I saw him at the store today." She'd also been seeing him a couple of evenings a week, after Dat had gone to sleep. Before that it had been Martin and before him Mervin. . . .

"Levi Rupp," Dat said. "Which family does he belong to?"

"A few miles out of Paradise, the other way."

Dat closed one eye, which meant he was thinking. "Is his youngest brother Ben?"

Betsy nodded. "That's the family."

"Hard workers, jah?" Dat dished up another helping of mashed potatoes. "Good attitudes?"

"That's what I hear." She smiled.

"I might be hiring in the shop. Tell him to stop by."

Technically, he wasn't hiring, at least not in the shop. He needed someone in the showroom—but it had to be the right someone.

Dat, like everyone else, just couldn't say no to Betsy.

"So is Levi looking to court you too?" I did my best to keep my expression neutral. It was a regular pattern, as predictable as an Amish quilt. Most of the young men who wanted to work for Dat also wanted to court Betsy.

She blushed, making her blond hair and fair skin appear even lighter. "Of course not. He likes to garden. He said he'd give me some tips."

Dat took another bite of potatoes, as if he hadn't heard our exchange.

I didn't believe a word Betsy said, but that wasn't why I pushed my plate away. How could I expect others to eat what I cooked when I couldn't even get it down? I supposed, with Betsy most likely marrying soon, I really would have to do something about my culinary skills.

"Cate's going to the singing with you on Sunday," Dat said to Betsy.

"No," I sputtered. "I didn't agree to that."

"We're going to get Cate married." Dat smiled broadly at her. "It's going to be a family effort."

Betsy's fork clattered to the table.

"Dat." I handed him the bowl of potatoes again, hoping he'd take thirds. "If marriage is so wonderful . . ." I paused, not wanting to overstep.

"Go on," he said, dishing up another serving of Betsy's fluffy clouds.

"Well, why didn't you remarry?" I swallowed hard after I'd said it.

A pained expression passed over his face. "Well, I had you girls and the business. Then the businesses." He wasn't making sense. That was exactly why an Amish man would remarry after his wife died, although because Dat wasn't a farmer, he wasn't as desperate for a helpmate as some would be. "I guess I was just too busy." He shrugged. "And now I'm too old."

Which wasn't true either. I hated to think it, but I knew there were single women just a little older than I who would marry him in a second, let alone the widows in their thirties and forties. I'd heard the gossip. "Tell us why, Dat. The real reason."

"No. That's it. Really."

I'd come across a book about remarrying not too long ago. "I read somewhere—"

Betsy groaned. "I hate it when you say that."

"What?" I turned my attention to her.

She mimicked my voice. "'I read somewhere . . .' It sounds so opinionated."

"Oh." So that was how she felt about the interesting facts I gleaned from books—apparently she'd confused sharing knowledge with opining.

In a sympathetic voice, Dat said, "Go on."

"It's nothing." My gaze fell on Mamm's rocker through the doorway in the living room.

"Tell us." Dat leaned toward me.

I took a deep breath. "Just that remarriage is a compliment to the spouse who died. That's all."

Betsy reached for my plate. "What's that supposed to mean?"

"That Dat and Mamm had a good marriage. For Dat to remarry wouldn't discredit Mamm—it would compliment her."

Dat didn't seem to have heard me. "That I didn't remarry is one of the reasons I want the two of you to turn out well."

"What?" Betsy sat up a little straighter.

"Well, there was talk that a widower raising two girls, especially two beautiful girls"—Dat sounded a little boastful for a Plain man—"wouldn't be able to keep them on the straight and narrow. But we've all done just fine. Don't you think?"

Betsy and I both nodded in agreement. I felt the same way as Dat—pleased that, even though she was flighty, I'd done a good job mothering my little Schwester and, for the most part, managing myself. Just before our grandmother died there had been an incident that raised the bishop's concern, but I'd responded with determination, keeping myself in line and working even harder at caring for Betsy to the best of my ability.

"Back to business," Dat said, rubbing his rough hands together, signaling it was time to reveal his latest edict.

I exhaled slowly.

"What I want"—Dat looked at Betsy and then at me, focused and intent—"is for both of you to experience marriage and motherhood, God willing. Your Mamm was the best wife any man could have. And the best mother too. That's what I want for my girls.

"So," he continued, "I'm implementing a new policy in our family, beginning tonight. Betsy doesn't go to the singing if Cate doesn't go."

"Dat, I'm a grown woman," I gasped.

"I'm not done." He squared his shoulders. "Betsy doesn't court unless Cate courts."

Betsy moaned.

It was a good thing I wasn't still trying to eat, or I might have choked.

Dat leaned forward. "And Betsy doesn't marry unless Cate marries first."

Betsy burst into tears—something she'd perfected through the years. When she was little she had been known to put her finger in her eye to make herself cry.

I fell back against my chair.

Dat boomed. "Understood?"

Betsy sobbed. I couldn't move. Neither one of us answered.

"That's the final word," Dat said. "I'll not budge an inch."

In shock, I watched as he stood and retrieved his Bible from the sideboard. Dat was a kind man, but when he made up his mind, he stuck to it. It made us love him even more because he usually acted in our best interest.

I couldn't think of a thing I wouldn't do for him—except get married.

Dat sat back in his chair and opened his Bible, holding it like a shield between him and me. "I finished Revelation this morning."

It seemed as if it had been a lifetime ago.

"So, tonight, Genesis one," he proclaimed.

Betsy whimpered. I stared straight ahead. Dat ignored us both. "'In the beginning,'" he read, "'God created . . .'"

The only other words I heard were "'Be fruitful and multiply.'"

"Cate, you have to find a husband." Betsy attacked the kitchen floor with the broom as she spoke. "Or I'll never be able to get married." Her tears had turned to anger, an emotion not usually displayed by my sweet sister.

I added more water to the dishwater, drowning out the sound of Betsy's voice.

Dat had gone out to the shop to meet the landscaper—jah, M&M were right about that—and then he said he would do the choring by himself. I would have rather been out in the barn too, visiting my horse, Thunder, than trying to ignore Betsy and her lament.

A new round of emotion overtook her an hour later as we readied ourselves for bed.

"Who are we going to find to court you?" She sat on her twin bed as I braided her fine hair by the light of our propane lamp.

I didn't answer.

"How about Joseph Koller?"

I didn't mean to yank. It just happened.

"Ouch!"

"Sorry," I muttered.

"He's not so bad."

"He's how old? Fifty?"

"Oh, I don't think he's more than forty-five," Betsy said.

That made him older than Dat. "And he has eight kids," I added.

"Half of them are grown."

I wrapped the tie around Betsy's braid, biting my tongue as I did. Two of Joseph Koller's kids were older than I. One of them had children. I had no desire to become a grandmother at twenty-three.

She turned on the bed and fixed her gaze on my face. "You know you've gotten really pretty in the last year or so."

I frowned.

"Your eyes are such a beautiful blue. And your hair is so dark now it's almost black. And your ears don't look so big anymore. And your temper's better than it used to be, although—"

"Stop!" I couldn't suffer her comments.

"No, it's true," she said. "I think you were just a late bloomer."

I hobbled off her bed, my right leg asleep, and limped across the room to my side, determined to distance myself from her.

"But you should smile more. That's when you look your—"

A pebble hit our window. Then another one. She quickly turned off the lamp and opened the curtain as a third pebble pinged against the glass.

I followed her, wondering if someone new might have made the late-night trek. She opened the window and stuck out her head. "It's Levi." She giggled.

I stared into the darkness, letting my eyes adjust. I could make out the outline of a man standing at the edge of the lawn. He stepped out of the shadows of the chestnut tree. I could see why Betsy thought him good-looking with his square jaw and broad shoulders. His hair was the color of his straw hat, and his smile grew brighter the longer he looked at her. He had a shyness about him that I found endearing, and he clearly adored her.

She called out, "I'm coming down." She plucked her robe off the end of her bed. "I'm just going to tell him to come by tomorrow, so Dat will hire him. That's all. It's not like we're courting or anything. Honest."

I put the brush on our bureau. "Don't worry about it." I couldn't seem to stop the sarcasm in my voice. "It's not like I'm going to tell Dat or anything. Honest."

She seemed to be unaware of my tone as she stepped across the room and grabbed my hand, squeezing it. "You're the best big sister . . ." Her voice trailed off. "Don't worry," she said. "Surely Dat's money will attract someone."

"Betsy." My entire body bristled. "I don't want 'someone.' Don't you remember? I tried that. It didn't work. He *was* only interested in Dat's money—I won't go through that again."

"But what about me?"

We stared at each other a minute. "Well, that's our dilemma, isn't it?" was all I could manage to say.

Another pebble hit the window.

"We'll find the right person." Betsy let go of my hand. "I'll put the word out. Tonight."

"Don't," I said as she dashed out of the room. I heard her steps on the stairs, and then the back screen door banged. "Please don't," I whispered, knowing it was already too late. I'd made peace with my being a *Maidel* for the rest of my life. Why couldn't Dat?

I turned off the lamp and climbed under my quilt, my book in one hand and my flashlight in the other, ready to finish off *Rural Country Medicine*. I'd already read all the other books I'd checked out. Thankfully I'd visit the bookmobile the next day. The driver, a Mennonite woman named Nan

Beiler, was becoming a friend of mine. Besides working for the Lancaster County Library, she also wrote for *The Budget*, a Plain newspaper, and a few magazines. I was interested in writing, but even more so in editing and eventually publishing. Dat said there wasn't much money in it, though.

All of the women entrepreneurs I knew were single, widowed, or had grown children. It was hard to run a business and raise a family at the same time. Being single would make it much easier. I would make *not* being married work for me. Now I just needed to figure out what kind of business I could make a living at.

And how to get around Dat's newest edict.

C H A P T E R

2

All the next day, Dat micromanaged my every move.

He knew it was bookmobile day—my stack of library books sat on the edge of my desk—yet he still delayed me. First with Levi's paperwork, then an unexpected billing, and finally a lecture on tracking our inventory. Granted, it wasn't as if I'd find a husband at the bookmobile, but I wasn't going to find one in my office either.

The bookmobile stop was just outside of Paradise, in a parking lot near a public school. By the time I reached the highway in my buggy, I knew chances were I'd be too late, but in case Nan tarried, I pressed on, snapping the reins, urging Thunder to go faster.

If my father had been along, I wouldn't have driven Thunder at more than a trot. Dat had heard too many reports of me racing my standard-bred horse along the back roads of Lancaster County.

But Dat wasn't with me today. "Giddy up!" I scooted to the edge of the bench seat.

I passed rich brown soil, freshly plowed and ready to plant. Then dark strips of alfalfa. Next, a light green pasture. I never grew tired of admiring the countryside. In the springtime, as well as in the summer and the fall, I longed to spread out a blanket and lose myself in a story. But not today.

I crested the hill just past Township Road. Ahead I saw the blue-and-white bookmobile van turning right out of the parking lot. I was practically standing now, willing my horse to go faster and yelling for Nan to stop. I couldn't survive without anything new to read.

The van accelerated, heading back toward Lancaster. As I slapped the reins again, Thunder lunged forward, and the bag of books beside me tumbled to the buggy floor. The van gained speed, leaving a growing gap of gray highway between us. Finally, in defeat, I sank back against the bench, slowing Thunder to a walk.

Tears of exasperation stung my eyes. I'd have to convince Dat I needed to go into Lancaster . . . for something. We were getting low on toner for the printer. I'd need to hire a driver. I'd need to figure out a way to make Dat think it was his idea.

In the distance, the panel van slowed, then pulled to the side of the road and stopped. I blinked back my tears. Nan must have seen me in her rearview mirror. By the time she pulled a U-turn, I was snapping the reins again, imploring Thunder to move, offering up a prayer of thanks that Nan had taken pity on me. By the time I reached the parking lot of the school, she had parked the van and was climbing out of the driver's seat.

She wore a floral dress and a sweater. Her light blond hair, mostly covered by her rounded Mennonite Kapp, glowed as if it were a halo. "Cate!" Her voice radiated warmth. "I thought I was going to miss you today."

I stuffed the books back into the bag and jumped from the buggy. She stepped forward and gave me a hug.

"Thank you for coming back." I was a little breathless as

I spoke, not from exertion, though, but solely from relief. "I had to work late."

I waited as Nan lowered the steps and opened the door. I followed her inside, handing her my returns, breathing in the peppery scent of the old books lining the van's walls.

It was my favorite place on earth. I loved the endless possibilities of the stories. I loved the places they took me. And I loved being with Nan. There was something so accepting, so kind and hopeful about her, that for a few minutes I'd forget how disappointing I was to others in my life.

It didn't take long to choose my books. Two on parenting teenagers, because I wasn't done with Betsy yet; three cookbooks to make Dat think the bookmobile would help make me a better *Haus Frau*; a book on quilting, again to keep Dat thinking good things about me; a how-to-write-articles handbook; a book on pregnancy, because medicine intrigued me, perhaps because of my mother's early death; and a book on gardening for Betsy.

Nan checked out the books, stamping each one in an efficient manner. "Oh, and here's the one you put on hold," she said, holding up the biography on Abraham Lincoln.

I put the book on pregnancy at the bottom of the bag and the biography on top and thanked her again for coming back. "You can't know how much I appreciate this," I gushed.

"Oh, I think I do." She smiled and led the way out of the bookmobile. Although reluctant to leave, I followed. After I reached the ground, she lifted the little staircase back into the van. As she did, Levi walked around the back. And then Mervin and Martin. I stifled a groan.

"Look who it is!" Martin whipped off his hat, nearly upsetting his ridiculous dark glasses.

Mervin started looking around, glancing from my buggy and back to the bookmobile. "Is Betsy with you?"

I shook my head as Nan asked if they wanted to check out some books, saying she'd be happy to give them a few minutes.

"Ah, thanks anyway," Mervin said, hooking his thumb into his suspenders. "We were just seeing if anyone was with Cate."

I glared from Mervin to Martin, and then my eyes landed on Levi. He was staring at the asphalt, the brim of his straw hat pointed downward. I guessed M&M didn't know he was courting Betsy.

"We were hoping her sister—Bitsy—would be with her," Martin said, grinning.

"They're looking for *Betsy*." I scowled from one to the other. The boys in our district used to call her Bitsy because she'd been the smallest girl in school for years and years. I, on the other hand, had been a certified giant. I was still taller than Betsy, but I no longer towered over her, or anyone else, for that matter, although everyone still seemed to think I was some sort of freak.

I thought her nickname had been abandoned, but apparently I was wrong.

Martin stepped closer to me. "We heard about your father's proclamation." He nodded toward Levi. "About Betsy not being able to court."

I balled my free hand into a fist, shoving it into the pocket of my apron. "Proclamation?" What a ridiculous word for him to use. I put out my foot as if I might trip him. He jumped back, obviously remembering our school days together too.

"Who's that?" Mervin asked, apparently unaware of my foot and its intention.

I turned toward the road. A car had stopped in front of the coffee hut on the other side of the highway, and a man climbed out of the back seat.

"I don't recognize him," Martin said.

As the car drove away, the stranger came toward us, calling out, "Hello!"

Nan stepped toward the road.

"He's not from around here," I said. His clothes were faded and worn. He was tall and wiry and carried a backpack in one hand and a wool coat in the other. He wore a straw hat, suspenders, a light blue shirt, and black pants, splattered with mud. Instead of shoes he wore brown hiking boots.

Nan was walking toward the newcomer now, her steps hurried. "Pete?"

Surprised, I focused on the two of them.

"Little Pete Treger?" she called out.

The man ambled across the road, squinting into the afternoon sun.

"Nan?"

She hugged him tightly.

Martin let out a laugh. "He's not so little."

It wasn't that he was *that* big, or *that* old, maybe midtwenties or so, but he had an air of independence and confidence to him that was anything but *little,* and he did tower over Nan.

He stepped away from her embrace. "I heard you were in Lancaster. In fact, I was going to look you up."

"What are you doing here?"

"Traveling." He flashed a grin, showing off the hint of dimples. "I've been all over. But I decided to stop in Paradise before I eventually head home."

I couldn't help but wonder where home was.

"Come meet my friends," Nan said, leading the man back to us.

Martin stepped forward, extending his hand. "*Welkom.*" He introduced himself and Mervin and then Levi.

"And this is Cate," Nan said, motioning toward me.

He shook my hand, holding it too long. His skin was rough and cracked, but his grip was firm. His hair was a little long, but it looked as if the last cut could have been in the Amish style. "Short for Catherine?" he asked.

"No, just Cate."

"Plain Cate?" His brown eyes danced.

I'd always known I was, in more ways than one. I jerked my hand away, not amused.

His eyes kept smiling. "Pete Treger from Cattaraugus County, New York."

"We knew each other back home," Nan said.

"Distant cousins, right?" Pete took off his hat and ran his fingers through his dark hair.

"Third or fourth, I think. On your mother's side," Nan clarified. "Of course, Pete was barely a teenager when I left."

"How long ago was that?" His expression was kind as he looked at Nan.

"Thirteen years." She sighed and then asked, "What brings you to Paradise?"

He put his hat back on his head. "Besides you?"

She laughed.

"I'm looking for work, for a man named Bob Miller, in particular. People in Ohio said to look him up."

Mervin's eyes twinkled as he said, "We've heard of the man."

"I was told he owns a cabinet shop." Pete lowered his backpack to the ground. "And that he has two beautiful daughters."

"You've got part of the equation right." Martin took off his sunglasses. "Two thirds of it, anyway."

Pete didn't seem to catch M&M's attempt at humor.

Mervin nudged me. I took a step backward, causing my book bag to slam against his leg. He yelped.

"I'm hoping to find a job—and a wife," Pete said, causing me to gasp at the brashness of his statement. He glanced around our small circle. "Where would I find Bob Miller?"

Martin nodded toward my buggy. "That rig right there could take you to him in no time."

I waved my hand a little, annoyed. "They're teasing you. Bob Miller is my father. But he's not hiring."

Levi stepped forward and blurted out, "But he is looking for a husband for a certain daughter."

I glared at Levi as his face reddened, desperate that he not say another word. "Ignore him," I ordered Pete.

Another grin spread across the stranger's face and he swept his hat off his head. "I see I put my foot in my mouth already. Cate, I'm doubly pleased to meet you," he said. "And I would be most grateful if I could hitch a ride to meet your Dat."

Our eyes locked. Nan knew and liked this man. I would try my best to not be rude. I bit my tongue, except to say again, "He's not hiring."

"Where are you staying?" Nan asked Pete, obviously trying to redirect the conversation.

He dug a piece of paper out of his coat pocket. "The Zooks' barn. On Mill Creek Road."

"It's not far from here."

"Is it close to Bob Miller's shop too?" He actually winked at me.

Appalled, I hoisted my heavy bag into my arms. "I need to go," I said and turned toward Nan. "See you next time."

"We'll have a chance to visit then." She patted my shoulder.

I hoped to. I'd wanted to ask her about her writing, but there was no way I was going to do that in front of M&M and Levi—and Pete. I waved to all of them, unable to force a smile, and then started toward my buggy.

Behind me, Martin laughed and then said, "One sister is known for her charming beauty and the other for her scolding tongue. . . ."

"We used to call her Cate the Cursed," Mervin added. "Still do when—"

Nan's voice drowned him out. "Boys!" Then she said something more I couldn't hear because I was practically running toward the buggy.

Pete spoke loudly. "Cate, could I at least meet your father?"

"I already told you—twice—he's not hiring," I called out, not daring to turn my face toward them.

"Are people always this friendly in these parts?" His sarcasm came through clearly, his comment obviously directed at me.

"Martin and Mervin can tell you how to reach the Zooks' barn," I yelled as I reached my buggy.

I jumped up to the bench seat, put the book bag on the floor, and grabbed the reins. Next I let go of the brake and pulled a quick U-turn out of the parking lot. In a minute I was speeding down the highway.

Obviously Betsy had told Levi about Dat's edict and he had told the evil twins. By now the whole county knew. My already humiliating life was growing even worse.

The rapid clop of Thunder's hooves on the highway drummed along with my anxious thoughts. Sure, I'd joined the Amish church. Sure, there were two given roles for an Amish woman: being a wife and mother. But there were a few single women who supported themselves. I could too. There was no reason for me to marry a forty-five-year-old widower to have a fulfilling life. Sure, I'd been responsible for Betsy her entire life, but I was not going to marry for her sake. She'd have to figure this one out on her own.

I turned off the highway onto our country lane. The closer

we got to home, the faster Thunder galloped. I couldn't stop smiling, in spite of my angst.

Until the back wheel fell off the axle of the buggy.

The buggy lurched and screeched as it crashed to a lopsided halt, catapulting the books out on to the lane as the wheel rolled into the ditch.

I immediately checked on Thunder, who whinnied and sidestepped away from me. It turned out he was spooked but fine. By the time I calmed him down and unhitched him, I heard faint whistling coming up the lane. The tune grew louder as I quickly gathered up the books and rolled the wheel back to the buggy. In the distance a man marched toward me.

"Need some help?"

I groaned.

"Oh, it's you." He was jogging now, his backpack bouncing on his shoulder.

"How'd you get here so fast?"

"Nan dropped me off at the end of the lane."

I felt a little betrayed. Hadn't I made it clear Dat wasn't hiring? But then again, Nan had known Pete since he was born. I couldn't blame her for wanting to help him.

But I could blame him for being such a pain. "I told you numerous times that Dat isn't hiring."

"Looks like you've had some trouble," he said, as if he hadn't heard a word I just said.

"Are you always so stubborn?"

"Ha," he said, shifting his backpack to his other shoulder as he stopped in front of me. "This doesn't come close to *stubborn.* I'd define it as *persistent.* And it's a good thing for you I am—looks like you could use some help."

"I'm fine."

31

"Do you have a jack?"

I nodded. "But I don't need your assistance."

He squinted down at the wheel, tilted his head, and pointed. "The boot's cracked."

I took a closer look. He was right. "I only have a half mile to go," I said. "I'm going to walk."

"You're lucky you weren't hurt."

I shrugged.

"Or the horse."

I turned toward Thunder. His head was up, and he was staring at me, his brown eyes as trusting as ever.

Pete stepped over and patted the horse's neck. "I'll walk with you."

"You just want to meet my father." I crossed my arms.

He smiled. "Well, sure . . ." His eyes danced under the brim of his hat. I imagined, after what M&M most likely told him after I left, that he also wanted to meet Betsy. "But I really would like to help you," he added.

What choice did I have? Obviously he was determined to meet the rest of my family, one way or the other.

He took my bag of books, slinging it across his free shoulder, while I led Thunder, keeping a few paces ahead. A lone blue jay, perched on a post, scolded us and then flew off over the field. In the distance Dat's handful of cows grazed, safe, secure, and solitary behind the white rail fence.

"Want my coat?" Pete offered. The late afternoon had grown cool.

"I'm fine," I answered.

We walked in silence for a few more minutes.

"Not much of a talker, are you?" he finally said.

I ignored him and quickened my steps, urging Thunder to speed up his pace.

"Okay, then I'll talk. I've been traveling for about six months."
I kept my eyes straight ahead. I wasn't interested in his bragging.

"I've spent time in different settlements, just passing through. Indiana. Colorado. Montana."
I slowed a little. I'd always wanted to travel.

"Then I hitchhiked back east and worked the last few weeks in Ohio. I hope to stay in Paradise for a good long stretch to save some money, then go on home, for a bit."
When I didn't respond, he peered into the bag of books.
"Mind if I take a look?"

Before I could say, *Jah! I do mind!* he'd pulled out the first one—the biography on Abraham Lincoln. I'd started with George Washington and was making my way through all the presidents and first ladies, although I hadn't found biographies on a few of the lesser-known wives.

"I stopped at Lincoln's birthplace when I went through Illinois," Pete said.
I raised my eyebrows.

"I toured the site with a group of schoolchildren. They made a big deal about the cabin not having an indoor toilet."
That made me smile.

He shook his head. "Who had indoor toilets in 1809?"
I rolled my eyes. He was only trying to impress me that he'd been to Illinois and knew the year Lincoln was born.

Changing the subject, I asked, "If you're rich enough to travel, why the interest in working for my Dat?"

"Oh, I'm not rich," he answered. "Far from it. In fact, I'm downright poor. Grew up that way and remain that way. I'm a genuine pauper, if you want to know the truth."
I raised my eyebrows again.

"'Tis a good thing it's the mind that makes a body rich.

I'm the fourteenth son—and the last. Believe me, there's not even a flowerpot of dirt left for me."

"Any sisters?"

He shook his head.

"Your poor Mamm."

"Indeed," he said.

"So why go back? If there's nothing there for you?"

"I have some unfinished business. I can't put it off forever—unless I find a really good reason to stay in Paradise." He grinned.

I quickened my pace.

The sun passed halfway behind a cloud, and the hill in front of us cast a long shadow. A breeze wafted through the row of birch trees lining the edge of the emerald-green field. In the distance a bird called out. On the slope of the hill, which was part of my uncle Cap's farm, a herd of Holsteins grazed, appearing as fancy black-and-white polka dots on green fabric. Beyond them a wooded area led down to the creek.

I hadn't traveled far, but I'd certainly read wide. Even though I hoped to see more of the world, I was sure the countryside around Paradise had to be the most beautiful place on earth—even when a braggart was pestering me.

"How long have you lived in these parts?" he asked.

"I have a feeling you probably already know that answer."

He chuckled again. "You're right. I was told your entire life."

My maternal grandfather, Dawdi Cramer, had left his son, Uncle Cap, his farm, except for a ten-acre strip with a second house and barn, which he'd left my Mamm. My Dat, whose Ohio family was probably poorer than Pete's, had used the property for his shop and to raise a few head of cattle and then to launch his businesses.

Uncle Cap did quite well with farming, with the aid of his

sons, six altogether, although the youngest two didn't do much yet at five and seven. He had one daughter, Addie, who was just older than Betsy, smack in the middle of the brood, and she practically ran the household, even though her Mamm and her aunt Nell were around to help. Addie was one of those practical girls who had always seemed much, much older than she was.

Still skittish, Thunder nudged up against me, knocking me off-balance. I stumbled and fell against Pete, bumping his shoulder.

He grabbed my elbow, but as soon as his hand touched me I jerked away, as if I'd been stung. I pulled Thunder closer, giving him less wiggle room.

Unable to contain my curiosity I asked, "Who in Ohio told you about us?"

"The Yoders."

"That takes care of about half of Holmes County." That was where my Dat hailed from. They tended to be more conservative than the Lancaster County Amish.

"Nathan Yoder. His wife is Miriam. I worked on their dairy farm."

He was Dat's cousin.

Pete asked how long I'd been out of school, and as I answered I knew he was guessing at my age.

I couldn't help but enjoy his attention, even though once he saw Betsy he'd have no interest in me.

Like all the rest, he'd be smitten.

The lane curved. To the right were the showroom, office, and shop, and then the big red barn. Straight ahead stood our three-story home with the covered porch, the sloping lawn, the white rail fence, the apple trees, and gardens. Pete whistled under his breath. I winced, thinking he was impressed by our property.

Pete stopped walking. I knew then he'd spotted Betsy.

Twenty yards away, she stood with her profile toward us. Wisps of blond hair had escaped from her heart-shaped Kapp and fell around her face. She had a basket in one hand, filled with April flowers—daffodils, tulips, and forsythia.

Pete froze. Betsy turned toward us, slowly. Her burgundy dress complemented her brown eyes.

"Who's with you, Cate?" she called out, her voice kind and sweet, the anger from the night before long gone. Her hand shielded her face from the afternoon sun.

Inwardly, I predicted it would be one of those moments she and Pete would talk about for the rest of their lives and pass down to their children and grandchildren. Because even I knew this stranger surpassed the men we knew, regardless of his arrogance. If Levi came around tonight, I doubted Betsy would go to the window.

"Who is it?" she asked again.

"It's just a vagabond I found along the lane," I responded, figuring I might as well make a joke of the whole sorry situation.

"Where's the buggy?" She moved toward us.

I stepped forward. Pete didn't. I elbowed him in the side. He lurched, awkwardly.

In a raspy whisper he managed to say, "That's Bitsy? Who Mervin and Martin were talking about?"

I poked him again, surprised at the sense of satisfaction I felt as my elbow connected with his ribs. "Her name is Betsy."

"And it's true your Dat won't let anyone court her until you're spoken for?" His voice was raw.

A twig snapped.

Pete spun around. Thunder snorted. Dat stood right behind us.

CHAPTER
3

As we'd walked up the lane, I'd harbored a small measure of hope that Pete might be different.

But he wasn't. So as he stared at my Dat, I elbowed him a third time. This one hard enough to make him yelp just as Dat boomed out, "Hello!"

After Pete's typical response to Betsy, I wished Dat would throw him off our property. I wished Dat would tell him never to come back. But Dat wasn't that kind of a man. He always welcomed a stranger.

As Pete introduced himself, Betsy floated toward us, holding a bouquet of tulips in one hand.

When she reached me, she smiled—brilliantly, of course—and then said, "Joe Koller is coming to dinner!" She beamed. "Isn't that great?"

"What?"

Dat and Pete conversed behind us.

"I saw him at the grocery store," Betsy said, "and asked him on a whim. I told him you'd be late tonight because it's bookmobile day, so he's coming at six."

"No." I choked on the word, feeling a surge of anger. It was useless to react, the invitation had already been both given and accepted, but I couldn't stop the emotion welling up inside me.

"All by himself. Without any of his kids. That was his idea."

"Betsy, how could you?"

She wrinkled her forehead. "I thought you'd be pleased."

My hand flew to the top of my Kapp as I bowed my head. "But after our talk last night, I thought . . ."

And I thought I'd made it clear I didn't want to court at all, let alone an old man. It was so like her to confuse what she wanted with what I wanted.

I didn't realize I was shaking my head until Dat put his hand on my shoulder. "You've met my older daughter, Cate," he said to Pete. "And this is my younger, Betsy." Dat nodded toward her.

I turned away. Still, I caught Betsy's radiant smile as Pete shook her hand.

"Looks like we'll have another guest for dinner," Dat said.

"Oh, that's wonderful-*gut*." Betsy's voice was all sweetness and light.

As I grabbed my bag from Pete and started for the house, Betsy reached out for my arm. "Could you take the flowers in? For the table." She thrust them in my face. I batted them away with my free hand, sending a red bloom bobbing back and forth, but then took them from her.

"And I'll need help getting dinner on the table," she added.

As I started toward the house a second time, Pete asked Dat about a job.

I slowed, straining to hear his answer.

"I might have a position in our showroom, now that you mention it."

I picked up my pace again. Dat must have thought Pete was something special. He wouldn't consider him for the showroom job unless he thought Pete could do it. He was big on first impressions.

"Cate, after you take care of those flowers, come back down to the office," Dat called out. "I might have some paperwork that needs to be done."

My back still to them, I held the flowers up in a wave to acknowledge I'd heard him. There was no way I was going to turn around and show all of them the look of disappointment on my face.

Stepping into the kitchen, my mouth began to water from the mingling smells of freshly baked bread, a beef dish, and an apple pie with a noticeable dose of cinnamon.

I fetched a vase from the top shelf of the pantry, filled it with water, and plopped the flowers into it. Just as I placed the vase on the table, Betsy came in the back door, humming a tune.

She stopped when she saw the flowers. "You didn't arrange them." She hurried over. "You have to trim the stems. And then put the tallest in the middle."

I gave her a blank stare. Although I'd read about arranging flowers, I'd never actually done it.

She threw up her hands in mock despair. "I'll do it."

"*Denki*," I muttered. Betsy appreciated beauty. Our simple home reflected our Amish values, but Betsy liked to add little touches, such as flowers and candles.

"Pete seems really nice," Betsy said. "And he's awfully handsome—don't you think?"

"I didn't notice."

"Even cuter than Levi . . ." She stepped toward the cupboard, pulling down another plate and glass. There was a time, up until about three years ago, when Betsy listened to me. Back then I'd told her, over and over, not to judge people by the way they looked. Or where they lived. Or by their horse or their buggy or their barn. But those days when I held such influence were long gone. I had to trust I'd taught her most of what she needed back then—had to hope she would remember it when the time came.

What I hadn't taught her, because I had no idea what to say, was about the birds and the bees. No one had taught me either—but I figured it out through library books. I tried to share what I'd learned with Betsy, by placing the books I'd read years before on her bedside table, then on her bed, then on her pillow. I know she saw them—but I never saw her actually read any of them, even though I kept renewing them, over and over.

After she'd added the fifth place to the table, she said, "Dat seems to like Pete a lot. He's sure to hire him. They were headed to the showroom. You'd better get down there."

Dat decided Pete would start on Monday, to give him time to settle in at the Zooks' place. I had him fill out a W-4 form, and after he was done, he and Dat headed down the lane to fix the buggy, taking Thunder along to pull it back home. I hoped when Joseph Koller reached them, on his way to our house, he would stop and help too, but the man came straight to the back door. Betsy poured him a glass of iced tea and insisted I sit with him in the living room while she finished the dinner preparations.

I led the way and directed Joseph to the couch. As he sat down, his hat in one hand and drink in the other, I asked how his business was going. He made wooden toys to sell—to tourists, mostly.

"*Gut*," he answered.

Gray hair fringed his bald spot. His beard nearly reached

his waist. I wondered if perhaps he was older than I thought, maybe past fifty.

I settled into Mamm's rocking chair. "How are your children?"

"*Gut*," he answered.

"How's business?" I asked.

"*Gut*," he said again.

"Any new designs?"

He shook his head. He'd been making wooden trains and trucks for as long as I could remember.

We suffered through a long, awkward pause. "My Dat will be in soon," I finally said, wishing he were there right now.

"Jah. I saw him down the lane with a young man fixing your buggy." He grimaced. "I figured the stranger was here to see your sister."

I started to shake my head but stopped myself. My face grew warm as I answered, "Jah, and to work for Dat too."

He didn't respond to that, so after a few more minutes of me silently stewing and him staring blankly toward the wall, I asked him if he'd read any good books lately.

"We're in Leviticus," he said.

"Oh."

"How about you?"

"I just started a biography of Abraham Lincoln."

He cleared his throat.

I stopped rocking. "Genesis. Chapter four this morning."

He smiled a little, as if he approved of my answer and nodded, his fringe of thin hair flying up a little. "What'd you do to your buggy?" He crossed his arms as he spoke.

"The boot cracked."

"Racing will do that."

Wondering what he'd heard about me, I gave him a cold stare as I stood. "I'm going to help Betsy."

I hurried into the kitchen. Betsy was humming "Amazing Grace," a favorite at the youth singings, and stirring the gravy. "It's your turn to talk with him," I whispered. "I'll stay in here."

"Everything's done." She put the whisk on a plate. Besides being a great cook, she was tidy too.

"All the more reason for me to be in the kitchen, then." I picked up the whisk.

"Oh, no," she said. "If I visit with him, he might get the wrong idea."

"Betsy." I plunged the whisk into the pan and began stirring, frenetically. "Go."

"He came to see you."

I hissed, "You're the one who invited him."

Betsy put her hands on her hips. No longer whispering, she said, just as the back door swung open, "You're the one we need to marry off."

I pretended to be intent on the gravy as I tried my best not to explode.

"Oh, look who's back," Betsy gushed. "That was fast."

"Many hands make light work," Dat said, hanging his hat on a peg by the door and then washing at the utility sink.

"I'll dish up," Betsy said. "Joseph Koller's in the living room."

"Alone?" There was a hint of disappointment to Dat's voice. I kept my focus on the stove.

"Cate?" Dat grabbed the towel as Pete stepped up to the sink.

"Seems that way," I answered. I concentrated on the gravy, and a minute later Dat and Pete's footsteps across the linoleum indicated they were going in to sit with the man.

"Let's get this over with," I growled at Betsy as I grabbed the gravy boat.

Without answering me, she opened the oven door and took

out a roast, surrounded by root vegetables. Her homemade rolls were already nestled in a basket atop a sky-blue cloth napkin. Next she heaped the mashed potatoes high in a pure white dish.

In a few minutes we had everything on the table, and Betsy stepped into the living room and politely called the men to the table.

I sat down at my usual place, and Betsy directed Joseph to sit beside me. Pete sat across the table, kitty-corner from me, next to Betsy.

After Dat led us in the blessing, he asked Joseph how his business was going. Unlike me, he was able to get the man to talk. A chain of toy stores in Germany was carrying his products, and he planned to branch into Sweden too.

The bouquet of flowers partly blocked my view of Pete, but not enough for me to miss him bending his head toward Betsy and making a comment. I couldn't hear what he said, but she laughed at it, quickly covering her mouth with her napkin.

I asked Joseph how the trade tariffs affected his profits. His face reddened. "I don't talk business with women."

I continued, saying, "I read somewhere—"

Dat cut me off. "Cate," he said.

I ignored him, keeping my attention on Joseph as I jumped to a new topic. "Who's your distributor?"

Dat tried a second time. "Cate . . ."

"We should look into the international market!" I exclaimed to Dat. Why hadn't I thought of it before? "It's the perfect next step."

"That might be so," Dat answered, "but Joseph doesn't want to discuss this."

I slumped down in my chair.

Pete winked at me. "Clearly Cate has a head for business."
I did my best not to smile, but I was pleased with the acknowledgment. Dat simply nodded and sighed.

"How long have you had your cabinet shop?" Pete's full attention was now on Dat.

"Eleven years," Dat said. "I started out in construction, framing houses for a local company. Then I moved on to finishing work. After a while I tried my hand at contracting."

It was a story I knew by heart. He wasn't saying anything that wasn't fact—the truth was, Dat had a gift for business. It was all about his relationships with people and the quality of his products and work. He was firm, but he bent over backward to take care of both his customers and his employees. He'd flourished as a contractor, adding more and more clients and employees. But contracting took him away from home and Betsy and me too often, and that's why he decided to sell that business and start the cabinet shop.

Cabinetmaking allowed him to be closer to us but applied the same principles as contracting. Great quality and excellent customer service. Plus, it turned out he had a knack for designing kitchens and bathrooms. He had orders from all over the country, from Maine to Hawaii. There was no reason we couldn't ship them all the way around the world.

"Once the cabinet business was on its feet, other entrepreneurs started asking for my advice. That's when I opened my consulting business." Dat took another helping of mashed potatoes and passed them on to Joseph. "That's it in a nutshell."

"And both your daughters work for you?" Pete asked.

"Just Cate. Betsy's in charge of the house"—Dat looked directly at Joseph —"although Cate helps with that too."

"So Cate has a lot of business experience?" Pete smiled at me through the tulips and daffodils.

"She's great with numbers," Dat said.

"And ideas," Pete added. "But I'm sure you're just as skilled when it comes to cooking, because the gravy's delicious."

I hesitated, confused, until I remembered I was stirring it when he came into the kitchen. In a daze, I said, "Oh, thanks." I pushed my plate away a little. "Except I didn't make it. Betsy did."

"What *did* you make?" Joseph asked.

"Nothing at all." I stood, intending to get the water pitcher off the sideboard, making a sweeping gesture as I did to indicate Betsy's vast accomplishments. But I accidently bumped the flowers, sending the bouquet off-balance. As it shifted, I lunged for the vase, but in doing so, I toppled it over, sending a mini tsunami of water toward Pete. He lurched back, but not soon enough. In a split second his lap was soaked.

After dinner, while I did the dishes and Betsy and Pete sat on the porch and chatted, Dat escorted Joseph Koller to his buggy. It was warm enough to have the window open, and I could hear both the clopping of his horse's hooves as he headed up our lane and Pete and Betsy's laughter. Fortunately, I couldn't hear their words.

Dat came back into the house, dished himself up a second piece of pie, and then practically collapsed back onto his chair.

"That was a disaster," he said.

I nodded, not wanting to rehash a single moment of the evening.

"I'll tell Betsy not to bring home any stray widowers from now on, unless they're under thirty."

"Denki," I said.

Dat chuckled a little. "Lucky for Pete, I'm tall."

I smiled. Dat's pants had fit in the length but were a little wide around the middle.

I turned back to the dish rack and pulled out the last plate, biting my lower lip as I did. I wanted Dat to understand my humiliation. I wanted him to lift his stupid edict.

"There's a volleyball game tomorrow night," he said. "At the Zooks'."

"Where Pete is staying?"

Dat nodded.

I definitely wouldn't be going. "Dat," I said, turning around. "Can we talk about this new rule of yours?"

He took another bite of pie, his face reddening a little as he chewed.

I sat down beside him. "I know humility is a good thing, but this is more than that—this is humiliating."

He nodded. "This evening was, but my intention isn't. You need a little nudge, Cate. That's all. I've been too soft on you in the past, too understanding. Not as strict as I should have been. It's made you neglect your future."

I exhaled slowly. "I know you want grandchildren, but think about me. I'm already the comic relief of the district. Do you want to turn me into an absolute fool?"

"You're not a fool, Cate—not at all. But it's the Amish way to marry. You just need some help." He put down his fork and reached for my hand, but I jerked it away. My father had never meddled in my life before. To keep from sharing my not so respectful thoughts, I headed straight to the open back door.

As I rushed through it, Betsy's laughter reached me again. I pounded down the stairs, scaring the two calicos that liked to hang around the house, and headed toward the shop, away from all the fun on the front porch. It wasn't fair. None of it was fair.

Why couldn't Dat leave me alone and let me be content with my lot in life?

I marched toward my favorite tree, the silver maple past the shop.

I don't remember having problems with my temper before my Mamm died, but afterward I did. When it would start to get the best of me, Dat would tell me to find a place to collect myself. The maple was where I went. Occasionally to think things through. Sometimes to pray. Oftentimes to read. Always to escape.

I grasped the lowest branch and pulled myself onto it, settling against the trunk, serenaded by the frogs down by the creek. Above, a canopy of new leaves swayed in the cool breeze. I could be as willful as Dat. I would simply refuse to court—no matter whom he chose for me. Surely Betsy's misery would eventually wear him down.

In the meantime, I would come up with a business plan for a publishing company that he'd be willing to finance . . . eventually. Once he accepted that Betsy would be his only source of grandchildren, he was bound to help me with my future.

When I heard Pete call out a good-bye to Dat and Betsy, that he'd see them soon, I craned my neck. It was a good thirty-minute walk to the Zooks' place, and the sun would soon be setting. A minute later Pete strolled by, reading as he walked.

I longed to know the title of his book. Forgetting my humiliation, and without thinking, I called out, "What are you reading?"

He startled and stopped all in the same moment. It took him a moment to find me in the tree, but when he did, he started toward me, saying, "You wouldn't tell me good-bye, but you'll scare me half to death? You are spirited, aren't you?"

Ignoring his comment, I strained to get a look at his book. He tucked it under his arm.

When he reached the tree, he asked, "Mind if I join you?"

"Jah, as a matter of fact I do."

He ignored me, dropped his backpack on the grass with the book on top, and quickly climbed to the other side of the tree. Leaning forward he said, "I was hoping to see you before I left."

"Why?"

"I enjoyed our talk."

"But you were laughing with Betsy."

He shrugged. "Well, sure . . ." He poked his head around the side of the trunk. "Are you always so defensive?"

I ignored him. "So what *are* you reading?"

"For the answer to that you'll have to wait, until tomorrow." He jumped from the branch and picked up his book, tucking it under his arm. "I hear there's a volleyball game at the Zooks'." He looked up at me in the waning light.

"I wouldn't know."

"Betsy would," he quipped.

"I'm sure."

"I'll see you soon." He picked up his backpack.

I didn't bother to respond. Clearly, he thought winning my trust would increase his chances of courting Betsy.

A moment later, as he reached the lane, he glanced back over his shoulder. "Good night!" He tipped his hat. "Sweet Cate."

I contemplated going to the volleyball match on Saturday with one goal in mind—to find out what Pete was reading. But even that wasn't incentive enough. By that afternoon I'd decided not to go, which meant Betsy didn't go either. She didn't speak to me for the rest of the day.

Late that night I feigned sleep through the ping of pebbles against our bedroom window. Our Plain courting ways likely seemed odd to outsiders, but that was often how it was done. Parents usually ignored the comings and goings, knowing it wouldn't last long. Either someone would lose interest or the courting would lead to marriage. Amish youth generally didn't court casually—if a young man called on a girl it meant he was serious—and parents relied on that. Not everyone who courted married, sure, but it wasn't our way to date a lot of different people.

Betsy scurried out of the room in a hurry. Regardless of her giggling on the porch the night before, it seemed she was still more interested in Levi than Pete. I could only hope Betsy and Levi were sitting in the kitchen, eating pie.

Although I tried to stay awake until she returned, I didn't, and the next morning it took me three tries to wake her for church. We ended up getting a late start, which made Dat grumpy. The service was at Mervin and Martin's farm, held in their Dat's shop. Their older brother, Seth, walked in front of us with his very pregnant wife as we arrived.

Most everyone was seated when Betsy and I crowded onto the back bench on the women's side and Dat walked toward the front on the men's side. I always felt sorry he didn't have a son to sit with at services. I was extra thankful for Betsy on Sundays, that I had someone beside me, but I wouldn't for long, not if she had her way. I was certain she would figure out some way to marry Levi, and then they'd most likely join his parents' district. Then again, Betsy might decide she was interested in someone besides Levi. Someone like Pete. It was hard to tell.

As Preacher Stoltz stood to lead the singing, a straggler sauntered by. It was Pete, without a book in his hand. The Zooks didn't live in our district. I could only guess his interest in Betsy had led him to our service. Even so, the sight of him made my heart beat faster.

Pete paused and then made his way down the center aisle and settled on the bench next to Dat. Betsy nudged me, but I didn't respond.

After forty-five minutes of singing, the sermon began. After a few minutes, Betsy leaned her head against my shoulder the way she had when she was little. If we hadn't been in the back, I would have made her sit up straight, but as it was I didn't mind.

Seth's wife sat in front of me, her back ramrod straight. She wasn't from our district and hadn't gone to school with us. I wondered if she had any idea what a cad her husband was.

Near the end of the sermon, my eyes began to droop too.

Preacher Stoltz read 2 Corinthians 12 and then, in conclusion, admonished all of us to turn our weaknesses over to God. For a moment my weaknesses overwhelmed me, but then I patted Betsy's leg as the preacher led all of us in a silent prayer. She sat up straight and adjusted her Kapp. Afterward we helped the women put out the food in the house while the men moved the benches inside. M&M seemed to be in charge of this task, and Dat and Pete helped.

Betsy yawned several times as we carried loaves of homemade bread to the food table in the living room and then began to slice them.

"You shouldn't stay up so late," I whispered.

She looked beyond me, and I turned.

Pete stood, smiling at us. "Good morrow, Cate," he said to me, his eyes sparkling. "Missed you at the volleyball game last night."

"We were busy," I answered. "Besides, aren't you a little old to be playing games with sixteen-year-olds?"

He laughed. "There was a wide range of ages present."

Betsy yawned, despite whose company she was in.

"Going to the singing tonight?" he asked.

I answered "no" as Betsy answered "yes."

Pete laughed. "Which is it?"

"We're going," Betsy said.

"We're not." Two years ago I'd vowed to never attend another singing in my life.

"So Betsy's going?" Pete had a confused look on his face.

"Not," I said again, turning toward the kitchen.

After lunch, I went to find Dat, hoping we could go home. I wanted to spend the rest of the afternoon reading. Pete, Mervin, Martin, and Seth were gathered in front of the barn, talking. Seth had the same hazel eyes as his brothers but had darker hair and broader shoulders. On the edge of the field, Dat stood with a group of men, one who was holding two of his grandsons in his arms.

As I walked toward Dat, Martin waved at me. "Come here!" I shook my head. I'd learned my lesson years ago.

"No, really," he said.

I turned my back to him and told Dat that Betsy and I were ready to leave.

He sighed. "Give me a while longer."

"We'll be in the buggy," I said, and started back toward my sister. I heard footsteps behind me but didn't turn. In a second I was overtaken by M&M, forcing me to a stop as they stepped in front of me.

"Please come to the singing tonight," they said in unison.

I shook my head and tried to dart around them.

Mervin shaded his eyes from the midday sun. "Cate, don't be so vindictive."

"Just because we've teased you a little . . ." Martin's sunglasses reflected my stern face.

I jerked away from him. "A *little?*" I barked. "Relentlessly is more like it." I stepped wide.

They hustled after me.

I stopped and turned. "Don't you know Betsy's seeing Levi?" There was no point mentioning she also seemed to be interested in Pete.

They looked at each other, and then at the same time said, "She's changed her mind before."

"Go away," I sneered, hurrying away from them again.

Betsy stood beside the fence. I made eye contact with her and pointed toward the buggy. As I followed, I glanced over my shoulder. Mervin and Martin were back with Seth and Pete, talking. I could only guess what about. Dat was walking toward them, his hand outstretched. He greeted M&M, Pete, and finally Seth.

As Dat stepped away, Seth looked toward me, a sad expression on his face. I couldn't help but remember a Sunday afternoon twelve years ago. I'd thought Seth was one of my few friends in all the world, until he turned into a bully that day and humiliated me in front of our entire district. Then, like a fool, I more than forgave him. I gave my heart to him, only to have him humiliate me again two years ago.

My face burned as I marched away. By the time I reached the buggy, Dat was behind me.

I escaped down to the creek after we reached the house, taking along the Abraham Lincoln biography and an old quilt. With my shoes off, I plopped on my stomach and, serenaded by the melody of the water lapping against the rocks, read for quite a while—until my cousin Addie interrupted me.

She and Betsy looked more alike than Betsy and I. Addie was taller and her blond hair was darker, but she had the same shapely figure and doelike brown eyes.

Although they lived next door, her family belonged to the district over from us. We didn't see a lot of them, so usually when Addie came around, I was thrilled to see her, but at that moment all I could manage was to do my best to be pleasant. I sat up, shaded my eyes as I said hello, and then noticed she had a book in her hand.

Now I was genuinely interested. "What are you reading?"

She held it up. "*Pride and Prejudice.*"

"Ah, Jane Austen."

She nodded.

Nan had recommended Austen, and I'd read all her books

by the time I was Addie's age. Nan said there were centuries of stories waiting for me, but I hadn't gone further back than the late 1700s, when Jane Austen started writing, except for the Bible and church history, of course.

As the only girl in the Cramer family, Addie was always busy with household chores. So, no matter how much she enjoyed it, and though she visited the bookmobile now and then, I couldn't imagine she had much time to read.

She sat down on the quilt beside me. "Ach, Cate," she said, her voice sympathetic, "I heard about your Dat's edict."

"Who from?" I held on to my book tightly.

"Betsy," she answered.

I gazed past her at the willows along the creek. The leaves turned in the breeze, one after the other, reflecting shades of light onto the water.

"I'm sorry," she said.

"Jah, well . . ." I closed my book. "The male gender doesn't seem to like me."

"Why do you think that?"

"I read too much." I held up my book.

She held up hers. "I read too."

I rolled my eyes. I knew there were boys who wanted to court Addie Cramer—Uncle Cap just wouldn't allow it yet. "Well, you look like Betsy."

She shook her head. "You're as pretty as anyone." She paused, and then said, as if it were an effort, "Maybe it's because you're prickly."

I wiggled to my knees, straightening my dress as I did. "You don't know what you're talking about."

Her eyes narrowed. "You're being prickly with me right now."

I swallowed hard. Addie was too nice, usually, to get defensive with. I did my best to keep my voice even. "Well, I'm a little stressed. About this whole edict of Dat's. About courting in general."

Addie tilted her head. "Didn't you used to court Seth Mosier?"

I groaned. "Please don't mention his name."

"What happened?"

"He was courting Dat's money—not me. Once I figured it out, I kicked him to the curb." I'd heard that line on the radio in an Englisch store one time and thought it fit the subject.

"Too bad."

I wrinkled my nose, surprised. There was some sort of rift between Addie's family and Seth's, although I could never quite figure it out.

She continued. "I always thought those Mosier boys seemed like fun, regardless of what my parents think."

"Well, they're not." I stood and motioned her off the quilt. "Believe me."

She stepped away, and I swung the quilt up into my arms, shook it, and had just started folding it when a little boy yelled, "Addie!"

It was her turn to groan. "Oh, no. They're going to find me."

"What's going on?"

"I told Billy and Joe-Joe"—they were her two youngest brothers—"I'd play hide and seek with them." She pointed downstream. "I'm going to keep walking." She tiptoed away, and as I headed toward the trail, the boys came crashing down the bank.

"Ah-hah!" Joe-Joe yelled.

I turned toward him.

"You're not Addie!"

"Where is she?" Billy demanded.

I shrugged and smiled.

They turned upstream, yelling their sister's name, their bare feet splashing through the water. She'd only have a few more minutes of peace unless she found a really good place to hide.

My resolve stronger than ever, I headed to the house, batting at the cattails along the path as I walked. A few minutes later I found Dat sitting at the table, staring at Mamm's rocking chair.

I decided to be up front with him and told him directly I wouldn't be going to the singing.

"What do you mean?" Dat flinched as if I'd insulted him. "It's one thing not to go to the volleyball game, but you are not too old for singings."

"I went to four years of those, Dat." Seth was the only boy who ever gave me a ride home in his buggy, and once I understood why, I vowed to never go to another singing in my life.

"What about Betsy?"

I shrugged. "She's still napping."

"Doesn't she want to go?"

"I'm sure she does." I hoped after another week of this, at the very most, Dat would realize what a horrible decision he'd made and change his mind.

"Cate," he said. "How can you?"

"How can *you*? You're the one who came up with this crazy plan."

He met my gaze but didn't respond. After a long minute, he took a drink of his coffee, and I went upstairs to wake Betsy to help with the choring.

As I entered, Betsy stirred.

"What time is it?" she asked.

"Five."

She sat up. "Let's get going."

"I'm serious about *not* going."

She plopped back down on her pillow. "Then I'm not helping with the choring."

"Fine."

"Or cooking supper."

I didn't answer. We usually had leftovers on Sunday evenings.

"And not just tonight. All week, if you don't go to the singing."

I sat down on my bed, not sure which I detested more—cooking or singings. I could sit in the back and sneak out before it was over. I could stay away from the *Youngie*. It wouldn't hurt to go, for Betsy's sake. I wouldn't even have to wait until it was over to leave. Levi would drive Betsy home.

"Okay," I said. "Let's go."

She flew across the room and knocked me flat on my bed.

"Get off me," I groaned.

"Denki, denki, denki," she squealed.

"Please don't," I answered.

"Let's hurry with the chores!"

Dat must have known something was up by the thundering of Betsy's feet on the stairs. By the time I reached the kitchen, they were standing side by side, beaming at me.

I shook my head. "Don't get any ideas."

"But doesn't it feel good to put your sister first?" Dat asked.

I shrugged. I'd been putting Betsy first my entire life.

By the time I turned Thunder off the highway and into the Bergs' driveway I felt sick to my stomach. I'd read one time that women don't remember the pain of childbirth until they start labor the next time. That's how it was for me and singings. Oh, I remembered that they made me miserable. I just didn't remember how badly—until I saw the gathering outside the barn. The boys were congregated in one group, having a pushing contest. The girls were congregated in another, having a gossip fest.

Betsy was already practically glowing, but she lit up like a firefly when she saw Levi. "Let me out!"

I pulled Thunder to a stop.

Levi walked toward us, a grin spreading across his face. "You're here!"

They locked arms and twirled around, the skirt of Betsy's dress poofing out a little.

My stomach tied itself into a knot.

Old Daniel Berg started to call the Youngie into the barn for the singing. *The youth.* I was anything but. I turned Thunder toward the line of buggies in the field, but then, instead of going straight, I swung wide and turned back toward the highway. Levi and Betsy were still outside. I called to her, but she ignored me. I called to Levi and he turned. "Can you give Betsy a ride home?"

He grinned again and nodded. Of course he could.

I turned right onto the highway, going in the direction opposite of home. It wouldn't do any good to show up early. Dat would be suspicious. I wasn't going to lie to him. But I wasn't going to be exactly forthcoming either—not if I could help it. I hoped I wasn't sliding down a slippery slope of deceit. It wasn't like me. In the meantime I had a good two hours to run Thunder on the back roads of the county. At least I would have if I hadn't run into Pete first.

He was ambling along the shoulder of the road, a book once again in his hand when I sped by him. Although he was reading, he still saw it was me. In my side mirror, I watched him leap the fence and run across the field. Ahead was a hairpin turn and then another, and by the time I reached the second, Pete was aiming to jump that fence too, waving as he did. I didn't slow—until he went sailing over the top rail. I couldn't tell for sure, but he must have tripped, because he landed in the gravel on the side of the road and rolled onto his shoulder. I thought maybe he hit his chin, too, but couldn't tell as I watched, again, in my mirror.

I'll admit there have been times in life when I've been cold-hearted, but never when someone is hurt. Besides, the Good Samaritan was my favorite story as a child, read to me over and over by my Mamm. I pulled Thunder to a stop, made sure there were no vehicles coming in either direction, and swung the buggy around. By the time I reached Pete, he was bent over the ditch that ran on the roadside of the fence. When he straightened, I saw he'd plucked his book out of the water.

I pulled Thunder to a stop, yanked on the brake, and grabbed the first-aid kit from under the seat. I'd put it together when I was sixteen after reading a book called *Everyday Safety*. Of course the author assumed the first-aid kit would be kept in a car, but I figured it was even more important in a buggy.

Blood oozed from the palm of Pete's left hand; plus it ran down the front of his chin. "Thanks for stopping," he said. I noted the book in his right hand was fairly thin and very worn. It didn't have a cover, and I couldn't make out the title at the top of the page.

"You really scraped yourself." I opened the box, taking out several antiseptic-wipe packets.

"It's not bad." He held his hand away. "I've had worse."

I handed him a wipe.

"I'm not usually so accident prone," he said, wiping his hand.

"You just said you've had worse."

He laughed. "Touché."

I opened another wipe and dabbed at his face, flicking away pieces of gravel. "I'll give you a ride back to the Zooks'."

"That's okay. I'm going to the singing."

"Then why the detour?"

"I was curious."

I narrowed my eyes. "You thought Betsy was in the buggy, right?"

He smiled, but before he answered, I proclaimed, "You *are* stubborn."

"*Persistent* is the word I prefer—remember?"

Funny how the difference between the two seemed to be solely in our perception. "You'll be happy to know my sister is at the singing. You can see her there." I wasn't going to bother telling him Levi would be giving her a ride home. He could find that out on his own.

"And why isn't Sweet Cate in the Bergs' barn?"

"Technically I am." I knew my smile was sarcastic.

His, in return, was even more so.

After I'd picked the gravel out of his hand and then his face, with him bending toward me, I reached for the bottle of antiseptic in my kit and squirted it liberally on his chin.

"Ouch!" He jerked away.

"Hold out your hand." I was enjoying myself with a man, for once.

For some reason he obeyed, and I squirted out another stream of liquid.

He flinched again.

"Would you rather have an infection?"

He didn't answer as he dabbed his palm against his pant leg.

"I read somewhere that staph usually starts in seemingly innocuous wounds."

He raised his eyebrows.

"You don't believe me?"

"I have no reason not to," he answered, an impish look on his face.

I ignored the expression and took a look at him. The red streaks on his chin were raw. He opened his mouth and scooted his lower jaw one way and then the other, then gingerly touched the scrape.

"Leave it alone," I commanded, pulling bandages from the kit. "How's your shoulder?"

He worked it back and forth. "It's okay."

After I affixed the bandages to his chin and hand, I wadded the wrappers in my fist, shoved them into my apron pocket, and started for my buggy.

"How about going back to the singing?"

"I'll give you a ride." I climbed in first, scooting the first-aid kit back under the seat.

As soon as Pete landed on the bench seat, Thunder took off, at my urging. Pete grabbed the side of the buggy as we sped around the corner. Ahead the sun was lowering in the sky, sending streaks of pink and orange along the horizon. I'd need to light the buggy lantern soon and turn on the flashing red lights on the back.

On the straight stretch, I drove the horse faster. Pete held his worn hat with his injured hand, the book still in his other.

I couldn't stand it any longer. "So what are you reading?"

He held the book up. "*The Pilgrim's Progress.* I found it in a thrift store outside of Cleveland. Ever read it?"

I nodded. "A few years ago." His copy looked much thinner than what I'd read, though. "Is that the condensed version?"

He laughed. "No, the consumed version. I buy old books and then use up what I've read as I travel."

I gasped. "For what?"

"Sometimes to start a fire," he said.

I must have had a horrified expression on my face, because he said, "Sorry. I'm a pragmatist at heart." He held up the thin, now wet, book. "Sometimes I just throw it away, section by section. It keeps my pack lighter."

I was shocked at the very idea of tearing pages out of a book. And even more so to burn them. Sure, if he was freezing to death, I'd understand, but to preplan it? "How could you?" I gasped.

"Books are heavy," he said. "On the road, an object that serves two purposes doubles in value for a pauper like me." He smiled as I pulled into the Bergs' driveway and stopped Thunder.

"That's horrid." I couldn't imagine he was that poor—although his hat and clothes, the same he'd been wearing on Friday, all had a shabby look to them. "Here you go." I stopped the buggy twenty feet from the barn, still aghast.

"Aren't you coming?"

"No."

"Ah, Cate," he said.

"Believe me," I answered. "If I were going to, I would have before, instead of just dropping Betsy off."

"Where are you going?"

"Driving."

"How about if I go with you?"

"How about if you don't." I nodded toward the barn.

"Why so angry?" he asked.

I gave him a wilting look.

"So waspish . . ." he muttered, gathering his things. "So stingish."

I couldn't help myself. "Beware," I sneered.

"Why do you push people away?"

"I don't."

"You do."

I scooted away from him. "You don't really want to know."

A pathetic expression crossed his face, and then he looked beyond me and pointed toward the fiery sky. The pink had disappeared and what was left looked like orange flames. His voice deepened as he spoke. "'Where two raging fires meet together, they do consume the thing that feeds their fury.'"

My face must have given away my confusion at his odd words, because he grinned and then quickly jumped down, tipping his hat. "See you tomorrow."

His stride was confident as he made his way toward the barn. I turned the buggy around. I couldn't figure out Pete Treger. I had no idea what he meant by his talk of fire and fury, but he intrigued me.

As I came back by, he stood in front of the closed door. He grinned again and waved. I kept a straight face but flicked my hand in his direction.

There was no doubt about it. Pete Treger was unlike anyone I'd ever met.

C H A P T E R

5

The next morning, over oatmeal with Dat, I pondered Pete's words again, wondering for the umpteenth time what he meant when he spoke of fire and fury.

"Cate?"

My head jerked up. "Jah?"

Dat had a pleased expression on his face. "Thinking about the singing last night?"

"Some," I answered, hoping to evade a more specific question.

"What time did you and Betsy get home?"

"I was here by nine," I said. "But Levi gave Betsy a ride home." I yawned. "I'm not sure exactly what time she came in."

"Oh." Dat put his spoon in his bowl. "So how was the singing?"

I took a deep breath and then exhaled slowly. "Dat," I said, meeting his gaze. I'd never lied to him. I wasn't going to start now. "I didn't actually go. I tried. Really I did."

His face fell as I spoke.

"It's just . . . once I got there and saw all the young people going into the barn, I couldn't."

He pushed his bowl away. "Cate." His voice had that tone of despair that made me feel an inch tall.

"I know, I know. You have every right to be disappointed in me."

"How am I ever going to be a grandfather if you won't even go to a singing?"

"Just let Betsy court. She'll be married within the year, and then you'll be a grandfather by the next."

Dat sighed. "That's what I'm afraid of."

"What?" I nearly choked on the word.

"Betsy's too young to decide who she'll spend the rest of her life with. And she's far too young to be a mother."

I shook my head. "She's so good at homemaking, though. And"—hard to believe, but I wasn't so sure of the word I was looking for—"relationships."

"Starting relationships, jah, but it's not as easy as that. Just a little more time can make a big difference when it comes to being a wife."

I stood and headed to the sink.

"You, on the other hand, are mature enough . . ."

I turned on the faucet, drowning out my father's words. He still didn't get it. No one wanted to court me. Why did he have to keep throwing it back in my face?

Fifteen minutes later, I was in my office, adding Pete's information to our payroll database. I used a computer and copy machine, powered by solar panels atop the building, for business purposes only. We also had Internet to e-mail our Englisch customers and distributors and to check to make sure our Web site, maintained by a designer with photos of the cabinets we sold, stayed in good order. Plus, I did some research for the business, mostly checking out competitors and ordering supplies.

The operation of the office and the management of our house remained in stark contrast to each other. With the population of our people in Lancaster County growing exponentially, there was less and less farmland for the younger generations. So, although farming was our community's preferred way of life, we had to adapt to support ourselves. Thankfully our family had the small property and could remain in the country—and make a living, thanks to Dat's business skills.

At seven o'clock, the shop crew arrived. Soon I was engrossed in the flyer Dat had asked me to make for his business-consulting clients. He was offering a free hour for every referral sent his way. As I wrote the ad copy, I toyed with an article idea about what a person needed to do to start a small business, an Amish person in particular, wondering if it was perhaps an article I could write for one of the Plain newspapers or magazines.

At seven forty-five, as I was proofing the flyer, someone knocked on my office door.

"Come in," I said absentmindedly, sure it was Dat with some new idea for me to implement.

It wasn't my father; it was Pete. My heart fluttered at the sight of him. He smelled fresh, like the cold spring air mixed with the scent of goat's milk soap, and wore a clean shirt and nicer pants than the ones he'd had on the other times I'd seen him, but they weren't anywhere close to new. The scrape on his chin was noticeable around the bandage but had started to scab over.

"Am I supposed to check in with you?"

I shook my head. "With Dat. He's in the shop, getting everyone going for the day. He'll show you where the time clock is."

He smiled sheepishly. "Okay. Have a good day."

"You too," I responded as he closed the door.

Throughout the entire morning, I was aware of Pete in the showroom. I imagined Dat explaining the products to him and the company's sales philosophy. I imagined Pete asking questions, intent on learning everything he could.

At eleven thirty I started up to the house for dinner.

On nice days, the crew members ate their lunches at a group of tables Dat had made and set up between the shop and the herb garden. The workers were already outside for the dinner break, and I saw Pete sitting at a table reading a book. I felt a little foolish for noticing him but couldn't help myself. He didn't look up. Beside him sat Mervin, and across the table, Martin, who wore his insufferable sunglasses. The twins stared at the house, most likely waiting for Betsy to appear, which she often did when the men were outside, coming out to the garden for a sprig of rosemary or a handful of chives.

Mervin nudged Pete as I approached, and at the same time Betsy came through the back door. She wore her mauve dress with a perfectly pressed apron over it. Her Kapp was bleached and starched. She'd looped her arm through the handle of a basket, making her look as if she'd just stepped out of a picture book.

She pulled out her kitchen scissors and snipped a clump of parsley and then a few stems of thyme. Next she turned toward the waning tulips along the border and cut the best of what was left.

As I approached the garden, she straightened up and greeted me, but in a half second it was clear she was looking beyond me, most likely at Levi. I turned. He was off in the doorway, talking to Dat. But Betsy wasn't looking at him. She had her eyes on Pete. But he, still engrossed in his book—one much thicker than last night's *Pilgrim's Progress*—didn't notice her. Martin did, though, and he nudged Pete again. This time he did look up, showing the bandage still on his chin, meeting Betsy's eyes and smiling.

A long moment later Betsy shifted her gaze to Levi. Poor thing, he had no idea just how short his courtship with Betsy would end up being. Dat must have felt the earth shift a little, because he turned toward us and started up the pathway.

I spun around and headed toward the house. The lone cloud in the sky drifted over the sun, casting a shadow over the yard. A single swift flew out of the barn window. The leanest of our calicos ran between my legs. I stepped wide and hurried on, my face growing warmer with each step, embarrassed that I'd wasted my time thinking about Pete.

"We'll eat in fifteen minutes," Betsy called after me. "After Levi takes a look at the roses."

I didn't answer. That gave me a little time to read. And at least Betsy had the courtesy to follow up with Levi's offer to give her some gardening tips.

When I reached the back steps, I turned again. Betsy ambled toward the rose garden with Levi at her side. Beyond them, Martin twirled his sunglasses between his thumb and index finger, stood, and pulled Pete up beside him. Mervin stepped around to the other side of Pete. And then both twins pointed at me.

Knowing they were up to no good, I hurried through the house and out the front door, circling through the far side yard and back around, willing to sacrifice a little reading time to figure out what was going on. I stopped behind an apple tree and held my breath as the white petals floated down around me.

Levi was bent down over a rosebush, gazing up at Betsy as he spoke.

Mervin and Martin stood on either side of Pete, whom I could barely see. Mervin slapped him on the back and then Martin shook his hand.

"All we ask is that you do your best," Mervin said.

"Well, right now, my best needs to be in the showroom," Pete answered, stepping away from the two, his book tucked under his arm. "But I appreciate your"—he hesitated—"interest in my future."

My eyes narrowed as Pete strode away.

I couldn't discern what was going on, exactly, but I knew the evil twins were up to no good, so as Pete stepped through the side door to the showroom, I marched from behind the tree and toward M&M.

"What are you scheming?"

Both of the twins froze.

"Tell me," I demanded.

"Nothing," Marvin sputtered.

Betsy's voice floated down from the rose garden. "Cate!" Her quick steps followed. "Let's go up to the house."

I ignored her. My hands landed on my hips. "Tell me now," I demanded of the twins.

Betsy reached me, linking her arm through mine. "Don't," she whispered. "You're making a fool out of yourself."

"I need to know." I pulled away from her.

"They're not up to anything." She turned toward Martin and Mervin. "Are you?"

They both shook their heads adamantly and then said in unison, "It's time to get back to work."

"Come on." She grabbed my hand and started dragging me toward the house, waving at Levi as he headed toward the shop, a concerned expression on his face. "You're not going to have much time to read before we eat if we don't hurry."

I cooperated then, following her obediently, desperate to escape, if only for a few minutes, knowing sooner or later I'd have to deal with M&M—and with Pete Treger.

The next day when it was time to go up to the house to eat, I slipped out the back door of the shop after the crew members had all gathered outside in the sunshine. I intended to circle around the barn to the house, avoiding Pete. I wasn't going to be made a fool of, not again.

Admittedly, before I had been feeling as if I could fall for Pete, but after yesterday's encounter between him and the twins, I willed myself to feel absolutely nothing for the newcomer.

As I stepped behind the apple trees again, one eye on the picnic tables, Pete scooted off the picnic bench and marched toward me. I increased my pace.

"Cate!" he called out.

I hid behind the next tree, my pulse quickening.

"Cate!" he called out again.

The back door opened and out came Betsy, carrying the same basket.

"Would you give me a minute," Pete yelled, presumably to me. "I have something to ask you."

I made it to the barn but then stopped, not wanting to draw any more attention to myself.

He caught up with me. "Would you take a look at my chin?" He jutted it out. "And my hand?"

His face looked fine—the bandage was off and the wound had completely scabbed over. He held out his hand but I didn't take it. Instead I motioned for him to raise it. The palm was red and looked sore. "Have you put more antiseptic on it?"

He shook his head. "But I'm thinking I should."

"Don't the Zooks have some you can use?"

"Not in their barn."

"They probably do. Try the bag balm. That will do."

"How about for today?"

I nodded my head toward our barn.

He frowned a little. I sighed. "Come on." I led the way to the house, figuring Betsy would be right behind us soon, wanting to hear what Pete might say. But she continued on toward the herb garden.

When we reached the back door, I instructed him to wash up in the utility sink while I opened the cupboard where we kept the antiseptic and bandages.

When he finished, I sprayed his hand and rebandaged the deepest cut while he kept his attention on the back door. Obviously he was anticipating Betsy's appearance too.

"All done," I said, tossing the wrappers into the woodstove. The coals, still hot from the chilly morning, consumed the paper in a second with a quick sizzle.

"I need to ask you something," he said. "Would you be interested in going on a hike Saturday afternoon? With me and a few others?"

"Such as?"

"Levi."

"And Betsy?" I crossed my arms.

He nodded. "And Mervin and Martin."

I may have been scowling by then.

"Think about it," he quickly said, holding up his injured hand. "Don't give me an answer right now. In fact there's no need to tell me until Friday. I promise I won't be"—his eyes sparkled—"*stubborn* about it."

I uncrossed my arms, and he turned and walked, in his usual

confident manner, toward the back door. But then he turned and said very sweetly, "Thank you for taking care of me."

I nodded curtly.

And then, his brown eyes dancing, he winked at me.

I crossed my arms again, but before I could respond, Betsy came banging into the kitchen, yelling, "Cate! Cate! You're never going to believe—" Her voice fell. "Oh, hi, Pete. What are you doing in here?"

"I was just leaving." He turned back toward me, smiled again, and slipped past her, out the back.

Betsy lowered her voice as she reached for my crossed hands, but couldn't contain her excitement. "Pete wants you to go on a hike with the rest of us."

I must have still had a scowl on my face.

"Please," she begged, pulling my hands apart and then swinging my arms. "You have to go. This is our lucky break."

I scowled, sure Martin and Mervin had put him up to it. There was no way a man like Pete would be interested in spending time with me.

After dinner, as I walked back down to the office, a car pulled into the parking lot of the showroom. The woman who got out of the car wore a Mennonite Kapp, and it wasn't until she turned toward me that I realized it was Nan.

"Hello," I called out, hurrying toward her, before it dawned on me she'd probably come to see Pete, not me.

She squinted up the hill, holding her hand above her eyes to shade them from the high sun. Even though she wasn't at work, she still had a pencil tucked behind her ear. "Oh, Cate," she said. "I hoped I'd see you."

Feeling a little awkward, I quickened my pace.

"You have a beautiful place here," she said, gesturing toward the yard, the house, and then the barn. "Do you garden?"

"My sister does most of it."

"Ah, the infamous Betsy."

I sighed. "Aren't you working today?"

"I have Tuesdays off," she said. "It's my writing day, but I thought I'd check on Pete."

"He's in here." I stepped toward the door and opened it.

Pete and my Dat stood at the counter, huddled over an open three-ring binder. They both looked up quickly.

Pete broke into a grin. "Bob," he said, "this is Nan Beiler. From back home, a distant cousin. Nan—Bob Miller."

He sounded both professional and enthusiastic.

Dat and Nan shook hands.

"I've known Cate for several years," she said. "I'm the bookmobile lady."

Dat beamed. "Then you're also the writer, jah? The scribe for *The Budget*?"

"That's right," she said. It was the first time I'd ever seen her blush.

I stepped toward the far door of the showroom, wanting to get back to my office. I'd been working on the inventory for the cabinet business and aimed to finish it by the end of the workday.

"Want to go on a hike on Saturday?" Pete asked. For a moment I thought he'd asked me again, but then I realized it was directed toward Nan.

"I haven't been on a hike in years." Her eyes shone.

He turned toward Dat. "We'd like to have you come along too," he said.

"Who's 'we'?" Dat stroked his beard.

Pete looked straight at me. "Levi, Mervin, Martin, and your daughters, if Cate agrees to come along."

Now Dat had his eyes on me too.

I stepped closer to the door.

Nan smiled at me. "I'll go if Cate goes."

Pete grinned.

I grabbed the doorknob.

"Looks like it's settled." Dat's happy face matched Pete's.

"Do you want to go?" Nan asked me. She wasn't grinning. Instead a look of concern spread across her face. She was probably remembering the way I'd been treated at the bookmobile just a few days before.

I didn't usually succumb to peer pressure, but in the moment I was feeling quite overwhelmed. "I suppose so," I managed to squeak.

Pete's eyes lit up even more. "Wonderful! I'll tell Martin to arrange for a van."

I opened the door and gave Nan a little wave as I slipped through. "See you," I sputtered, sure I could come up with a good excuse not to go on the hike by Saturday morning. If Dat and Nan were going, Betsy would be well chaperoned. The thought of not going disappointed me, sure—that part of me that longed for Pete's invitation to be genuine and sincere. But I knew the whole thing had to be a setup.

Friday evening I plopped down on my bed beside Betsy as she brushed her hair. It was time for me to put myself first for once.

"He really does want to court you," she said, as if she could read my mind. "Honest to Pete." Her face went blank and then she began to laugh, once she realized her accidental pun.

"But why?"

Betsy shrugged. If she knew, she obviously wasn't going to tell me.

I swallowed hard. "It feels like I'm coming down with a sore throat."

"Don't," she said.

"What?" I feigned ignorance.

"Fake being sick."

It was true that I'd used that technique in the past to get out of events in which I didn't want to participate. I swallowed again. "I'm not. It's been sore all evening." Alone in the buggy that afternoon I'd shouted into the wind as loudly as I could, hoping to make myself hoarse.

Betsy moved away from me and bounced onto her knees, facing me. "Cate Miller, don't you dare do this to me."

I wrinkled my nose. "Dat and Nan are going. You won't have to stay home."

"I'm not talking about the hike. I'm talking about Pete. He's the best chance we're going to get, that you're ever going to get."

"Ouch." I leaned away from her. "I can't help it if his motives are suspicious."

A puzzled expression settled on her face. I couldn't tell if she was trying to hide something or if she was confused. "How can you say that?"

I shrugged. "He's poor, right? He's been all buddy-buddy with Dat. At first he was interested in you, like everyone else. And I thought you were interested in him."

She shook her head. "Half the time I don't have any idea what Pete's talking about—like that night he and I sat on the porch. That's why I kept laughing. I always get what Levi's saying."

I slumped against the wall, relieved she wasn't interested in Pete but still not sure why he wasn't interested in her. Perhaps my original suspicion that he planned to win her through me was correct. "Well," I said, "he clearly wasn't interested in me at the beginning, but now it seems, after spending time with Martin and Mervin, he is. What do you think his intentions are?"

She stopped smiling. "Who cares what his intentions are! Do you have to overthink everything! Can't you just enjoy life for once!" Her legs flew out from under her and she scampered off my bed, flinging herself across the room and onto her own. "You are going to ruin my life. Absolutely destroy it." She pulled her pillow over her head.

I waited a long moment, wondering at how badly I was being manipulated. Finally I ventured across the room and sat on the edge of her bed and began to rub her back. "Want me to braid your hair?"

The pillow shook.

I rubbed her back some more.

"I want you to go on the hike. Can't you just do that?" came her muffled response.

I didn't answer. Betsy had always been poised and confident, even as a toddler. From the beginning it was obvious that she was much different than I. She was mostly all sweetness and light, like the early summer sun, while I was moody and dark, like the winter twilight.

She would marry and have a houseful of kids. I would be their *Aenti* Cate. I had Dat and Betsy—and her future family. That was it. No matter how much she irritated me, I loved her. It wasn't that I loved her more than I loved Dat, but I did love her differently. I was used to putting her needs first.

I swallowed hard. "My throat's feeling better," I said.

The pillow moved again. "You'll go?"

"Jah. But only for you." With Dat and Nan along, I

assumed Martin and Mervin—and Pete—would be on their best behavior.

The pillow fell away, and Betsy's head appeared. She turned toward me, her brown eyes rimmed with red. "You won't change your mind in the morning?"

"I promise not to."

Her arms flew around my neck, the way she used to hold on to me as a child.

I patted her back, willing her to let go of me. I loved her, yes, but not to the point of being strangled. Finally she released me, dabbing at her eyes after she did.

I turned off the lamp and climbed straight into bed, retrieving my flashlight from my bedside table. I was dying to get started on my new stack of books, including a biography of Mary Todd Lincoln. I desperately wanted to distract myself from thinking about the next day. I desperately wanted to keep from hoping that Pete Treger might want to—genuinely— court me.

C H A P T E R

6

I focused on appearing as calm and collected as I could, drawing as little attention to myself as possible as we rode in the van to the trailhead. After a few tense minutes of trying to act normal, I decided to pretend I was dozing instead.

Betsy and Levi sat on the first bench seat, Mervin, Martin, and Pete on the second, and then Nan and I. Dat sat up front with the driver, who turned out to be a Mennonite man from Nan's district.

The colloquial term for what he was doing was "hauling Amish." Some people made a career out of it in Lancaster County, and the saying got a chuckle out of tourists. For us, it was just part of how we got around when we needed to travel farther or faster than our buggies could take us. In this case we were headed west, nearly two hours away.

I could make out bits and pieces of the others' conversations, my interest piqued the most by Pete's voice, but it was all small talk, mostly comments about the lush vegetation, the light traffic, and the long hike ahead of us—ten miles round trip—and what the guys had packed for lunch.

I didn't open my eyes until the van slowed when we pulled off the main highway. A minute later the driver parked in a lot half filled with cars.

The men, including Dat, all had small packs they positioned on their backs. After I stepped out of the van, I pulled my dress tight around my legs, kneeled down, and retied my walking shoes. Betsy and Levi were already at the trailhead, ready to go. I caught a glimpse of the driver, reclining his seat, a book in his hand.

Dat asked him again if he was sure he didn't want to come with us. He just smiled and waved.

I wished I could curl up with a book too.

We planned to hike to the Chimney Rock vista, eat our lunch, and then hike back. The morning had started out bright and sunny, although cool, but now clouds were forming to the south, so I slipped my arms into my sweatshirt.

An Englisch couple, dressed in pants and fancy jackets made out of synthetic material and carrying sleek packs, stood beside their car and gawked at us. I squinted to read their license plate. *New Mexico.* There weren't Plain people out that way, I was sure. I smiled at them, and they turned their heads abruptly. The woman wore a baseball cap that looked rather masculine. I couldn't help but speculate that my feminine prayer Kapp looked like something from two centuries ago to her.

"Come on," Nan said to me.

I gave the Englisch couple one more glance and then fell in step with Nan. I knew we were quite a sight to strangers. Most Englisch women hardly wore dresses and stockings at all, let alone to go hiking.

Levi and Betsy took off quickly, with Martin and Mervin close behind. The twins had been quiet all morning—most likely because their boss was along, which was exactly what I'd hoped for.

Dat and Pete motioned for Nan and me to go ahead, and

then they took up the rear. The scent of new-growth pine and damp soil, saturated from the spring runoff, filled the air. The trail wound its way through a glistening field of ferns. We climbed over several downed trees, likely from the winter storms. Soon we were completely in the forest.

Nan asked if I'd hiked the trail before.

I answered no but that I had hiked a nearby one several years ago, on a youth outing.

"I used to hike quite a bit back in New York," she said. "When I was your age."

I hadn't heard much of her story and asked when she'd come to Lancaster County. "I was twenty-eight," she said. "I'd just left the Amish."

"Why?" I'd assumed she'd always been Mennonite.

"Long story," she said. "Sure you want to hear it?"

I nodded.

"I joined the Amish church when I was seventeen. I never questioned it. Then I taught school for several years. I didn't court anyone special, and by the time I was twenty-seven I'd resigned myself to being single."

The one thing I'd known about Nan was that she'd never married. I really liked that about her.

"But then a Mennonite man from Lancaster County showed up in our district. Mark was a carpenter and drove an old Chevy truck. He'd come to rebuild the school I taught in. The old one was literally falling off its foundation. I kept my distance at first, but he was personable and easy to talk to."

She explained she gradually fell in love with him and he with her. They were in a quandary about what to do. He said he'd join the Amish, but she was afraid he wouldn't make much of a living as a carpenter where she lived. Finally, she decided she would leave the Amish.

"And be shunned?" I asked, even though I knew the answer.

"Yes," she said.

We'd come to a boulder field now and slowed as we picked our way across it. The wind had picked up and was twisting our dresses around our legs.

Nan continued with her story as we watched our footing. "As soon as he finished the school, we went to my parents and told them our plan. It was wrenching, but when we left, I knew it was the right thing. I felt at peace with God. I was ready to start a new life with the man I loved. We planned to be married as soon as we reached Lancaster."

"What happened?" I imagined him changing his mind. Or his family not accepting her.

"Outside of Harrisburg, a semi turned into the pickup, on Mark's side."

I gasped and slipped on a rock, catching myself before I fell.

"For two weeks, he was in a coma, with his family and me at his side."

"Oh, Nan," I said, heavy with sadness. I knew what was coming.

"He squeezed my hand once, but never regained consciousness. He died in the middle of the night, with me beside him."

"How long ago?"

"Thirteen years now."

We reached the end of the boulder field, and I stepped gratefully back onto the soft trail. "And you didn't think about going back to New York?"

"Oh, I thought about it. I even intended to. I just never did."

We strolled along in silence for a moment, taking a turn in the path onto a straight stretch. Up the hill, Betsy and M&M were laughing, while Levi stood a pace away with an awkward expression on his face. Because he wasn't from our district and didn't go to our school, he probably hadn't realized how close Betsy was to the twins.

"Mark's family has been so good to me," Nan continued. "Before his Dat passed away he taught me how to drive. And I joined their church. There's a little cottage on their property that I rent, and I watch out after Mark's Mamm. Take her to doctor's appointments, do her grocery shopping. That sort of thing."

"So you ended up an old maid after all." As soon as I said it I realized how rude it sounded and wished I could cross my words out with a big red pen.

Nan didn't seem to be offended, although her voice was firm. "I don't think of it that way. I just think of it as being in the place in life God has for me. It's as simple as that."

I nodded, my face warm. "That's how I try to think about my life too."

"Ach, Cate. Don't be thinking that way yet." She sighed. "You're still so young."

When we reached the Chimney Rock overlook, we all stood on the slanting shale and took in the view of the endless forest and faraway hills. Mervin and Martin scampered down to the tree line, while the rest of us stayed above. Cumulus clouds scudded across the darkening sky as a springtime storm sailed toward us.

A few minutes later, we found a spot off the trail to eat lunch. The wind blew through the tops of the pines, showering needles and twigs. I pulled the hood of my sweatshirt over my Kapp to keep it clean. The entire sky had turned gray, but the day was still warm. We ate two large sticks of salami Dat had brought, bread torn straight from the loaves

Levi had packed, M&M's family's homemade cheese, and nuts and dried fruit contributed by Pete. I got the feeling he ate a lot of that sort of thing while on the road. I imagined him huddled too close to a fire, a handful of trail mix in one hand and a book in the other, feeding the fire each page as he finished it. I shuddered at the thought.

Dat pulled a plastic container of Betsy's oatmeal cookies, a large thermos of coffee, and a stack of paper cups from his backpack after we finished eating.

After dessert, Dat climbed on top of a boulder. "It would be fun to camp somewhere up here." He stood with one foot forward and his arms crossed, as if he were king of the hill. "We'd have to backpack in. And stay for a few days."

I wondered how many books I could carry.

"The girls would have to take over the cooking, though," Mervin said. "I couldn't live off salami and cheese for that long."

"Then you'd have to pack in the meat and vegetables," I said. "And the pots and pans."

Mervin flexed his biceps. "No problem."

"You jest," I retorted.

"And you don't cook," Martin said, peering over his sunglasses.

I pretended not to have heard him. "I've read that cooking on a stove and cooking over a fire are two entirely different things."

"And you think if you can't do one you could do the other?" Martin asked.

I crossed my arms. Who told him I couldn't cook? I glared at Betsy.

She shrugged. Levi grimaced.

I turned my attention to Pete. He held up his hands, as if he were innocent.

Nan stood to the side of him, and I couldn't help but notice a hint of concern in her eyes.

Nevertheless, I lunged forward, face-to-face with Martin, yanked his silly sunglasses from his face, and glared into his beady eyes. "Believe me, if I wanted to cook I could." But even as I said the words, I wasn't entirely convinced they were true.

He snatched the glasses from my hand and positioned them back atop the bridge of his nose.

In a near whisper, not wanting anyone else to hear me but determined to change the subject, I hissed, "Is there something you're trying to hide? Or something you don't want to see?"

Even with his eyes covered, I could tell my words had wounded him. For a moment I considered apologizing but spun away instead. He'd never apologized to me for far, far worse. If I said I was sorry for asking an honest question, he'd never think any of the hurtful things he'd said to me were wrong.

I caught sight of Pete as I retreated. An expression of disapproval lingered on his face.

I turned from him abruptly as Dat said, in his diplomatic voice, "Well, well, obviously if we go on a backpacking trip, it will take a lot of thought and planning. I think that's something to leave to the future."

Betsy's recent anger with me returned as she said, an edge of sarcasm to her voice, "Maybe Cate can read up on it for all of us."

"That's enough," Dat said firmly. "Let's get back on the trail." With that the others began scrambling around to clean up the site.

A few minutes later, Levi, Betsy, and M&M led the way again. Pete started off next, but Dat stepped to the side, allowing me to go ahead of him. I trailed Pete, still smarting from my encounter with M&M, and listened to Dat and Nan talk. It turned out he knew the woman who was her almost-mother-in-law and was inquiring about her health and then about the state of her house.

Nan said some repairs needed to be done, including replacing a leaky pipe and a kitchen cabinet.

"I'll send a crew over," Dat said. "Maybe Pete could head it up."

I doubted if Pete was good with tools. He didn't seem the type.

We hiked the next stretch of downhill at a pretty quick pace, and as I rounded a bend, Pete was waiting. I started to breeze on by, but he fell into step with me. "Mind if I join you?" he asked.

"Actually," I answered, "I was enjoying the silence."

He feigned surprise and then said, "I was told you were aloof."

I shrugged.

"And rude."

I winced. "And you didn't believe them?"

"Not from our encounters so far."

Dumbfounded, I ventured, "What about what just happened?"

"They were teasing you," he said. "That was all. And you took it to heart."

His words jabbed at me like a hot poker in a woodstove. I retorted, "Aren't you the opinionated one."

A sarcastic, "Look who's talking," tumbled from his mouth.

"What? You think I'm opinionated?"

"Actually, jah."

I quickened my pace.

"It's no wonder." He was speaking rapidly. "And you're

right, I'm opinionated too, which isn't surprising, considering how much we both read."

Nan's and Dat's voices were not far behind us.

Pete caught up to me and grasped my elbow, matching my stride. It hurt that he agreed with Betsy, claiming I was opinionated. I'd been doing my best not to be a know-it-all.

He released his grip on my elbow and forced a smile. "I was told you were rude, jah, and sullen, but I think they're wrong."

I crossed my arms as I marched along. "Go on . . ."

Pete took a deep breath and then exhaled slowly. "I've found you adventurous." He paused. "And nearly as pleasant as"—he swept his arm wide, toward the meadow to his right, scattered with purple phlox—"the springtime flowers."

I groaned at his odd speech. "Please change the topic or stop talking." I had no interest in listening to such nonsense.

He complied, not uttering another inane word, and we walked in stone silence for a time.

Once we reached the creek, he asked what I was currently reading. Relieved at his choice of a new subject, I told him a biography on Mary Todd Lincoln.

"So you finished Abe already?"

I nodded.

"Being from New York and an outdoorsman, I'm rather partial to the Roosevelts."

"I haven't gotten that far yet," I said.

"I like their wives too," he added, as if he hadn't heard me. "Edith Roosevelt wasn't as vocal as Eleanor Roosevelt, but she had a lot of admirable qualities too. She loved books. She loved her husband. They had eight kids. Their youngest was named—"

"Quentin," I said.

He nodded. "He had a pony named—"

"Algonquin." I interrupted again. "Quentin took the pony up the elevator to his ill brother's room to cheer him up."

He laughed. "Sounds like we read the same book."

"A kids' book?"

He nodded again. "They seemed at home in the White House—what a great place for that family." He sighed. "Isn't that what everyone wants, whether Plain or Englisch? A home. A family. A way to make a living."

I didn't answer.

"I know that's what I want. I think *home* is the most beautiful word in the world—no matter what language one speaks."

Inwardly I groaned. Who knew where his thoughts were headed?

"What do you want, Cate?"

The question surprised me. No one had ever asked me about what I wanted. "I like the idea of a business."

He laughed. "What about a home and family—and a husband first, of course?"

I shrugged.

After a moment he broke the silence. "What kind of business?"

I hesitated to answer, sure he'd ridicule me, but then I decided I really didn't have anything to lose. "A publishing business."

"Magazines?" he asked.

"Perhaps. Or maybe books."

"My uncle Wes works in publishing."

My heart quickened. "He's Plain?"

"Mennonite."

"And he makes a living at it?"

"Jah, so it seems. I haven't talked with him in several years, though."

Ahead, Betsy and the boys had stopped for a break. All four were sitting on a fallen log on the side of the trail. It was big enough that Betsy's feet didn't reach the ground. She kicked her legs back and forth as if she were a child, her dress lifting up and down a little with the motion. They were laughing and all talking at once, except for Levi. Pete and I quieted as we passed them.

When we were farther down the trail, Pete looked back and then cleared his throat. "May I ask you something?"

"As long as it isn't personal."

"Martin and Mervin said you aren't courting anyone."

The pitch of my voice grew shrill. "That's personal."

He ignored me. "I was wondering"—he took a deep breath and then continued—"if you would, you know . . ."

He was nervous, it seemed. Was there a chance he was sincere?

"Let me court you," he stated, his voice back to its usual confident level. "Starting with the singing tomorrow night."

My heart raced as if it wanted to gallop down the trail all by itself. I didn't know what to say, and even if I had known, I was pretty sure I wouldn't have been able to speak.

When I failed to answer, he added, his voice low and soothing, "You can think about it."

"Okay," I chirped.

"Okay?" His voice held a hint of eagerness.

I regained my composure. "I'll think about it."

I gave him a sassy look. He returned it with a sarcastic smile, which added to my growing sense of camaraderie as we hiked along in silence, increasing our speed with the downhill slope. I couldn't ignore the odd feeling welling up inside as I wondered if I could actually court Pete—for Betsy's sake, of course. If I did, maybe Dat would change his mind, allowing her to marry even if I didn't.

As much as he annoyed me, Pete was far more interesting than the other young men I knew, far more my style. But, besides M&M's possible influence on him, something else was bothering me.

"You said you came to Lancaster County looking for a wife."

He blushed. "And to find a job."

"But also to find a wife, jah?" It certainly seemed to be the priority.

"Ach, Cate," he said. "I'm twenty-seven. I want a family. What's wrong with being intentional about it?"

I evaded his question and asked another of my own. "So why not court back home?"

"I tried that. Let's just say I got burned."

"Where two fires meet?" *They do consume the thing that feeds their fury.*

He chuckled. "Ah yes, my attempt at profundity when you abandoned me at the singing."

I nodded but wasn't going to admit I had no idea what his words had meant.

"No, it wasn't fire. More like acid. Splashed unexpectedly."

"Ouch."

"Jah," he said. "It hurt me, for sure."

"But you're over it?"

He didn't answer at first, causing my heart to skip a beat. Maybe he wasn't as available as he thought.

Finally he said, "I wouldn't be asking you to court if I wasn't."

Not sure I believed him, I continued my questions. "But

why me? There are lots of"—I almost said *wealthy*—"eligible women in Lancaster County." I turned to meet his gaze, intending to say *Like Betsy*, but he responded before I could.

"Why *not* you?" His eyes danced.

I had no idea where to start. Just then, there was a thundering of feet behind us. We turned together. Betsy was leading the boys, running out ahead, the ties of her Kapp flying behind her. She grabbed my waist as she reached me, spinning me around.

"Isn't this fun?" She whispered, but the giggles that followed were heard by all. "Thank you so much."

She kept on going, M&M following, and then Levi, who still had a worried look on his sweet face. I couldn't help but smile. It looked as if Levi wasn't as aware as I was of how much Betsy favored him.

Pete began whistling, and I realized I was still smiling. What would it hurt to court Pete? Dat would be happy. Betsy would be that much closer to marrying. I would feel halfway normal for once, as if I sort of belonged.

For some reason I trusted Pete, at least a little. Maybe it was his bookish ways. Maybe it was because he was poor. I could always break the courtship if it turned out he wasn't the sort of man I wanted to marry.

I glanced at Pete again. Still whistling, he lifted his face, his hand on the top of his hat, intent on the rustling trees. I looked up too, trying to see what he saw, and as I did a smattering of rain hit my forehead.

"Oh dear."

Ahead, Betsy shrieked, and the four began to run again.

Pete slipped his pack from his back and unzipped it quickly, pulling out a blue object. In a second he shook it out. "It's a poncho," he said.

"You should wear it."

"No, I insist." He handed it to me.

I slipped it over my head and pulled the top over my sweat-shirt hood and Kapp as the rain pummeled us.

In a couple of minutes the rain had soaked him.

I suggested we stand under a tree and wait for Dat and Nan, thinking I would give her the poncho, but when we caught sight of them, they were engrossed in conversation, even in the downpour, Nan tightly wrapped in Dat's coat.

"Come on," Pete whispered, nudging me along.

I matched Pete's stride as the rain continued, and when it slowed, he asked me how old Betsy had been when our Mamm passed.

"Less than a day." My voice wavered.

Tenderness filled his tone. "So you raised her, then?"

I nodded. "She's been a good girl. Everyone's always adored her."

He smiled through the water dripping down his face.

"Other kids, all the parents, our relatives—everyone has always liked Betsy." I wasn't going to emphasize how little everyone cared for me. "She has a kind heart—toward me too."

"Really?"

I shrugged. "Well, we've had a few bumps lately. But mostly she has." I mulled over Betsy's behavior toward me ever since Dat's edict, wondering how much Pete had noticed.

He changed the subject, interrupting my thoughts. "So why don't you like Martin and Mervin?"

"A long time ago, I did. They were cute boys. I was friends with their brother, Seth." In fact, for a while he'd been my only friend. "But then Seth turned into a bully and M&M followed his example."

"What happened?"

"It started when Seth tackled me at first base." Actually it started the day before, after church, but I wasn't going to share that story with someone I barely knew.

"Tackle baseball?" Pete laughed. "We used to play it all the time."

I shook my head. "He literally took me out. Plowed me over. It was definitely on purpose. And it was ongoing after that. A jab here. An insult there. And then Martin and Mervin followed his example." I took a deep breath. "Then, once we were grown, Seth asked for a second chance and I gave it to him, because I'd been so fond of him when we were young, before the bullying. But he made a fool of me . . . again. And M&M have been keeping it up ever since."

I glanced at Pete as I finished.

He had a sympathetic look on his face. "That's really sad," he said, slowing his pace a little, probably to match my mood.

My heart somersaulted at his kindness. I stepped faster on the downhill, and Pete followed my lead. The rain stopped. In the distance the sun shone through the clouds. Rays of light streaked through the trees.

We didn't speak another word until we reached the end of the trail. I reached out my hand then and pulled him to a stop. "Jah," I said.

"Jah?" He swiped at the water trickling over his brow.

"I'll go to the singing."

He broke out into a smile. "I'll pick you up at—"

"How about if we meet there."

"That will do just fine." He grinned. "I'm looking forward to it."

I was surprised to admit, although only to myself, that I was too.

CHAPTER
7

Once I was at the singing—trying not to look at Pete, who sat on the other side of the room with the other men—I came to my senses once again. I truly hadn't been looking forward to the singing. What I had looked forward to was being with Pete, after the singing.

I endured the next two hours, singing along but not thinking about the words to the songs, sitting as straight as I could with Betsy at my side, doing my best to keep my eyes on my side of the room.

As soon as the event ended, Betsy snuck away with Levi. As Pete and I stood side by side I could feel the stares of others on us, until the warmth rising up my neck forced me outside. Pete followed, and I asked if he wanted to come by our house. That was customary. The man came to the woman's home for a snack, one that Betsy and I had already prepared.

"Sure," he said. "And then I'll walk back to the Zooks'."

"Or I can take you."

He shook his head, a grimace on his face. "Believe me, not having my own transportation is hard enough as it is."

When we reached the buggy, after we lit the lantern against

the darkness of the night and hitched up Thunder, I walked to the right side, bundled under my cape.

He grinned and helped me up, and then hurried around to the driver's side. We spread the wool blanket over our laps and then he took up the reins. Once we reached the road, he barely drove Thunder at a walk. He was either a much more cautious driver than I was or he wanted our time together to last longer. I hoped for the latter. Still, I couldn't help but have some fun. I clucked my tongue and Thunder took off.

"Hey!" Pete held on to his straw hat with one hand and the reins with the other. I began to laugh and then he joined me. Thunder turned when Pete wasn't expecting it, taking the shortcut. The buggy lurched to the side. Pete yelled. I laughed harder, bouncing on the bench as the swinging lantern cast circles of light around us.

Finally, nearly worn out, Thunder slowed, and Pete wagged a finger at me. "The rumors are right," he said.

I flashed a mock expression of surprise.

"About you racing the back roads."

"A girl's gotta have a little fun," I said, coming as close as I ever had, in my entire life, to flirting.

"So it's Wild Cate, then?"

I didn't answer, afraid perhaps I'd given him the wrong impression.

"Just kidding," he said, giving me a sideways look. "But I'm impressed. You read. You talk. You think. You race." He looked straight ahead and muttered something under his breath.

"What did you say?" I leaned a little closer to him.

"What more could a guy want?" His dimples flashed.

I could think of quite a lot. "Cooking. Gardening. House-keeping."

He laughed. "So those rumors are true too?"

I blushed, thinking of Martin on the hike. "They're not my favorite things," I said.

"Well, all you have to do to learn to cook is read. The same for gardening." He waved his hand, dismissing the thought. "I'm sure you could figure out all the rest and become Conforming Cate once the need arises."

I bristled. Conforming Cate—even though I was Plain, I didn't like the sound of it. I much preferred Sweet Cate. Even Wild Cate was better.

Pete clucked his tongue and off Thunder went again. It was my turn to yell—and Pete's to laugh.

Amish parents usually stayed in the shadows when a courting couple came home from a singing, but not Dat. He was smiling like a two-year-old with a lollipop, fussing over the snacks, rearranging the Ritz crackers and slices of cheese on the tray, and then pouring us glasses of lemonade, even though we each already had one.

"Ach," he said, standing in front of us in the living room, the full glasses in his hands. "I'll save these for Betsy and Levi." He started for the kitchen and then over his shoulder said, "They should be along shortly, *jah?*"

"I think so," I said, settling into Mamm's rocking chair.

I didn't bother to tell him they'd left quite a while before we did. I didn't want to think of what they might be doing, my mind picturing the unread books still sitting on Betsy's nightstand.

When Dat reached the doorway to the kitchen he turned back toward us, a smile on his face.

"What is it?" I asked.

"Oh, nothing." He sighed. "I'm just so happy."

I put my hand to my face.

"I'll leave you two alone." He seemed to be remembering his place. "I'll be in the sunroom if you need me." He left quickly.

I picked up a cracker. "He's . . ." I paused, at a loss for words.

"Great," Pete said, sitting in the chair next to me. "He's a good man. And so young. My oldest brother is probably older than your Dat."

"He's forty-two."

Pete laughed. "Burt's fifty-one. My Mamm had all of us within twenty-five years," Pete said.

I remembered there were fourteen boys—who could forget that? "She must be worn out."

Pete nodded.

"How old is she now?" I asked.

"Seventy-two. But my father turns eighty-one this year." Pete looked off toward the dark window. "They seem older than that, and my Dat's health isn't good."

We chatted awhile longer, landing on the topic of books.

"Have you returned the Lincoln biography yet?"

I answered that I hadn't. I'd held on to it in case I wanted to compare parts of his story to his wife's.

He asked if he could borrow it.

"Only if you promise not to burn it." I intended my tone to be light. "Because if you're going to amount to anything in life, you should start acting in a civilized manner."

The expression on his face, which had been happy, wilted.

Still I pressed on. "Because that would be hard to explain to Nan. It's probably a federal offense or something. Burning library property."

He froze for a moment and then stood.

I couldn't seem to help myself, suddenly aware of how much his lack of respect for books bothered me. "Personally, I think burning any—"

"I'm going to ask your father if I can spend some time in the showroom, getting ready for tomorrow."

He'd flat out interrupted me. My face reddened. "Now?"

He nodded.

Had I offended him with my joke? "Dat's in the sunroom." I pointed toward the hall, and Pete headed that way while I gathered up our half-empty glasses.

A few moments later, he met me in the kitchen. He opened his mouth as if to say something, maybe to apologize for being so sensitive.

But then he closed it.

I crossed my arms. "Do you want the book?"

He shook his head. "I changed my mind."

He started for the door and then turned back around as if he'd changed his mind again.

Dumbfounded by his behavior, I blurted out, "What's going on?"

"I had a question I wanted to ask you."

"Wanted?" Had he changed his mind again?

"I meant *want*."

"Well?"

He took a deep breath. "I found a place that rents kayaks," he said. "Would you like to go on Saturday? On the Susquehanna River."

I was a little taken aback. Was he upset with me or not?

"It's perfectly safe. I've gone before, back in New York."

"That's not my worry," I said. Because he'd just turned defensive on me—after I thought he had a sense of humor—

I wasn't sure about going, not at all. "Can I let you know tomorrow?"

"Sure," he said.

As he walked down the back steps, Levi's buggy turned the corner. Pete kept on going, into the dark night, toward the showroom.

By the time I was back inside, pulling the door closed behind me, Betsy was bounding up the stairs and then throwing the door wide open.

She burst through. "Why'd you let him leave already?" Her Kapp was askew and her face was red.

"He wanted to get some work done," I answered, starting the hot water for the glasses.

"I was hoping we could all visit."

"I'm going to bed after I finish these dishes. Dat poured lemonade for you and Levi." I gestured toward the table, but Betsy wasn't interested.

"So did you have a good time?" Betsy's eyes shone brightly as she turned her attention back to me.

"Jah," I answered.

"And you two are courting? Right?"

I frowned. "He asked me to go kayaking on Saturday, so . . . maybe." If he got over his little fit.

Betsy gave me a quick hug and then rushed out the back door to find Levi. After I finished washing the glasses, I told Dat good night.

"Pete's a hard worker, jah? Wanting to get a head start on tomorrow. That's admirable."

I nodded.

"He's a good man, Cate." Dat stood. "I'm sure he's the one."

"Ach, don't say that." I stepped away. "You can't know."

"We'll see," he answered, a smile spreading across his face.

My feet landed heavily on the stairs on my way to bed, still disturbed at the way Pete had reacted and then by his escape down to the showroom to work. I hadn't expected him to be so thin-skinned.

I continued to mull over Pete's behavior the next morning, but I didn't seek him out to see how he was. Dat had gone into Lancaster for a business meeting, leaving Pete alone on the showroom floor. Several contractors stopped in during the morning, mostly doing remodels, which he seemed to handle just fine. Unlike me, he was gifted at small talk. He also wasn't afraid to offer his ideas, whether it saved the customer money or cost a little more.

Just before noon he knocked on my office door, opening it quickly. "Can you help me out?"

I tucked my pencil behind my ear, pushed the spreadsheet to the center of my desk, and followed him into the showroom.

An Englisch woman, probably in her midthirties, was leaned over the counter, scanning a catalog. She wore a tight pair of jeans and a skimpy shirt.

"This is Cate," Pete said. "She knows a whole lot more about this than I do."

"What can I help you with?" I stepped to the other side of the counter.

"Oh." She looked from me to Pete and then stood up straight, pulling her handbag to her side.

"I'll be back in a minute," Pete said, striding out the back door. I watched him until, to my surprise, he turned and smiled at me. Then he pulled the door shut.

The woman cleared her throat, and I turned my attention

to her, feeling a little flustered. "I wondered if these came with a pullout pantry," she said, flipping the catalog pages to the maple cabinets.

They all did. Pete knew that. I turned the binder around. "Yes, they do. We can customize these shelves to your exact specifications as far as the widths and heights of the shelves, how many you want, how deep you want them, and what type."

She leaned a little closer, but not as far as she had been.

"We have several pullouts in our kitchen," I said.

"You live here?"

"Jah," I answered.

She smiled a little. "So you and Pete are married."

"Oh, no." My face grew warm.

She smiled more. "Oh, I see. Well, then, you look at him like you'd like to be. And he's obviously fond of you."

I blushed and glanced toward the closed door, hoping Pete wasn't on the other side, listening to our conversation.

She shrugged. "I thought maybe you and he were the owners."

I shook my head.

"Cute guy."

My face grew even warmer. I wasn't used to a stranger being so forward. I stuttered, "W-w-ould . . ." I swallowed hard and got my sentence out on the second try. "Would you like me to show you anything else?"

"This is good for now. I'll be back once I'm ready to make a decision." She headed toward the exit as I closed the binder. I glanced up, expecting her to be gone. Instead she stood in the doorway. "If I was a nice young Amish woman like you, I'd snag that guy in a heartbeat. You'd be crazy not to."

I put my hand to my face to hide my smile, but I think she

saw it anyway because she grinned back at me, then flicked her long hair over her shoulder and strode out to the parking lot. I liked her—and felt a little sorry for her too. There were so many things I appreciated about being Amish, and the way we dressed was definitely one of them. Being immodest was never a consideration. Or using the way we dressed to push ourselves on others.

Pete must have been waiting for her to leave because he came in through the back a minute later.

"Denki," he said.

"You seem to have a way with the ladies."

He stepped past me, saying, "Only certain ones, I'm afraid."

I wanted to tell him I wouldn't be too sure of that but decided that seemed too forward.

"I'm grateful for your help." He dipped his head.

"She'll probably be back."

He groaned.

"Maybe my Dat can help her," I said.

He laughed. "She'd probably hit on him too."

As I left the showroom, I couldn't help but think of the story of Joseph in the Bible and how he fled from Potiphar's wife. It was hard for me to admit it, but Pete seemed more and more trustworthy each day.

A half hour later, as I walked up to the house for lunch, Addie stood with Betsy on the edge of the herb garden, chatting away. Uncle Cap, in his overprotective role, didn't like her to come over when the crew was around.

Just as I reached the girls, the shop door opened and Mervin and Martin spilled out, followed by a few of the other crew members. It was a chilly day, a little too cold to eat outside, with dark clouds threatening more April showers.

Mervin and Marvin came to a halt at the sight of Addie

and Betsy together. I could guess what they were thinking. Another girl as cute as Betsy. Even though Addie was seventeen, her parents didn't allow her to go to singings yet, and because they were in different districts, and their families were at odds, M&M probably hadn't seen her in quite a while.

Personally I thought my aunt and uncle were asking for trouble by prohibiting Addie from having a normal social life. No one talked about it much, but when it came to Addie, they were the most controlling parents I knew.

Mervin turned to Pete, who was coming around the exterior of the showroom. "What were you saying about going kayaking on Saturday?"

Pete shot me a glance and I shrugged.

"Could we make it an outing? Like the hike?" Mervin clenched his hands together, as if pleading.

"What do you say, Cate?"

I shrugged again. Two weeks ago I wouldn't have wanted to go anywhere with M&M, but the hike hadn't been that bad, except for the comments about my cooking. And Pete seemed entirely over his odd episode after the singing. I was willing to give it another try.

"I guess," I said, intentionally sounding noncommittal. I didn't want all of them to think I was too eager.

Mervin clapped his hands together. "Levi!" he called out, heading back into the shop.

Betsy whispered something to Addie, and then the two laughed. It looked as if there would be three of us couples going. Pete and me. Betsy and Levi. And Mervin and Addie, if Uncle Cap would allow it. That left Martin as the odd man out, or perhaps he'd come along on his own.

The thought of going kayaking made me both nervous and excited. The river was probably high and fast. I'd never been kayaking, although I had seen one on top of a buggy before. I wondered if paddling down the river would give me the same thrill as racing Thunder. That, I was excited about. Going on another outing without Dat and Nan was what made me nervous.

For the first time in my life I felt close to belonging to a group, but I couldn't shake the nagging feeling that it wouldn't last.

My anticipation built as the week passed by. Pete continued to be kind and attentive, greeting me every morning and seeking me out every evening after he put in a couple of hours of work after quitting time. When I checked his time card, I discovered he'd been clocking out at the normal time and then going back to the showroom to teach himself more about the business.

By Thursday morning, I admitted to myself that I'd reached a stage of cautious optimism, something I hadn't felt for the last two years. I longed for it to keep growing.

That afternoon, Levi announced he had to go with his father and brothers to a barn raising in their district on Saturday so he couldn't go kayaking with us. Several times that afternoon he and Betsy conversed by the rose garden. Levi was supposedly teaching her how to take care of the bushes, but it was obvious as they stared into each other's eyes they were talking about other things. After work she told me Levi was fine with her going with the group, and that Martin would be going too.

That evening Dat and Pete went over to the property where Nan lived, to repair the leaky pipe and fix the cabinets in the main house. When Dat got home, he said Pete was as handy with tools as he was good at sales. "He continues to impress me," Dat said, his voice full of cheer.

I hid my smile, not wanting to add to my father's hopes. But I couldn't help but feel the same way about Pete.

On Friday Uncle Cap came over to talk with Dat about the outing. I could hear them outside my open office door. Dat assured him Pete was responsible and that all of us would be wearing life jackets.

"I don't know about those twins," Uncle Cap said.

"They've been working for me for nearly a year," Dat said. "I haven't had a bit of trouble with them."

Then Uncle Cap asked three times if I would be going along, and then a fourth time said, "You're sure Cate will be there?"

"Jah," Dat said. "She enjoyed the hike last Saturday with the same people. I can't see any reason why she wouldn't go tomorrow."

A second later the two bustled into my office. Dat was tall but my uncle was nearly a giant. He was at least six and a half feet tall and almost as broad as our barn. His gray hair stuck up around his head, making his face look even rounder than usual. Although he was my Mamm's brother, I couldn't imagine the two ever looked anything alike. He was only a few years older than Dat but looked as if he were a decade older, at least.

"You're going tomorrow, right?" Dat asked.

I nodded.

"For sure, Cate?" Uncle Cap stepped around Dat.

"Jah."

"And you think it's fine if I let Addie go? These boys—"

"They're fine," I said, hardly believing I was vouching for M&M. "I'll look after her."

"Denki," Uncle Cap said, although his voice still sounded a little unsure. "I'll let her go, then."

He followed Dat back out and shut the door. I wasn't sure if Uncle Cap's motivation to worry was because he had a grudge against M&M's family or because his older boys were wild. His oldest three had quite a reputation for raising trouble. I understood why he would worry about how boys might treat his daughter.

The next day, we left after lunch. Again Pete and M&M carried backpacks, and I carried a bag with a change of clothes for myself, Betsy, and Addie wrapped in plastic bags, just in case we capsized. I assumed the men each carried an extra change of clothes too. And perhaps a snack. We had the same van and driver as before, but this time he sat up front alone and we paired off on the three benches, with Pete and me on the first one. With Levi not along, now that he had the chance, Martin sat by Betsy in the back, leaving Mervin and Addie in the middle. We bypassed the city of Lancaster, heading south and then west toward the river. Betsy and Addie did most of the talking, although M&M interrupted from time to time.

The morning had been overcast with a drizzle of rain, but as we traveled the sun poked through the clouds. The leaves of the trees fluttered, displaying every shade of green imaginable. The faded tulips bent toward colorful annuals lining flowerbeds and spilling over pots and window boxes. Garden after garden showcased rows of seedlings, and the calves danced around their mothers, across the brilliant green grass in the pastures. The landscape sparkled with new life in a way I didn't remember from other springs.

We passed a campground and then a state park. The driver slowed and pulled into a parking lot.

Pete handled the details of renting the three kayaks, the helmets, and the life jackets. He then asked the van driver to return at nine o'clock.

"Does Uncle Cap know?" I asked, a little alarmed.

"Oh, jah. Of course," Pete said. "We cleared it with your Dat too." Then he explained as we all headed down to the dock that the man from the rental place would pick us up downriver and bring us back to meet our driver.

After strapping on a life jacket and then the helmet over my Kapp, I eyed the vessel, wondering how hard it would be to step into it in a dress, but as I watched the man get Betsy and Martin situated in the first kayak it didn't look too difficult. Next Addie and Mervin stepped into theirs, and then Pete and I, with my bag over my shoulder, climbed into the last kayak on the other side of the dock. I quickly slid my free hand down the back of my skirt and tucked the length of it under my legs as I sat, covering the seat. Then I positioned the bag of clothes at my feet.

Between the man from the rental place and Pete, we had all sorts of information coming at us.

We were to keep our weight centered in the craft. If we capsized, we were supposed to not panic, stay with the kayak, find our paddle, and float on our backs.

We told the man good-bye and started on our way.

The other two couples began to paddle in circles ahead of us. Pete told them to wait. On our first try the paddles moved in sync, from left to right. In the water on one side and out; in on the other side and then out. Back to the left; back to the right again. Our movement felt practically effortless.

Once we caught up with the others, Pete coached them through the strokes, telling Betsy she needed to let Martin, who was in the back, take the lead. And then telling Mervin he needed to take charge too.

Addie and Mervin moved ahead a little ways, but we soon caught up with and then passed them. I felt like Sacagawea, leading the way on an epic expedition. The spring sunshine warmed my face and hands. Ahead a blue heron took off from the shore, flying low, his talons dangling over the water. Pete asked if I saw it.

"Jah," I said. "He's beautiful."

The current grew faster. An otter splashed to the right of us, and a flock of returning geese flew overhead.

I looked back at Pete. His shirtsleeves were rolled to the elbow and then pushed up on his arm. With each stroke, his muscles rippled, contracting and then relaxing. The geese began to honk as their leader started toward the marshy area on the other side of the river.

When I turned back to face the front, I couldn't help but smile, with no one to see me.

"Pete!" Martin shouted from behind. I looked back again. He and Betsy were getting the hang of the kayak and paddling hard. Not far behind them were Addie and Mervin. "Wait for us—and then we can have a proper race, down to the bend."

"That okay with you?" Pete asked.

I nodded, pleased he asked my opinion.

We slowed until they all caught up, and we formed a line straight across the river, as best we could.

Betsy called out, "On your mark. Ready? Set. Go!"

Off we went. It was obvious within a few strokes that Pete and I were going to win. I knew the others would chalk it up to the fact that Pete had kayaked before. Or maybe that I loved to race. But the truth was, we made a good team. Plus we were probably both a little more competitive than we should have been.

As we reached the bend, Pete shouted in victory. I turned toward him, and he reached forward with his paddle. I raised mine and he tapped it, a huge smile on his face. "Way to go!" His eyes locked on mine. "You're a great sportswoman."

I blushed but took it as a compliment.

We both looked behind us. Addie and Mervin were gaining on Betsy and Martin, and when they pulled up beside them, Martin poked at Mervin with his oar. Mervin grabbed it and yanked it out of his hands.

"Let's go," Pete said.

"What if they knock each other over?"

"They have life jackets."

"I told Uncle Cap I'd watch out for Addie."

"Knock it off!" Betsy's voice was harsh.

"I'll have to tell Levi he didn't have to worry about Betsy going off without him." Pete laughed. "I think she's getting annoyed with M&M."

I smiled that he used my nickname for the twins and rowed all the harder.

As it turned out, the kayaks stayed upright—at least for a while.

Around four o'clock, we docked for a snack at a state park. A group of Englisch having a picnic gawked at us the whole time, so we soon headed back to the kayaks for the last leg of our journey. Addie fed a few crackers to the ducks paddling along, while both Martin and Mervin flirted with Betsy.

"You take the back," Pete said as we strapped our life vests back on.

I did, gladly, stepping in quickly and again slipping my hands under my skirt to pull it beneath my legs. Pete handed me the bag with the change of clothes, and I pushed it down between my feet. I easily steered us away from the dock before the others were back in their kayaks.

"I like it up here," Pete said after we'd been on the river for a few minutes.

"And I like it back here," I shot back, picking up the pace. And I did—especially watching the muscles in his triceps flex over and over with each stroke.

When we neared our final stop, he told me to slow down and let the others go first. I dug my paddle into the current, pulling against it, spinning us around. The others were lolly-gagging along, chatting and laughing. The air had cooled, but I was still warm from the exercise.

"Want some water?" Pete held a bottle out to me and I took it, taking a long drink. When I handed it back to him, he finished it off.

"So what's for supper?"

"It's a surprise." He put the empty bottle in his backpack and zipped it, grinning as he did. "Are you having a good time?"

I nodded. The peacefulness of the water, the natural beauty all around, and Pete's company all soothed me. I couldn't remember the last time I felt such harmony.

By the time we neared the dock, I was looking forward to dinner, though. And to sitting around a campfire, next to Pete.

"We'll have to carry the kayaks up to the park," he said as Mervin and Addie paddled up to the dock. "And then to the road later."

Martin and Betsy maneuvered to the other side.

"Move all the way up," Pete instructed.

I paddled our kayak behind Betsy's. By the time I started to climb out, with the bag over my shoulder, Martin stood on the dock.

"Let me help." He extended a hand.

"I'm fine." I was okay going on an outing with him, but I wasn't ready to actually trust him.

"Let me get out first," Pete said to me.

Mervin stepped onto the dock and stumbled a little. Addie gave a little shriek. I started to step out of the kayak as Pete put his second foot on the dock. At the same time Mervin slipped and stumbled toward Martin. My plan was to sit back down in the kayak as quickly as I could, but Martin swung his arm wide and knocked me off-balance.

I did my best to land back in the seat, but my center was off, and I landed to the right, on the side of the kayak with a hard knock to my thigh and then a bounce into the river in a very unladylike tumble. I didn't go under—in fact the life jacket buoyed me from midchest up—but the water was icy cold. To make matters worse, the bag slung over my shoulder floated for half a second and then filled with water.

Of course my fight-or-flight reaction kicked in, and because I couldn't flee, my natural inclination was to lash out.

"You idiot," I screeched at Martin.

I knew it had been an accident, but it didn't feel as if it had been. I was back on the playground, shoved away from first base by Seth and landing with my leg twisted under me while M&M pointed and laughed along the sideline.

Martin hollered, "I'm so sorry! Are you all right?"

Pete scrambled toward me, grabbed the rope to the kayak, handed it to Martin, and then stepped in front of him.

"It really was an accident," he mouthed to me. "He didn't do it on purpose."

I exhaled and bobbed around a little, taking in everyone on the dock. They all looked as if they were holding their breath, as if waiting for me to completely explode.

Pete started to take off his boot, as if he planned to jump in after me.

"Don't be ridiculous." As I spoke, I tried my hardest not to bark, but it probably sounded a little harsh, nonetheless. He stopped—his leg bent at the knee, his hand on his bootlace—hopped once, and then landed on both feet. All of them appeared frozen on the dock, their row of faces staring down at me.

"I may freeze, though," I said through my now chattering teeth, "if someone doesn't give me a hand."

Pete quickly stepped forward, grabbed my outstretched hands, and pulled with hardly any visible effort.

I stumbled onto the dock, water pouring off me. Everyone except Pete took a step backward. I turned the heavy bag upside down. A small river cascaded out, along with the sleeve of a dress. I reached inside. The plastic bags had come undone. All of our clothes were soaked.

Pete seemed to recover. "Take my pack," he said to Betsy, "and get Cate up to the restroom. I have a towel in there, besides clothes. Get her dried off." He turned to Addie. "You go with them—but get the matches. And then gather twigs and wood. Start a fire. We'll be up with the kayaks in just a minute."

I followed Betsy and Addie into the restroom, my shoes squeaking as I went. Betsy gave me a few funny looks and, after Addie took the matches out of the pack, expertly zipped in plastic, started to laugh.

"What's so funny?" I stepped toward the biggest stall.

"You."

I frowned.

"I didn't think you'd lose it in front of Pete—but you did."

I took a deep breath.

Betsy kept talking. "But not as badly as you would have

otherwise. If Pete hadn't been here, you would have jumped out of the river and sent both Martin and Mervin over the other side of the dock." She started laughing again. "Now that would have been a sight."

I held out my hand and spoke through my chattering teeth. "Give me the backpack. Go help Addie."

"You don't need my help?" She went from laughing to sounding hurt.

"No." I grabbed the backpack and pulled.

She let go, sending me stumbling backward, bumping against the metal door.

"You know"—Betsy stood at the exit—"Pete's really good for you. You're a whole lot nicer when he's around."

I pretended as if I didn't hear and stepped into the stall.

"Cate?"

"I'm freezing." I fumbled with the zipper and mumbled, "Go away." I wasn't sure if she heard me or not, but a second later the door closed.

I was too cold to cry, but that didn't mean I wasn't overcome with hurt. Betsy's words stung, almost as much as the icy water running down my legs. Maybe hanging out with M&M had made her mean.

But I had to acknowledge there was truth to what she said. In the past I would have lashed out at Martin. And she was right, I would have said more today if Pete hadn't stopped me. The reality of that stung almost as much as the icy water.

I pulled the towel and clothes out of Pete's bag. Below them was a cold pack of food, which I didn't bother to look inside. At this point I didn't care what we were having for dinner.

There was a long-underwear shirt, a pair of sweatpants, a pair of socks, and men's sandals. I smelled the clothes, wary of Pete's vagabond ways, but all of it was freshly washed.

I was going to look like a fool, but I didn't care. I stripped out of my wet things, dried off, and pulled on his clothes. I wrung out mine, over and over, getting every last drop of water out of them and then rolled them all inside the towel.

When I stepped outside the restroom, I said a little prayer, asking God to help me be nice. I was cold, tired, hurt, and hungry, plus I was feeling out of sorts wearing sweatpants and a man's long-underwear shirt. At least I still had my Kapp covering my head.

I followed the smoke to the fire pit closest to the river. The boys had hauled the kayaks up and arranged them around the camping area. My river-logged bag with all our wet clothes had been left close to the fire. I wrung out the clothes and then put them back in, adding the rolled-up towel to the bag.

There weren't any other groups around—probably because it was growing cold.

"Get close to the fire," Pete said, taking the backpack from me.

I obeyed.

"I really didn't mean to do that," Martin said. He was scraping a stick with his knife, his sunglasses still on, his head down.

"I know." My teeth chattered.

"No hard feelings?" He turned toward me.

"None." I clamped my teeth shut, not wanting to waste any more energy on talking.

Pete took the cold pack from his bag and pulled out hot dogs and squished buns. "Give me the stick," he said to Martin, who obliged. He pushed a hot dog onto it and handed it to me. "Eating will help warm you."

By the time my hot dog was cooked, Betsy's and Addie's were also nearly finished, and the boys had started on theirs.

Pete had everyone stop what they were doing while he led us in a silent prayer.

M&M had brought catsup, mustard, and relish, and although sauerkraut would have been nice, it was still the best hot dog I'd ever eaten. I started cooking a second one as soon as I finished eating the first, and took a handful of the broken chips Martin offered me as I held the stick over the fire.

Pete sat down next to me after I finished with my supper, and then inched a little closer until our legs touched. I shivered at the contact but didn't scoot away. In a split second, probably in response to sensing how cold I still was, he wrapped his arm around me and drew me even closer. I leaned against him, my heart thumping, wondering if he could really care for me, especially after the way I'd just acted.

Even though I wasn't certain, a warmth began to grow inside of me. I couldn't help but hope, after all my resolve to be happy single, that I'd been wrong about the direction my life would take.

Betsy and Addie sat next to each other, with M&M on either side. None of them reacted to Pete and me. They must have decided he was merely trying to keep me warm.

"That was good advice to bring extra clothes." Martin nodded toward me as he went on to question Pete. "Are you always so prepared?"

"Jah, I try." He squeezed my shoulder.

"Ach, that seems to be your way," Martin said.

I must have looked puzzled because Martin continued, now focused on me.

"You know, he's pragmatic. Thinking ahead. Considering his future." Martin pushed his sunglasses higher on his nose, even though it was dusk, and Mervin nodded in agreement.

I began to blush. Was Pete courting me for my father's

money after all? I inched away from him, pulling his hand from my shoulder.

"What do you mean, Martin?" I stammered.

"Nothing." He quickly turned his attention to Pete. "Tell us about a time when you didn't think ahead. When you weren't prepared."

Pete answered immediately. "I didn't plan very well when I left home."

"Do tell," Betsy said, leaning forward.

As I listened, I still pondered what Martin had been talking about.

"I let some circumstances get the best of me." Pete made eye contact with me, but I averted my gaze, my eyes landing on the orange flames of the fire.

"How's that?" Martin stirred the coals, and the smoke went this way and that and then chose me.

I held my breath as I waved the pungent smoke away and anticipated him talking about a lost love. I couldn't imagine why anyone wouldn't want to marry him, unless she learned he was after her father's money.

But he didn't elaborate. "I had some problems, with my brother in particular. He'd always been a bit of a sneak, but he took it to a new level."

"We have a brother we had problems with," Mervin said. "But he was more of a bully."

My head shot up.

"Jah. He was always picking on us, something fierce." Martin took his sunglasses off. "We were such nice boys too." He was dead serious—or else more of a deadpan comedian than I ever would have guessed. "Although he's better now that he's married."

"Maybe my brother got better after he married. . . ."

Suddenly I was more interested in Pete's story than M&M's revisionist account. I inched back toward him but not close enough that we touched again.

He continued, "You could say I was a bit of a surprise to my folks. My Mamm thought my brother would be her last, and she spoiled him. Then along I came, six years later, and she was worn out by then. The last thing my next older brother wanted was someone to replace his position, and the last thing my mother wanted was another baby—especially another boy."

He stirred the fire more and then, as if it were a joke, said, "I don't think she ever quite forgave me. Plus to add to the mix, I have a stubborn streak wider than"—he paused and glanced at me—"the Susquehanna. I keep trying to put a positive spin on it and convince Cate I'm persistent, not stubborn. But the truth is, there have been times in my life when I've been downright difficult, through and through."

At the moment, it was hard for me to believe he was all *that* stubborn. I was pretty sure he was doing a humble-pie routine. Maybe *persistent* was the better word choice after all.

I leaned forward, a little surprised at the empathy I felt toward him, especially because I couldn't quite shake my fear that his intentions to court me might not be as straightforward as he claimed.

He continued. "When I left I just didn't think things fully through. Although"—he looked straight at me—"it looks as if it was all for the best." He smiled. "Anyway, back to the story, I was mad one night and gone the next. I'd felt like a failure before in my life but never as bad as then. I did stop to talk to the bishop on the way out of town, and I left a note for my folks . . ."

"What exactly did your brother do?" Betsy was sitting on

the edge of the log now, leaning toward Pete. I was glad she asked. Better her than me.

"Ah, well." Pete seemed a little embarrassed, which M&M must have picked up on. Perhaps he'd already told them.

"That's quite the outfit," Mervin said to me, his voice loud and familiar.

The sudden change of subject caught me off guard.

Martin snickered, his glasses still on in the waning light, and said, "You've never looked so smashing, Cate."

I felt the old defensiveness build, but then, determined not to give in to it, I put one hand at the back of my head, as I'd seen women do in old illustrations, and batted my eyes as I flopped my other wrist and the sleeve of the long underwear, which had fallen over the back of my hand. "Why, thank you, young man."

Both Martin and Mervin laughed. My face grew warm, and not from the fire. I wasn't sure if they thought my attempt at humor was funny—or ridiculous.

The smoke shifted toward me again. I turned to Pete and asked what time it was.

He glanced at his watch. "Eight fifteen. We should get going."

I stood and stepped away from the smoke, over the log and toward our kayak, glancing back at M&M over my shoulder as I did—still wondering at their laughter. Goofy grins had spread across both their faces as Mervin and Martin both made thumbs-up signs and then pointed to Pete, whose back was still toward me.

Flustered, I stepped quickly into the shadows under the trees and then froze, my eyes still on the twins.

Surely I was misunderstanding what was going on.

"Our plan is working," Martin whispered. "She's really buying it."

I held my breath, not sure I'd heard correctly.

"Jah," Mervin added. "She's practically in love with you already."

The fire crackled behind them. My heart lurched as the smoke changed course again and filled my lungs, stealing my breath with its pungency.

I gasped for air as I stumbled back against a tree, stepping on a twig that cracked loudly as I did.

Martin, Mervin, and Pete all turned toward me, momentarily paralyzed. I did my best to act as if I hadn't seen or heard a thing, averting my gaze until Pete's movement caught my eye.

He calmly dumped a bottle of water on the fire. It sizzled and then sputtered. He stood, picked up a stick, and began raking it across the embers, pushing them around the pit.

In a split second, as if coming back to life, Martin and Mervin jumped to their feet and began scurrying around, collecting our garbage while Pete continued to put out the fire. Betsy and Addie stood off to the side, seemingly oblivious to what had just transpired.

I didn't budge until Pete announced it was time for all of us to head up to the parking lot. Forcing myself to move, I scooped up my still-wet bag and then helped him lift our kayak, upside down, holding it with our arms above our heads. On the way I concentrated on the trail in the dim light as the coldness inside of me spread with each step.

Pete's voice echoed inside the craft, sounding a little hesitant. "Want to go to the singing tomorrow?"

So that was how he was going to handle the situation—as if nothing had happened. "Planning ahead?" I answered, my hurt voice bouncing between us. "That's what you're good at, jah?"

CHAPTER

9

Regardless of the fact that I'd read many different times that getting a chill doesn't cause a cold, I had one the next day. And I was thankful for it.

Maybe it wasn't from the chill of falling in the water. Maybe it was from the chill of watching M&M reveal what was behind Pete's interest. Maybe it was from the feeling inside me, one that hurt far more than the worst loneliness I'd ever felt. Whatever the reason, I was too ill to go to church or to the singing that night. Because Dat assumed I was still courting Pete, he let Betsy go without me while I curled up in bed, listening to the rain against my window and trying to concentrate on a book—something I couldn't, for the life of me, seem to manage.

For the first time since I taught myself to read, my mind continued to wander to other things, mainly the image of M&M giving Pete their identical thumbs-up alongside their stupid grins.

I pretended to be asleep when Betsy finally came to bed, and I didn't go to work the next day. In the afternoon, Betsy traipsed up to our room with a card from Pete that he'd given her when she'd returned his freshly laundered clothes. There was a river scene on the front of the card.

"Isn't that sweet?" Betsy said as she handed it to me.

I took it but didn't open it.

"I know you're faking it," she said, sitting on the end of my bed.

I assured her that, even though I'd done such things in the past, I wasn't this time.

I turned the card over. It was handmade.

"Pete's so persistent," she said. "Ignore Martin and Mervin—they're just silly boys—and stop imagining things."

I met her gaze.

"Cate Miller, Pete Treger is the best thing that ever happened to you." She stood, placing her hands on each hip, looking as if she were five. "Don't you dare blow this." She turned and stormed from our room.

I opened the card. *Hope you're feeling better soon. I miss you. Pete*

His handwriting was small and neat, and there was a blue heron drawn on the inside.

I pressed the heels of my hands against my eyes, managing to stop the tears that threatened to fall.

I worked shorter hours the next couple of days, but by Friday I'd recovered, physically at least, and planned to make my regular visit to the bookmobile. After lunch, Pete knocked on my office door and asked if he could go with me. I was a little surprised—enough so that I agreed.

I didn't offer to let him drive. The day was hot and a little humid. I pushed Thunder down the lane. Pete tried to get a conversation going, but I kept my answers short and to the point.

Once we reached the bookmobile, Nan handed me a few books she thought I might enjoy, including a romance.

I frowned.

"What?" she asked.

I shook my head, putting it back on her small desk. She knew I'd sworn off romances two years before.

After Pete checked out a few books, he said he was going across the street to the coffee hut.

"So how's it going?" Nan nodded toward Pete, who was jogging across the highway.

Tears filled my eyes.

"Ach, Cate." She put her hand on my shoulder. "What is it?"

I hadn't planned to tell her, but her sympathy encouraged me. I told her about the kayaking trip and what had happened as far as M&M's thumbs-up gestures and the two saying Pete was doing a great job and the plan was working. . . . My throat thickened. I couldn't say any more.

"What's happened since?"

I managed to tell her about Pete's card.

"And you think he would be manipulated by those two to court you? And then send you a sweet note."

I nodded.

"Oh, Cate. I don't think Pete would do that. Do you?"

"He's poor. He admitted he's looking for a wife. He was interested in Betsy when he first met her—then a few days later he switched his interest to me. I think Martin and Mervin talked him into it."

Nan was shaking her head. "I'm sure he wouldn't do that." Nan's tone was adamant. "I think he's interested in you—for you." She reached out and touched my face in a tender gesture.

I swallowed hard.

"But you should talk with him," she said. "If there's one thing I'm sure of, it's that Pete Treger would tell you the truth. Please give him a chance. He's trustworthy. I'm sure of it."

And *I* was sure Nan was wrong. I stepped toward the door. He stood at the little coffee stand talking to the barista. I turned back toward Nan and asked her what she was reading.

She gave me a rundown of the children's books she'd reviewed for the magazine she wrote for but stopped midsentence. "Look." She pointed behind me.

I spun around. Pete was crossing the highway, holding three iced coffees, in a triangle, straight out ahead of him. He smiled under his straw hat when he saw us, holding the drinks up in a salute.

"I'm telling you, Cate, he cares about you." Nan put her arm around me and squeezed my shoulder. "And I think you feel the same way about him."

"*Felt*," I answered.

Nan shook her head, her mouth turned down in sadness.

A pickup truck that was going too fast blew its horn at Pete. He just grinned and picked up his pace a little faster. When he reached us, he extended the first coffee to me.

"A treat for my Sweet Cate." His eyes met mine.

I blinked as I took the plastic cup.

Nan nudged me as he handed her the second one.

"Denki." I took a sip. Maybe Nan was right. But could I risk thinking, once again, that he cared for me?

I didn't get a chance to ask him about M&M on the way home because he decided to ride into Lancaster with Nan.

That evening at supper Dat asked if I was feeling up to company on Sunday.

"Perhaps."

"I thought we could ask Cap and his family for dinner, although I doubt the older boys will come." None of them had joined the church yet and they pretty much avoided family gatherings. "And Nell too." Addie's aunt, on her mother's side, had been living with the Cramer family since Addie was a *Bobli.*

Betsy brightened. I frowned. That was a lot of people for dinner.

"And Martin and Mervin's family." Dat took a bite of his sandwich. "Because Cap let Addie go on the kayaking trip, I think maybe he's ready to let some hard feelings go with the Mosiers."

I started to ask for more details about the hard feelings but decided to let it go.

Dat held his sandwich in front of his mouth. "As long as we're at it, I thought we should ask Pete and his cousin Nan too." He took a bite.

My face grew warm. "That's a lot of people."

"Everyone will offer to bring something. Take them up on it. We'll do a couple of roasts and make the potatoes." He chewed as he spoke. "I'll run over to Cap's. And I'll ask the others too. Cate, could you call Nan in the morning?"

I nodded, wondering what Dat was up to.

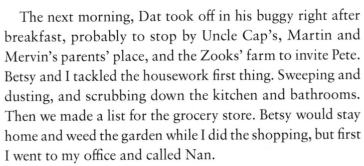

The next morning, Dat took off in his buggy right after breakfast, probably to stop by Uncle Cap's, Martin and Mervin's parents' place, and the Zooks' farm to invite Pete. Betsy and I tackled the housework first thing. Sweeping and dusting, and scrubbing down the kitchen and bathrooms. Then we made a list for the grocery store. Betsy would stay home and weed the garden while I did the shopping, but first I went to my office and called Nan.

She was delighted by the invitation and said she would bring two pies, a lemon cream and a chocolate cream.

Feeling much more optimistic than I had earlier in the week, I hitched Thunder to the buggy and headed to the grocery store. I didn't drive him hard, partly because the tourist traffic clogged the highway.

When I pulled into the grocery parking lot, Hannah Lapp, who was a cousin of Addie's on their mothers' side, and Molly Zook, from the family Pete was boarding with, were walking into the store. The girls were a year apart, nineteen and twenty, and had been inseparable for as long as I could remember. They hadn't gone to the same school as me, but I'd seen them at singings and volleyball matches through the years and at the farmers' market at times.

I tied Thunder to the hitching post and entered the store, my purse slipping off my shoulder as I did. I hoisted it back up and grabbed a shopping cart from the corral, heading down the first aisle, which happened to be the condiments. Betsy wanted to make an apple and walnut salad for the next day, and it called for a mayonnaise dressing. Next I headed to the baking aisle and grabbed a bag of walnuts. We'd used all of ours from last fall already, thanks to Betsy's baking. Next I headed to the produce section for the apples. I saw Hannah and Molly's kapped heads to the right of me as I stopped the cart.

Molly was saying something, but I only caught the name "Bob Miller." And then, "It must be working. He was just over at our place this morning, inviting Pete to dinner tomorrow."

"Did you ask Pete what's going on?" Hannah asked.

"Jah, but he ignored me."

"So what did Martin say?" Hannah's back was toward me as she and Molly picked over the grapes.

I strained to hear.

"He said he and Mervin offered Pete money to court Cate."

My hand shook as it hovered over the apples. It was worse

than I'd suspected! Not only had Pete been talked into courting me, he was being paid to do it.

"And she doesn't know?" Hannah's voice was loud.

"No," Molly said. "But Betsy does."

My heart fell.

"So did Pete take the money?" Hannah's voice was lower now.

Molly giggled. "Not yet. But he's dirt poor. He will." Then
she sighed. "To think Martin still thinks he has a chance
with Betsy."

"Really? Even after she leaves the singings with Levi every
time? If she was sitting any closer to him, she'd be sitting on
his lap. I—"

My hand slipped, knocking over an apple, which nearly
started an avalanche, and I quickly scrambled to shove them
back into place. I didn't dare look at Hannah and Molly, but
a second later, they were pushing their cart toward the front,
both a little hunched over as I picked up the apples that had
hit the floor.

I took a deep breath, willing myself not to cry. I'd been
won back by Nan's optimism and an iced coffee, but I should
have known better. How many times would I let myself be
made a fool?

I grabbed the last few items on my list, including fancy
creamer for the next day, and went to check out the bulk
foods at the other end of the store, away from Molly and
Hannah, but as it turned out, we all ended up leaving the
store at the same time.

"Oh, hi," I said, as if I'd just seen them for the first time
that day. "How are you two?"

"*Gut,*" Hannah answered, a guilty expression spreading
across her face. Molly waved.

"Tell Pete hi," I said to her. "And that I'm really looking

forward to seeing him tomorrow." My voice was incredibly calm, under the circumstances.

Molly's neck reddened and the color quickly spread to her face.

I pushed my cart past them and loaded my bag of groceries into the buggy. I let them leave first, and by the time I turned back onto the highway, I didn't care about the tourist traffic. I pushed Thunder hard again, feeling more like my old coldhearted self each time his hooves pounded against the pavement, beating out the rhythm of *un-lov-able, un-lov-able, un-lov-able,* each syllable taking me another step back to the truth I'd always known.

Betsy claimed not to know what I was talking about when I confronted her as she put the groceries away. "That's ridiculous," she said.

"Are you denying it?"

She shrugged and turned back to the bag.

"How could you? After all I've done for you!"

"Whoa, Cate." Betsy held out the jar of mayo. "Mervin and Martin were probably joking but Molly believed them." Her voice trailed off. "And what do you mean all you've done for me?"

"Taken care of you. Put your every need before my own. Raised you."

She had the bag of apples in her hand now. "Yeah, well, we can talk about that later, after you've calmed down."

"No, let's talk about it now." I held the empty paper bag in my hand as if I were about to stuff her inside it.

"Talk about what?" Dat stood in the kitchen doorway. I'd thought he was out in his office.

"Nothing," I barked.

Betsy put the apples in the fruit bowl, one at a time. "Cate was just having a little . . . relapse. But she's better now."

"*Gut*," Dat said. "Glad to hear it." He headed to the back door. "I'm going to spend some time in the shop today. Sure am looking forward to tomorrow . . ." The screen door slammed shut behind him.

I crossed my arms as the old familiar rage grew.

Betsy hissed, "Don't you dare mess this up." Her eyes were barely slits, her back was hunched, and her mouth was pursed. "The best thing you can do for all of us is forget what Hannah and Molly said. They're just a couple of silly girls."

"M&M are silly. And now H&M are too? My, there's a lot of silliness going on, isn't there? And it sounds like you've known about it all along." I met her gaze. "How could you?" I demanded.

When she only shrugged in response, I spun around in a fury. I marched out of the kitchen through the living room, and up the staircase, wounded to the core by the conspiracy that had been swirling around me. Why, oh, why hadn't I heeded my suspicions? Why had I agreed to play along when I knew I couldn't trust any of them?

I wasn't sure what to do about the next day, so I decided to hole up in my room. I didn't usually read on a Saturday afternoon, but today was an exception. I'd renewed the pregnancy book and decided to skim through it. Ironic, *jah*, considering I'd never experience it for myself. I read about signs of pregnancy and prenatal care. Health care choices and complications. Weight gain and fetal development. Every bit of it was fascinating, except I couldn't quite fathom why I was torturing myself.

Betsy and I didn't talk the rest of the day. I went down for supper—barley and beef soup—but we didn't go to the volleyball game. She didn't ask to, and I didn't offer. Levi was helping to finish up the barn that had been started the weekend before, so I figured she didn't have much of an incentive to go. It was becoming clear that he was the young man she would choose to marry or, more accurately, would have chosen to if the deal wasn't null and void now.

The next morning, I still didn't know what to do about dinner, but I knew it was too late to cancel. After a silent breakfast, Dat escaped to the shop again. Betsy began readying the roasts to pop in the oven, and after I made a trip to the root cellar to gather the potatoes, I started peeling them, something I could manage.

I held a peeled one in my hand. It was cold with flecks of dirt on its white flesh. It looked exactly like I felt. I plunged it into the bowl of water, swishing it around. That was what I needed. To be cleansed of all the scheming around me.

I swallowed hard, knowing this would be a good time to say a prayer, but I was too hurt. Why had God allowed this to happen? I picked up another potato, grabbed the paring knife, and cut all the eyes off, one by one, digging deep.

Betsy stood on the other side of the sink, glancing at me now and then. "How are you feeling?" she finally asked.

"Fine."

"About yesterday—"

"I said I'm fine."

"You're not planning to make a scene or anything, are you? With Mervin and Martin? And Pete? Because if you are, I think we need to tell Dat what's going—"

"I said I was fine." The paring knife slipped from my hand, clattering to the counter and then falling to the floor. I jumped back.

Even though I was a peace-loving Amish girl, I wasn't going to go down without a fight.

I continued to stew over the best way to confront Pete as our guests arrived. Surprisingly, Addie's aunt Nell, who was known as a bit of a gossip and usually visited as much as she could, didn't tag along. She sent her regrets, saying she needed a day of rest. The way Addie's youngest brothers were running around, I didn't blame her.

Pete, along with Nan, who wore a yellow floral dress with a blue sweater and looked even prettier than usual, arrived last. She immediately cornered me in the kitchen and asked me what was wrong. I evaded her question.

The twins' mother, Eliza, pitched in to help while Aunt Laurel stood back and watched. She soon struck up a conversation with Nan. Pete asked what he could do to help, and I bit my tongue to keep myself from saying, *Get lost.*

"Would you go tell Dat everyone's here?" I managed to say. "He's out back with the other men."

Fifteen minutes later we were all seated around the big table. Addie's little brothers poked at each other at the far end, and Dat, Uncle Cap, and M&M's father, Amos, sat together at the other end. Dat led us all in prayer, and then we started passing the food. Eliza oohed and aahed over each dish, pleased that Betsy had made almost all of it, except for the rolls, which Addie had brought, and the pies Eliza and Nan had contributed. I couldn't help but wonder if Eliza thought Martin had a chance at Betsy. Finally she asked what I'd made.

"Nothing," I answered, dreading the rest of the conversation.

"She peeled the potatoes," Betsy offered up sweetly.

Eliza didn't seem to know how to respond.

"Well, they're delicious," Pete said, a glob on his fork.

"Betsy whipped them." I looked away from Pete as I spoke. He sat across the table and down several spaces, and I kept my eyes averted, not wanting to make contact.

Nan, who was sitting in the direction I turned, started to say something but then stopped. I dropped my eyes away from her too and kept them mostly on my plate for the rest of the meal.

Afterward Dat suggested that we have dessert outside. He had the horseshoes ready to play, and there was also croquet. Addie's little brothers practically fell over each other to get out the door. I was pretty sure they planned to make a contact sport out of our croquet set.

The women offered to help clean up, but I insisted they go out. Betsy too. She'd already washed the pots and pans before we ate.

"I'll come out with the pies when I'm done," I said. I knew it went against our principles of community for them not to help, but the day was gorgeous, and the thought of lounging outside in the sunshine must have been much more appealing than spending time in a hot kitchen with a shrew like me.

"I'll start a pot of coffee," I said. "And bring it out as soon as it's done. And I bought creamer yesterday at the store." That was a special treat.

That seemed to do it, because they filed out, one by one. However, Pete lagged behind.

One of the calico cats had slipped into the kitchen, and I brushed it with my leg, turning it toward the door. As it scooted away from me, I knocked the step stool over.

Pete jumped.

It may or may not have appeared as if I'd kicked the stool on purpose. I didn't take the time to upright it, but went after the cat, who had headed under the table. I caught it quickly as Pete righted the stool. I tossed the calico out the door, yelling, "Scram."

Pete jumped again as he stood at the door of the pantry and then laughed. "I thought you were talking to me," he said.

"I was," I answered, holding the door wide for him too, directing him outside. "Go play horseshoes with the men."

"I'd rather help you."

My eyes narrowed as I gestured toward the yard. "Go."

"No," he responded, standing his ground.

I decided to ignore him and go on with my work, turning my attention to the stove. I grabbed a potholder and lifted the teakettle, pouring the boiling water through the coffee press into the carafe.

As I did, Pete scraped the leftover food on the plates into the compost bucket, stacking them beside the sink. When he finished, I ran the hot water, adding soap and stirring the bubbles. Next I plunged the glasses into the suds.

"Cate." He grabbed a towel and stepped closer. "Can we talk?"

"No."

I quickly washed the sink full of glasses, rinsed them, and placed them in the rack. He dried them quickly and put them away, one after the other.

I checked the coffee, gathered up a tray of mugs, grabbed the creamer from the fridge, headed outside without saying a word to Pete, and placed everything on the picnic table. He didn't follow me.

"I'll be out in a jiffy with the pies," I announced. No one answered me, but the croquet mallets cracked ominously behind the apple trees. When I returned to the kitchen Pete was washing the plates, so I started another pot of coffee and turned my attention to the dessert, gathering forks from the drawer and then pulling down a stack of small plates.

As I placed them on the tray, Pete turned from the sink and said, "Let me carry that."

"No thanks."

He started to reach for it.

"I said no."

His hands gripped the sides, bumping into mine.

I flinched, pulling away as if I'd touched a hot burner. "I'd hate to have to pay you for your services."

The tray wobbled, but he steadied it.

His eyes narrowed, locking on mine. "What are you talking about?"

"M&M might be foolish enough to pay for your help, but I'm not."

His face began to redden.

I stepped wide, opened the fridge and took out the whipped cream Nan had brought, then headed for the pies.

"Cate." Pete was behind me, the tray still in his hands. "We really need to talk."

I grabbed a spoon, plunged it into the whipped cream, and then yanked it out, my back to him. "So you know what I'm referring to?"

"Look at me," he pled.

I spun around, the scoop of whipped cream clinging to the spoon in my hand, which I may have been holding in a threatening manner.

He stepped back, balancing the tray.

I held the spoon higher. "I am not a source of income. Or a project. Or a joke." My voice was clear and steady, but my knees shook. More than anything, I wanted to fling the cream into his face.

The timing couldn't have been worse when M&M came stumbling through the back door, laughing. "We're going to walk down to the creek. Want to come?" Martin had his sunglasses in his hand.

"No!" Pete and I said in unison.

"You go," I said to Pete. "But first take out the tray." I pointed to the cream pies and then to Mervin. "You take those." He reached for them.

"Martin, you take your Mamm's pies." I turned around and flung the whipped cream back into the bowl, as if it were Pete's face. "And this." I spun back around, as Pete put the tray back on the counter. I thrust the bowl at him and started toward the living room.

"Cate?" Pete's voice had a frantic edge I hadn't heard before.

I ignored him and headed to the stairway.

"Are you going to the singing?" Martin called out from the hallway.

"Nope," I said. "Not even if you paid me."

Their silence said it all.

Pete's voice grew louder. "Cate! Give me a chance."

I stopped on the landing. Pete stood on the bottom stair, looking up at me, the bowl of whipped cream still in his hands.

"Wasn't the payment from M&M just a stepping stone to what you were really after?"

He shook his head. "I can explain, honest."

"Why would I believe a single word of it? You will amount to nothing—absolutely nothing—without my Dat's money. Which is clearly what you were after all along."

He locked eyes on me one more time, and then he stepped out of my view. A moment later the back door opened and then closed.

By the time I reached my room, tears poured down my face. My heart might have been as cold as a potato straight from the cellar, but my grief was real. It was my comeuppance for thinking I had a chance at love.

It wasn't Dat or Betsy or Addie who came to check on me. It was Nan. I knew by the knock on the door. It was kind, just like her. "Cate?" she softly said.

"I'm fine," I squeaked.

"May I come in?"

"There's not anything you can do," I answered.

There was a long moment of silence. Finally she said, "Ach, Cate. Let me in. I won't stay but a minute."

I rolled off the bed and trudged to the door, opening it quickly, hoping to get the encounter over as soon as possible.

Nan's fair face was flushed, probably from the heat of the day. "Pete asked me to come up. He's worried about you."

"More likely worried about his bleak future," I muttered, heading back to my bed where I settled on the edge.

Nan followed me. "He'd really like to talk with you."

I shrugged. "It's too late for that."

"He said it's not."

"No, it definitely is," I said, meeting her eyes. "And it's worse than I thought. Mervin and Martin are paying him to court me. No. Correction. They were paying him to court Dat's money."

She shook her head slightly. "He said he has a good explanation." Nan's face was full of pain. "If you'll only listen."

"It's too late."

She sat down beside me, one hand flat against the bed, the other on my shoulder, bringing me a measure of comfort.

"I can't put myself through any more of this," I said. The pain was nearly unbearable.

"Love can be scary, sure, but sometimes you have to take a risk, before—"

"You haven't taken a risk again—not in all these years."

"I'm waiting for the right man," she responded. "Which I think Pete is for you."

"No, he's not." I was done with men.

After a moment of silence, she spoke again. "Just know Pete can be stubborn." Even though she didn't say it, I was sure she was thinking *too*. "He gets it from his mother. I just hope the two of you don't let a misunderstanding"—clearly she didn't fully comprehend the situation—"get in the way of your future."

"We have no future."

She pulled me close, our kapped heads touching. "I'll be praying," she said. "For both of you."

She left after that, as peacefully as she'd arrived. If anyone else had told me the same thing, I would have been offended, but I knew Nan meant well. She just didn't know what she was talking about.

I slipped the Mary Todd Lincoln biography from my nightstand and curled up on my bed, ready to escape. I'd survived before after my heart was broken. I would again. One last time.

I longed for a good sleep that night, but Betsy's sobbing kept me from it. I pulled my pillow over my head, but still the sound of it filled my ears. Finally, after what seemed like an eternity, there was a ping on the window. She must have stopped to breathe, because otherwise we both would have missed it.

I was pretty sure it wasn't Pete.

I peeked out from under my pillow. Betsy sat up, took a ragged breath, exhaled, and then hurried to the window. I could tell from the expression on her face it was Levi. It wasn't one of bliss or happiness or even contentment. It was pure pain.

She waved at him, pointed to the back of the house, and then grabbed her robe, her hair bouncing on her back.

I sat up in bed. "Stop."

She glared at me. "He's waiting for me."

"I know you're mad at me. But this is the way it has to be."

She stepped toward the door.

I stood. "You had no right to encourage Mervin and Martin—to not tell me what was going on."

She turned her profile toward me. "I know," she whispered. "I'm sorry. It's just that I truly love Levi. I want to marry him."

I chose my words carefully. "I'll talk to Dat again, but even if by some miracle he agrees, promise me you'll wait awhile. You're still too young."

She shook her head. "I'll be eighteen soon." In two steps she was at the door.

As I called out, "Betsy!" her footsteps fell on the stairs, in quick succession. I turned toward the window. A moment later, she was running into Levi's arms.

I crawled back into my bed, my flashlight in one hand and a book in the other.

I'd taught myself to read, but it was my Mamm who had taught me how to pray.

She told me God wanted me to talk to him, tell him about the little things, and the big things. Silently. Respectfully. Consistently. But for the last two years, since I overheard Seth tell Martin and Mervin—and everyone else gathered around—that once he married me his money worries would be over, praying had been a struggle for me. Tonight was no different.

Betsy returned a half hour later. I shone my flashlight in her direction, and she shielded her red-rimmed eyes.

"Sorry." I turned it off, ready to try to sleep.

Betsy's steps fell across the wood floor, coming toward me. "Scoot over," she said.

I did.

She lay down, bumping against my legs, and pulled the quilt around her. I tugged it back my way. I expected her to lash out at me again, but she didn't.

"Tell me about Mamm," she whispered.

It was what I used to do, through the years, when she crawled in bed with me at night.

Happy with the change of subject, I started at the beginning. "Mamm liked to garden and cook. She was happy and content." Her personality was far more like Betsy's than mine. She always looked on the bright side. I didn't find out until after Mamm died that she'd had several miscarriages and a stillbirth between Betsy and me.

"She trusted God—and she was a really good mother, the best." That's what Dat always said, but I knew both Uncle Cap and Aunt Laurel felt my Mamm had spoiled me.

Betsy scooted closer to me as I continued the story. "As you know, most Amish mothers don't talk about their pregnancies to anyone, let alone their children, and Mamm didn't until that last month. Then she talked about the Bobli—about you—every day. She told me how to bathe and dress an infant, how to change a diaper—even how to give a Bobli a bottle if needed."

We practiced everything on my faceless doll. Because I liked to learn, even then, about anything and everything, I soaked up every detail. The funny thing was, Mamm kept me home from school a year after I should have started. She said I already knew how to add and subtract, and because I was reading, I was mastering English too. She couldn't imagine what I would learn that I didn't already know. She said I had plenty of years to be a scholar, but this was her last year to spend with just me.

Later, once I'd read about premonitions, I wondered if Mamm had had one. If that was why she'd kept me home—because, as it turned out, it was our last year together at all.

"Go on," Betsy said. I was at her favorite part.

"The day you were born started out as the happiest day of my life. Because of all her complications, Mamm delivered in the hospital. Our grandmother hired a driver, and we went to visit the two of you. I held you the entire time I was there. You were so lovely, right from the beginning. Dat was beside himself with joy, and although Mamm seemed weak, I'd never seen her—the happiest person I knew—as joyful. When it was time for me to leave, Mamm said she and you would be home in a few days."

Betsy sighed. Now came the hard part. "But only I came home, with Dat," she whispered.

I nodded in the darkness. The next morning he climbed out of a car holding Betsy. I knew before he reached the house that Mamm wasn't coming home. "I met him in the driveway and took you from him."

That was the day I became a mother. I was the one who fed Betsy that day, even giving her a bottle in the middle of the night. At first everyone was in such shock they didn't realize who was feeding and diapering her and keeping her clean. When Dat walked into the kitchen and saw me giving Betsy a bath on the table, he gasped and called for *Mammi* as he stepped slowly toward me, as if he might startle me and make me hurt the Bobli.

Because her cord hadn't fallen off, I wasn't giving her a tub bath, just a sponge one. I'd told him earlier she had stuff under her chin, like cottage cheese, and my grandmother too, but they'd been talking about the funeral.

"You bonded to me," I said to Betsy. "I've never been more thankful for anything in my life than having you as my Schwester."

I felt her body tense a little beside me. "So what happened that time after church, before grandmother died? When you tackled Seth. When you were still in school."

I'd been eleven. The incident wasn't part of our usual story.

Betsy added, "Is that what Dat was referring to? When he said people thought he should remarry."

"Ach, Betsy, that was a long time ago."

"Jah, but I can't remember the details."

I scooted closer to the wall, until my arm pressed against it. "I'd made you a new apron—back when I used to try to sew. After church, while we were still in the Mosiers' barn, Grandmother yanked it off you and said I'd done a horrible job, that I needed to rip out the hem and redo it. I left the barn." Fled, actually, in absolute humiliation as my grandmother called out, *"You're going to make an awful frau."* "I kind of bumped into Seth on the way out."

"Bumped?"

I cleared my throat. "Well, *knocked* into might better describe it." He'd been standing in the doorway with a group of his friends, watching my grandmother berate me. When I turned toward the door, he laughed and pointed at me.

"So that started your problems with Seth?"

"Basically." The next day was when he tackled me at first base, sending me into the mud.

"And it made the bishop think Dat should remarry. . . ."

I turned toward her. "Jah, but after that I was on my best behavior. And because Grandmother couldn't sew for us anymore, Dat hired that out. We made it all work."

Betsy yawned. I hoped she was done with her questions.

She wasn't. "So why did you court Seth, once you were grown, if he'd been mean to you?"

"I thought he'd changed."

Betsy's voice was matter-of-fact. "He probably had."

Annoyed, I answered, "He hadn't."

"People do, you know." She reached for my hand.

I didn't answer. I was pretty sure they didn't.

Betsy yawned again, and after a few moments her body relaxed beside me. A minute later she released my hand.

My thoughts traipsed through what we'd talked about. Through the years, I went from thinking in Pennsylvania Dutch, my first language, to English. Maybe because of how much I read. But there were a handful of words I continued to think of only in my mother tongue. *Dat. Mamm. Bobli. Schwester.*

Shahm was another one of them. That was what I felt after my grandmother's diatribe—shame—something I'd experienced plenty of times since.

The whole episode with Pete had filled me with Shahm again, the kind that made it hard for me to think, to reason, let alone pray. The kind that made me feel as if I were a child again.

I loved Betsy, but I couldn't subject myself to more shame just to make her happy.

CHAPTER

11

I held my head high and squared my shoulders as I marched down the hill to the shop the next morning.

The crew parted, making a path to the entrance. I unlocked the door and held it open. Martin and Mervin were the first to go through. They kept their heads down. Levi was the last. He looked at me but didn't speak.

After I filled my coffee cup, I retreated to my office and stayed there all morning, not even leaving for a refill.

I heard noises a couple of times from the showroom and made out the sounds of a few cars pulling into and then leaving the parking lot. I assumed Pete was working but hadn't actually seen him. Nor did I want to.

In the afternoon, Dat knocked on my door and entered before I said anything.

"Fess up," he said. "Tell me what's going on."

"About?"

"Well, Betsy has been moping around the house all day, for one thing. And I think you know the reason. And then Pete tells me, just now, that he's giving his two-weeks' notice. He's going back to New York."

I kept my face as blank as I possibly could.

"Did you know about this?"

I shook my head.

"Are you surprised?"

I shrugged.

He put both hands on my desk and leaned forward. "How did you and Pete go from being a couple to this?"

"Technically we never were a couple. We were hardly even courting." I met Dat's eyes. "And if Pete wants to go home, who am I to stop him?"

"Is that what this is all about—you not wanting to leave Lancaster County?"

I shook my head, but he didn't seem to notice.

"I moved from Ohio to marry your Mamm. It was the best decision I ever made, for lots of different reasons. Don't be afraid of change."

"That's not it at all. Pete and I aren't right for each other. We never got as far as talking about . . . any of that stuff."

He pushed back from my desk and stood up straight. "Could you talk to someone about all of this? Your aunt Laurel?"

I shook my head.

"Nan?"

My voice was a near whisper. "We did. Yesterday."

"And she's okay with this?"

I shrugged.

"How about if I talk to Pete?" Dat had his arms crossed now.

"That won't do any good. Believe me." I took a deep breath. "How about if you help me start a business instead?"

He ran his hand through his beard. For a moment I hoped he was considering my request, but then he said, "No." His voice wasn't loud—just firm. "It's too soon to think about anything that drastic." Without another word he left my office, bumping against the door on the way out.

Not able to concentrate, I quit work early, deciding to go for a walk. Pete must have seen me out the window of the showroom because he came to the door and called out to me, asking me one more time if we could talk.

"We did," I answered, meeting his gaze and then continuing on my way through the parking lot. A car pulled in behind me and I turned, half hoping it would be Nan. It wasn't. It was the woman from two weeks before, the one who in my naïveté made me think Pete was a man of integrity. I darted behind the silver maple tree and then to the path that led down to the creek, feeling as if a tourniquet were being tightened around my heart.

As I neared the water, I heard voices. One was Betsy's. I expected the other to be Levi's, but it was much softer. I took a few more steps, then stopped and listened. Finally the second person spoke again. It was a woman.

I kept going along the path, coming around the corner. Betsy sat on a log and beside her was Addie.

I greeted them immediately, not wanting to eavesdrop.

Addie said hello and stood. "You should talk to her, Betsy. Now."

Betsy shivered, even though it was as warm as usual for the last day of April.

"Cate?" Addie motioned to me. "I need to say something to you first."

I followed her under the willow.

She took my hand. "I've been wanting to say this for a while, but I have to say it now. You need to stand up to Betsy."

I whispered. "What's going on?"

"That's for her to tell you. I just want you to know that

you've been letting her get away with too much. You need to stop—"

"What?" Sure things had been rough just lately, but Betsy had never been any trouble.

"You need to think about your own life. . . ."

I nodded. I had been. "But if something's wrong with Betsy . . ." I glanced back toward my Schwester. "I need to help her." No matter what had happened, Betsy was my top priority. I hadn't finished raising her—not yet.

"Cate?" Betsy stepped toward the pathway. "I'm going to head back to the house."

"Just remember what I said." Addie shoved me forward and then left.

I stepped to Betsy's side. "What's going on?"

"You wouldn't understand."

"Try me."

She sighed. "I think," she said. "I think I might be in some trouble."

"Trouble?"

She turned toward me, her hand on her midsection.

Time froze. I thought of the library books on her bedside table that I kept renewing. Had she read them? Were they to blame? Had she not read them? Was I to blame for not forcing her to? "Why didn't you tell me last night?"

"I wasn't sure."

"How can you be sure now?"

"I'm late. Really late."

Betsy was never late. I sat down on a log, hard. "How did this happen?"

"How do you think?"

"Levi?"

She nodded, as if she were about to cry.

"What were you thinking?"

Her eyes narrowed. "That I was going to marry him. But you've wrecked that for me—you've ruined everything!"

I felt sweaty and cold at the same time. "I should make you an appointment."

"I don't want to go to the doctor."

I knew from my reading that it was important for the mother to get prenatal care from the beginning, something most Amish women didn't do. In the end it didn't matter so much because our diet and lifestyle were so healthy, but Betsy was young.

"You need to—sometime soon."

"I want to get married."

I put my head in my hands.

"I'm sorry," she wailed.

"We need to talk to Dat."

She shook her head. "I don't want to talk to Dat. I just want to marry Levi. And then figure everything out."

Although it wasn't common, it wasn't unheard of for an Amish bride to be pregnant when she took her vows. Sometimes the couple confessed and were put under a six-week *Bann*, but other times the wedding took place in a hurry. Betsy and Levi had both already joined the church. It was plausible they could marry. Except for—

"If only you hadn't broken things off with Pete." She was crying now. "Think of how this is going to break Dat's heart." And then abruptly her voice became angry. "If only you'd explained things better to me."

"I tried," I said.

"Not hard enough. You knew all about all of this, right?"

My voice grew shrill. "I gave you the books."

Her full gaze fell on me. Her usual sweet disposition had disappeared. But I knew fear drove her anger. I understood.

She swiped both her hands under her eyes. "Everything was going so well. Everything would have worked out just fine until you decided to take the high road and dump Pete. Now the whole family will be disgraced."

"You don't know that."

"Dat will be devastated. Remember what he said about wanting to show everyone he could keep us on the straight and narrow? That we didn't need a mother to raise us? Remember how you tried so hard to raise me right?"

I took a deep breath. The old familiar Shahm started to wind its way around my throat like a woolen winter scarf.

"You think you've done such a good job with me, but I have to disagree," she said. "And now the entire community will know how you failed."

I wasn't sure if I wanted to laugh or cry. "I never said I did a good job," I answered in my own defense. "I said I always put you first. What I didn't say is how much I love you, and how much your love has given me."

My declaration of affection took some of the tension out of the air, and she scooted closer to me, taking my hand.

"Everyone will blame Dat," she said.

"What are you talking about?"

"For not remarrying. If I'd had a mother, this wouldn't have happened."

For once, I didn't know how to respond.

She squeezed my hand and said, "Would you reconsider marrying Pete?"

I knew I couldn't marry Pete—or anyone—just because Betsy wanted me to. But could I if I thought it was what was best for my family . . . ?

Tears blurred my vision as I stood and started back toward the house, with Betsy beside me.

C H A P T E R
12

Under the circumstances, the best thing for Betsy was to marry Levi as soon as possible. The sooner they married the better.

And Betsy marrying Levi without letting Dat know why was entirely contingent on me marrying someone, and sadly, Pete was my best—and only viable—option.

That evening I sat on my bed and made a list of pros and cons. Besides allowing Betsy to marry, the only real pro for my marrying Pete was that I would avoid shaming Dat. I wanted to protect him. Betsy was right, if our neighbors found out what was going on, we'd be the talk of the district.

I had a whole list of cons. Deceiving Dat. Entering a loveless marriage. Spending the rest of my life with Pete.

I wrinkled up the piece of paper and tossed it into the wastebasket. I knew of a couple of marriages that seemed as if they were for practical purposes mostly. I'd even been to a couple of weddings where I was sure the couple didn't love each other. But it also seemed that none of them despised the other.

I chewed on the end of the pencil. I wasn't sure exactly what happened to those marriages, though, because all of those couples now had a mess of kids.

I'd been determined not to marry just to make Dat happy, but this was different. This was to shield him from Shahm. This was to protect him from gossip and ridicule. This was to keep him from regretting raising us alone.

I headed down the stairs to find Betsy. To my surprise, she and Levi were sitting in the living room talking to Dat. She held an early daylily in her hands, most likely from Levi, but looked pale. I motioned her into the kitchen.

I whispered. "What's Levi doing here?"

"He stopped by to see me, and Dat asked him in." Betsy put the flower on the counter and wrapped her arms around her waist.

"Have him ask Dat if he can marry you."

"That's not going to work." Her voice squeaked as she whispered.

"It's worth a try."

I stayed in the kitchen. We hadn't had dessert, so I started to cut the apple pie Betsy had made that afternoon, once she was feeling better.

"Dat," Betsy said, "Levi has something to ask you."

"Oh."

There was a long pause, and I imagined Betsy trying to communicate silently what she wanted Levi to do.

Finally, the young man stammered, "Betsy and I, we're looking to get married."

Betsy's words overlapped the end of Levi's sentence. "Want to get married!"

"Want!" Levi echoed.

"We love each other." Betsy's voice was back to a normal tone. "And since Cate broke things off with Pete, I think you should allow us to marry."

"Cate broke things off with Pete?" Dat's voice was low.

"Jah," Betsy said. "That's what Pete said."

"I thought Pete broke things off with her." Now his voice was raw.

"Who knows?" Betsy said.

"Cate?" Dat's voice was coming toward me, and in an instant he was in the kitchen doorway. "What's going on?"

"It was mutual, Dat. It just wasn't meant to be."

"He was perfect for you."

My face reddened, but not as much as Dat's.

"I want you to be happy," he stammered.

"I am." But then I started to cry. Tears cascaded down my face, one after the other. I couldn't stop them. I'd cried more in the last few days than I had in years. "I couldn't be happier."

"Bull," Dat answered. It was the closest I'd ever heard him come to cussing. He wrapped his arm around me, squeezed, and then tromped back into the living room, dragging me along with him.

We stopped, facing Betsy and Levi. "The answer, to the two of you, is 'yes,' even though I think you're too young," Dat said.

Betsy whooped.

I knew there was more and stood straight as a pole, bracing myself.

Dat held up his hand. "Wait a minute. I'm saying 'yes,' but not until Cate is married. That was the original plan. And it still stands."

That night, there were no pings of gravel against the glass panes of our window. Around midnight, Betsy pushed against me, and I rolled toward the wall again.

"I'm sorry," she said.

"Thanks," I answered.

"But I just want you to know, I'm sure Pete would take you back."

I didn't respond.

"He's poor. There's not much for him in New York. He'd like to start a business. You know Dat would set him up right away. You might even be able to convince him to start a publishing house—like you've always wanted." It was obvious Betsy had been listening more closely than I'd imagined. "Levi said his parents don't really like each other, but they've had nine kids."

"Betsy . . ."

"What? Maybe you've read too many novels. Maybe average people aren't really all that happy."

I knew she didn't consider herself average.

"What would be so bad about being married to Pete? He's handsome. Smart. A hard worker. Dat's right. Pete's perfect for you."

I frowned.

She kept talking. "Honestly, Cate, you'd have a whole lot more opportunity with him than without him."

Again, I didn't respond.

Finally, she whispered, "Thank you."

I could feel her breath against my ear. I turned toward her, finding her eyes in the dim light of the stars shining on the curtains. "For what?"

"Reconsidering . . ."

"Who said I was?"

She smiled. A moment later her eyes fell heavy and closed. Soon her head was on my shoulder. Then she pressed against me, sending me flat up against the wall.

Love and jealousy wrestled inside me. Levi adored her— and if he didn't there would be any number of young men to step up to the front of the line. I thought of the Bobli growing inside of her, and even though being jealous of an unwed mother was probably a worse sin than being just plain jealous, I couldn't help myself.

I was.

Betsy began to snore—gently, of course. I pushed her a little, sending her on her side, reclaiming a small portion of my bed. I must have slept a little that night, but mostly I thought, rehashing everything over and over and over, from Betsy as a Bobli to the butterflies-in-my chest way I'd felt about Pete before I knew the truth, to the ache I felt now.

For a while my mind landed on Joseph Koller. Was that what I wanted five or ten or fifteen years in my future? It wouldn't be Joseph—but another widower or perhaps a bachelor who would be even more set in his ways. I shivered, and Betsy flung her arm over the top of me, as if to keep me warm.

I speculated about how soon Bishop Eicher would let Pete and me marry. The sheer shock of learning someone wanted me might speed things along considerably—theoretically speaking, of course.

Just before I finally drifted off to sleep, I found a measure of peace with what I needed to do.

"Get out of bed, sleepyheads," Dat called out. Our door was ajar, and a minute later he was standing in the doorway. "Ach," he said. "Are you two ill?"

"No," I groaned, gently pushing Betsy.

"Well, I'm glad to see my daughters still love each other, regardless of all the strife." He grinned. He'd always been a morning person, and an afternoon person, and an evening person. Always happy, except for when Mamm died. The grief had been heavy on him then for several years.

"Up, up, up!" He turned to go. "I fed the horses and cows, but the chickens are hungry." He closed the door behind him.

I pushed Betsy a little harder, and she stumbled from the bed, with me right behind her.

"Go start breakfast." I took off my nightgown. "I'll go feed the chickens." I wanted to be done before the crew arrived.

Betsy yawned and stepped over to the wall, where her clothes hung. "So what are you going to do about Pete?"

I inhaled. For a minute, probably the only one in the last month, I hadn't thought about the man. "You'll see," I said, stepping into my dress.

Even though I knew what I needed to do, I was miserable all day long. Nothing felt right. Not the straight pins in my Kapp. Not the red pen in my hand. Not the thoughts in my head.

I tried to talk about it with God, tried my very best as I stared at the spreadsheet in front of me, to converse with him, to make sure I was doing the right thing. I'd get started all right, but soon my mind would wander, playing over the last month, then the last ten years, then back to Betsy as a Bobli and my Mamm's death. To Dat, stricken with grief. To my failures. To my—our—Shahm. I knew I didn't want all of us to have to go through that again.

I'd decided to broach the subject with Pete. I was certain he'd say no, but I could ask. He was leaving in two weeks anyway, and besides, he already saw me as a fool. At least I'd know I'd done what I could to try to protect my Dat and my Schwester, and they would know that too.

Once Pete said no, we'd weather our storm as a family and get Betsy married. Then I could go back to being a spinster, Nan and I could be on good terms again, and I could eventually bask in my new role as *Aenti* Cate.

The only drawback would be the continued fuss over my single state and the bachelors and widowers who would be paraded through the house.

I sighed. I'd just have to figure that out later.

On my way back to the office from lunch I swung into the showroom. Pete's eyes sparked—obviously he hadn't expected me.

"I was wondering if we could talk after work," I said.

He shook his head, concentrating on the binder in front of him. "Too late," he answered. The day had turned warm, and his sleeves were rolled up to his biceps.

I tried to concentrate on what I wanted to say. "I have a proposition for you."

He actually rolled his eyes.

"I was thinking we could talk in the buggy." It was the only place I could be sure no one would eavesdrop.

"We already talked. Remember?" He flipped the page.

I stepped out the back door of the showroom without saying good-bye. The grief that fell across my shoulders like a soaked wool cape surprised me. Not grief for how things turned out, but grief—again—for what I thought I had with Pete for that short time.

But I'd tried—that's what mattered.

As it turned out, it counted for far more than I could have ever imagined.

As I left the office at the end of the day, fully resigned to being a Maidel, I heard the showroom door open and close.

My desire to turn around and see if it was Pete caught me by surprise. I resisted and kept my eyes focused straight ahead.

"Your offer still good?" he called out.

I stumbled a little on the path.

"To go for a ride." He cleared his throat. "And talk."

I pivoted around, slowly. "Sure," I answered as my stomach churned.

"I have another half hour of work."

"I'll hitch up Thunder."

First I went into the house for a strong cup of tea.

Betsy was working on dinner. Meatballs, mashed potatoes, gravy, a green salad, and applesauce that she and I had canned last fall. Once I sat down at the table, I told her Pete and I were going to go for a ride, to talk.

Her face lit up.

"If he says no, though, I'm calling the doctor tomorrow," I said. "And then depending on what the outcome of that is, we'll talk to Dat and then Preacher Stoltz."

Her face fell.

After I'd rinsed my teacup, she stepped over and gave me a quick hug. "Thanks," she said. "I don't deserve a sister like you."

"Don't say that." I squeezed her. No matter what, our life together was changing. It would never be the same.

By the time I brushed Thunder, led him out of the barn, and hitched him to the buggy, Pete was approaching.

"Ready?" I asked.

He nodded.

I climbed up onto the driver's side, and Pete jumped up to the passenger side. As I drove Thunder down the lane, Dat stepped out of the shop, followed by Levi. Behind him were M&M. I thought the boys had all gone home, but Dat must have kept them late.

Dat smiled and waved. I looked away before I could discern the expressions on their faces, but I was sure Dat's was hopeful.

Once we reached the lane, Thunder began to trot. The pastures on either side looked as if they'd been painted a vivid emerald. Dat's few head of cattle looked up as we drove by. Next was Uncle Cap's freshly seeded field. As we crested the hill of the lane, with a view of the broad valley ahead, to the right I took in the whitewashed farmhouses and barns, appearing as sails on a sea of green.

Once we reached the highway, I turned away from Paradise and headed toward the covered bridge.

"So what's your proposition?"

"Give me a minute. . . ." I couldn't seem to find the words.

"Does this have anything to do with Betsy?"

"Sort of."

"So she can marry Levi?"

I glanced at him, trying to guess what he knew.

"I'm just speculating by the way Betsy's been acting," he said. "But don't worry, I won't tell anyone. Especially your Dat."

I still couldn't seem to speak.

He took off his hat and ran his hand through his hair. "Shall I start guessing?"

"No," I answered, getting Thunder to go a little faster on the highway. I summoned my courage and said, "Have you ever thought about a marriage of convenience?"

He repositioned his hat. "Is this something you got from one of your books?"

I shook my head. "You would benefit from Dat's resources. It would be a win-win situation."

"You're proposing a business deal?"

"Jah, as long as I'm included in the business."

"Say again?"

"A family business."

"Doesn't love make a family?" he asked.

"I'm told marriages—for other reasons—can be long lasting."

"But can two people create a true home, under those conditions?"

I shrugged.

He was silent for a minute but then said, "I see what Betsy gets out of it. Not quite so sure what's in it for the two of us."

"You'd have a secure future."

Pete seemed deep in thought. Finally he said, "And what's in it for you?"

I shrugged. I couldn't explain to him the part about wanting to protect Dat from Shahm without making my father sound prideful. Nor could I explain my fear of the future widowers and bachelors I would be forced to consider. "Well," I said, borrowing Betsy's logic, which was probably a foolish thing to do, "I'd have more opportunities married than not."

That made him laugh. "That's assuming I'd be a *gut* husband, jah?"

The lowering sun blinded me for a moment. "Women are made to bear—"

"Bear or bare?" he asked.

"Their husbands," I sneered.

"And babies?" His eyes were dancing again, as they so often did.

I squinted. "Hah. Not in this case."

The teasing in his voice was gone. "Two days ago you hated me."

I held my breath for a moment and then managed to say, "Hate's such a strong word."

His voice took on a pleading tone again. "We still need to talk about what Mervin and—"

"No!" I could only endure so much humiliation. "I can't revisit that."

He took a deep ragged breath and then leaned forward, as if examining the covered bridge ahead of us.

I drove Thunder over the planks, his hooves drumming a hollow beat over the wood. The light dimmed, and a dove flew out of the rafters, startling me. I slowed the buggy at the turnaround on the other side. We'd gone far enough.

I headed toward home. I couldn't think of anything else that needed to be said, so I asked if I should drop him off at the Zooks'.

"At the grocery is *gut*. I have a few things to pick up."

After I pulled into the parking lot and stopped, Pete jumped down.

I cleared my throat.

"Do you need something?" He nodded toward the store.

"An answer."

"Ah." He walked around to my side of the buggy and looked at me, his eyes searching my face.

I looked away.

"Can you give me until tomorrow?" he asked.

"Sure," I said, snapping the reins.

Pete jumped away.

I fought back tears as I pulled back onto the road, trying not to think about the fun Pete and I'd had before I knew the truth. My mind kept playing it over though, again and again.

When I reached our driveway, Betsy came running down from the garden. I stopped the buggy and she jumped in, riding along to the barn.

"So?" she asked.

"He's going to tell me tomorrow."

Her face fell. "What do you think his answer will be?"

"I don't know," I said, parking the buggy. A week ago, I thought I could read Pete, but now I had no idea what he might decide.

Betsy walked back toward the house, stooping over to pick a couple of sweet pea blossoms growing along the fence, and then twirling them in her hand as she continued. I watched her for a couple of minutes, and then unhitched Thunder and led him to the barn.

When we reached his stall I buried my head against his neck, breathing in the musty smell of horse mixed with the scents of hay and oats and dust and leather. I longed for the way my life used to be. Before Dat's edict.

Before Pete Treger came to Lancaster County.

C H A P T E R
13

As much as I wanted Pete's answer, I didn't have the courage to seek him out the next morning. Instead I wallowed in my misery as I went about my work. Not only did I feel sick to my stomach about Pete's possible answer, but just the thought of Betsy's predicament made me feel queasy too. At eleven thirty, I hurried up to the house, ate my dinner quickly, and then snuck into the sunroom and finished the biography on Mary Todd Lincoln.

I felt even more despondent after turning the last page. She wore black from the time President Lincoln was assassinated until the day she died, living in perpetual grief. All of her children except her oldest son, Robert, passed away before she did, and her relationship with him was strained until the very end. Her life turned out to be one of despondency and despair. I couldn't help but wonder how much better off she would have been if she would have married someone else, say Stephen Douglas. Or not married at all. Even if two people loved each other, there was no guarantee of happiness.

The back door slammed, and footsteps fell across the kitchen floor. I could tell by the soft landings it was Betsy, even though I couldn't see her.

"Pete wants to talk with you!" She called out, her voice full of cheer.

I clutched the book to my chest, paralyzed by fear at the thought of both a "yes" from him and the resulting loveless marriage and a "no" and our family's shaming. If only I knew how my life would end up—if only I could read my biography now—I'd know which one to hope for.

"Cate?!"

"Back here," I managed to answer.

In a second, she stood in the doorway, beaming. "He's waiting. Come on!"

The book slipped from my hands to the couch. I left it there and let Betsy drag me through the house, chatting as she did. "Remember to smile. And be pleasant."

"Did he tell you what he's decided?" We were halfway through the kitchen.

"No. But I have a good feeling about this." She practically shoved me out the back door, closing it behind me. I was certain her positive impression was wishful thinking.

Pete stood beside the vegetable garden, gazing down at the pumpkin seedlings.

I approached. He didn't raise his head. I cleared my throat.

His straw hat was pulled down on his forehead, but even under its shadow he looked pale.

"Betsy said you were looking for me."

He crossed his arms. "Yes."

My voice quavered as I spoke. "Yes, you are looking for me?"

"That too. But, yes . . ." His face was as stoic as could be, giving off absolutely no emotion. "I'll marry you."

I swallowed hard and then managed to sputter, "Are you sure?"

He dipped his head, enough that the brim of his hat nearly hid his eyes. "Sure enough."

My throat thickened. I hadn't considered how I would respond if he agreed, but with no joy involved it felt hollow. "Okay. So, then . . ." My voice trailed off.

Pete rubbed the side of his face with his hand. "I already wrote to my bishop back home. Mailed it this morning. I asked him to send the letter."

It was called the *Zeugnis*, and it affirmed that the groom-to-be was a church member in good standing.

"When I deliver it to your bishop, I'll say we want to marry as soon as possible."

"Because?"

"I need to get back to New York. I want to take you with me."

I couldn't leave. I needed to help with Dat's business. And get Betsy married. Besides, Lancaster County was home.

"You want to live in New York?" I sputtered.

"Probably not." His gaze shifted beyond me. "I'll figure that part out later."

I couldn't help but note his use of the singular pronoun *I* instead of the plural *we*.

"I told my bishop I was eager to get back home. I imagine he'll send the letter within a couple of days." He met my eyes.

I dropped my gaze, saying, "I'll make sure the guest list is small. I won't let Dat go hog-wild."

He shrugged. "Do what you want. It doesn't matter to me. I'll talk with your Dat soon, though. To ask him if I can stay on until we leave for New York. And to ask his permission."

My eyes narrowed. "What will you tell him?"

"The truth. That we'd like to marry."

"The partial truth?"

He shrugged again.

The whole truth was stranger than fiction and would break Dat's heart. For a moment I didn't know whether I wanted to laugh or cry. I opted for neither and instead asked again, "Are you sure?"

"Jah," he said. "I might be stubborn, but I'm a pragmatist at heart."

I cocked my head, remembering he'd said that before, about tossing—or burning—the pages he'd read. I supposed a man who could burn books might be audacious enough to agree to a marriage of convenience. I couldn't help but ask, even though I had a hard time getting the words out, "Enough to . . . you know . . . Because it'll strictly be a marriage of convenience."

"Enough to live a life of celibacy?"

I gave him a half nod, thankful he caught on quickly.

He looked off into the distance. "I have thus far. And I know other men who manage to do it." He shrugged, his eyes still focused in the distance. "So I guess so."

I wasn't sure how to respond to that. From what I'd read, I didn't think most men would agree to such an arrangement. Obviously he didn't want an intimate relationship with me, but I was surprised he was willing to give up hope of having a conventional marriage with someone else. I blushed.

"I need to get back to work," I finally said.

"Me too," Pete replied, rubbing his mostly healed chin. Soon it would be covered with a beard. He still didn't look me in the eye. "I'll talk to your Dat this afternoon."

We walked side by side down the brick pathway as a cloud drifted away from the sun, brightening the day even more. The scent of blooming lilacs filled the air from the bush beyond the garden. A robin flew toward the silver maple, a worm dangling from her beak. I was certain I could make out the chirping of baby birds.

I stopped abruptly, wanting to shake my fist at all that was good and true and right. At the hope of spring. At the natural order of the world—that I wasn't part of.

Pete didn't seem to notice my angst at all and veered off toward the showroom without saying good-bye.

By the time I reached my desk, my legs shook. By the time I collapsed in my chair, my heart raced. Had I really just committed to marrying a man I didn't love? I'd be sharing a home—but at least not a bed—with a husband who didn't love me. I'd been so sure I was making a rational choice, but now I wasn't sure if altruism or stupidity drove my buggy. Only time would tell.

Of course Betsy was in my office a few minutes later, grilling me for information. I told her I would talk with her later. I didn't want to discuss it before Pete had spoken with Dat.

Betsy left with a pout on her face, while I did the best I could to concentrate on my work.

Just as I was filing my last report of the day, Dat eased open my office door. "Got a minute?" he asked.

"Sure." My heart began to race again.

His brows were drawn together and his forehead wrinkled. He pulled the folding metal chair from against the wall up to my desk, sat, and placed both of his palms down on the wood, between the two of us. "Pete just spoke with me." His voice was solemn.

I nodded.

"Cate, what's going on?"

I did my best to sound cheery. "We want to get married."

"That's what Pete said. He asked my permission."

"And?"

Dat stared at me for a long moment. "You've been acting funny."

I responded quickly. "I'm fine."

He stroked his beard, searching my face.

"It's just nerves," I said.

"Just a few days ago you told me the two of you were never a couple. That you hadn't even been courting and—"

"That was nerves too."

He closed one eye, as if he were sizing a piece of wood.

"You said once you and Mamm knew after you'd only known each other a week."

He nodded. "That's true."

I tried to smile, but it felt more like a grimace.

The mention of Mamm must have convinced him, because he stood and stepped around the side of my desk, wrapping me in a hug and pulling me from my chair. "As long as you're sure . . ."

"Jah," I managed to squeak.

"Well, then, I'll stop my worrying and give Pete my blessing." He released me as he spoke. "Have you told Betsy?"

"Not yet."

"Let me. At dinner. Tonight." As the door swung shut behind him, I sank back in my chair.

Unable to concentrate on work any longer, I closed the files on my desk and placed them atop my inbox. I took out a legal pad and wrote *Wedding* at the top. Amish weddings were anything but simple. Sure, there was no fancy dress to purchase or five-tiered cake to order. But the average bride and groom invited three to six hundred guests. Ours, however, wouldn't be that big—not anywhere close. I started to jot down names. Uncle Cap and Aunt Laurel and their brood, the families in our district . . . I wrote down *Pete's parents* and *13 brothers.* That meant he probably had thirteen sisters-in-law and lots and lots of nieces and nephews. I wondered if they would all come. I guessed not. Probably just his folks and one or two brothers.

I put my pencil down and rubbed my eyes. If Mamm were alive she would help me with all of the preparation. She would ask relatives and friends to cook the chickens and make the potatoes. She would round up teenage boys to be the *Hoestlers* for the guests' horses and men to set up the benches and tables. If Mamm were alive . . . I probably wouldn't be in this predicament at all. I swiped at a tear.

An hour later Dat, Betsy, and I sat around our big table as Dat led us in a silent prayer. Betsy had fixed meatloaf and baked potatoes, carrot and raisin salad, and green beans and pickled beets from what we'd canned last summer. The delicious smells and my anxious thoughts distracted me from the prayer, and before I knew it, Dat said, "Amen."

Immediately, Betsy said, "So?" Her eyes were as bright as her smile.

I plunged the serving spoon into the salad.

Dat leaned back in his chair and beamed. "Your sister is getting married."

Betsy jumped from her chair and wrapped her arms around me. "Denki," she whispered, her mouth against my ear. Then she squealed, "I'm so happy for you!"

I patted her arm.

Dat frowned. "Why is it, Cate, that we're all more excited than you are?"

"It's just my way, I guess," I said, patting Betsy's arm again, this time with a little more enthusiasm.

"You're absolutely sure?"

"Of course she is." Betsy scooted back on to her chair.

"What girl wouldn't be thrilled to marry Pete Treger?" After a quick breath, Betsy said, "We need to start planning. I'll help," she said. "You know, do everything a mother would do. Ask people. All of that." Betsy dished up a spoonful of beets. My cheerful Schwester was back.

"I want it small, so—"

"Why?" Betsy passed the bowl on to Dat.

"Well, you know. We want it to be soon."

"Oh." Betsy blushed.

"Pete wants to go to New York. . . ."

"To live?" Betsy gasped.

Dat put the bowl of beets down hard, and a little splashed over the side. Betsy was on her feet in a split second, retrieving the dishcloth to wipe it up before it stained the table.

"I don't think so," I said.

"Just to visit, probably," Dat said, "is what Pete said."

"Oh, thank goodness." Betsy gave me a wary look.

It didn't make sense for Pete to want to stay in New York. Not if he wanted Dat to set us up in a business here. I hadn't taken a bite of food. I mashed the end of my baked potato with my fork and then pushed it around my plate a bit. I didn't think I could manage to swallow.

Thankfully Betsy chattered away about the wedding. "I've been thinking about it all day. You won't have to worry about a thing."

If only it were that simple.

The days slowly crept by, one by one. Betsy seemed to be doing better, buoyed by the upcoming wedding and the hope that her problems would soon be over. A couple of times I asked her how she felt, and she simply answered, "Fine."

Pete was cordial with me but didn't make an effort to talk. I figured he wouldn't until the letter arrived from his bishop. Then we could speak with Bishop Eicher and have the wedding published—announced at church—as soon as possible.

By Friday I was as restless as I'd ever been in my entire life, but for once I was leery of going to the bookmobile. I wasn't sure I could face Nan and not tell her what was going on. But by midafternoon, I talked myself into it. Surely she wouldn't have heard anything unless Pete had told her, and I couldn't quite imagine that.

It was the Friday for her to be north of Paradise, not the location closest to us. As I left my office, Dat called for me from his.

"Off for some books?" he asked.

"Jah."

"Tell Nan hello," he said.

I told him I would.

"Is Pete going with you?"

I shook my head.

"He can if he wants to. Tell him the boss says he can leave an hour early. I can cover the showroom."

"Okay." I told Dat good-bye and then started for the barn, intending to ignore Dat's instructions, but my conscience got the best of me. I backtracked and then veered left, into the showroom. Pete stood at the counter, filling out a form. His face seemed paler than usual, and he appeared tired.

"Want to go to the bookmobile? Dat said he'd cover the showroom."

He put his pen down. "Do you want me to go?"

I shrugged. "It was Dat's idea."

He held my gaze. I shifted my feet and then looked away.

Finally he said, in a subdued voice, "I think your Dat has enough to do without adding my work to his load."

"Suit yourself," I said, relieved not to have to spend the time with him.

I arrived just as Nan was pulling down the steps to the panel van. I returned my books, including the biography of Mary Todd Lincoln.

She handed me biographies of Andrew and Eliza Johnson.

I thanked her and started browsing through the shelves as she tucked a pencil behind her ear.

Nan cleared her throat. I turned toward her.

"I had a phone call last night," she said. "From New York."

My heart began to race. "Oh?"

"From Pete's mother."

I hugged the books against my chest.

"Is it true?" Nan's voice was low. "That you and Pete are getting married."

I nodded my head like a marionette.

"I thought you two stopped courting."

"We changed our minds," I squeaked.

"Do you love him?"

I didn't answer. The truth was, at one point I thought I might, or at least thought I could. But now I knew I wouldn't love someone who didn't love me. I certainly wasn't going to confess to Nan that we'd decided on a marriage of convenience, a decision based on a bribe, Betsy's needs, honoring Dat, and Pete's destitution.

"Cate?"

My eyes filled with tears, and I quickly stepped away.

"I have a verse for you," she said. "It's in Proverbs, from a modern translation. It goes something like this, 'Under three things the earth trembles, under four it cannot bear up . . .

including an unloved woman who is married. . . . '" She took a step closer to me. Her eyes were kind and sincere. "I don't know what's going on with you and Pete, but if either of you doesn't love the other, please don't marry."

I averted my gaze and pretended to be looking at the top shelf of books. "What did you tell his mother?"

Nan didn't answer, and for a long moment I could only imagine what she'd relayed. Finally, she said, "Well, I couldn't answer any of her questions about your relationship with Pete, because I don't know. I concentrated on what I do know. That you are a smart, resourceful, and beautiful young woman."

I leaned my forehead against the metal bookcase.

"And that, yes, your father is quite wealthy." Nan sighed. "That was actually her first question."

"Pete must have told her." I imagined him calling his folks or perhaps writing a note. My heart dropped, again, at my ongoing realization of being nothing more than a dowry to Pete.

I managed to ask if Pete's mother said whether or not his family would come to the wedding.

"She said she and Pete's father would like to, and perhaps one of his brothers." She took her pencil out from behind her ear and gripped it tightly.

I thanked Nan for the information and continued my search for books, although it was a lackluster hunt for once. Nan sat at the little desk and did paperwork while I browsed the shelves. I ended up checking out only half a dozen books.

As I got ready to leave, she said, "See you next week."

"I don't think so," I answered. "I've got a lot to do."

"Wedding preparations?"

"Jah." I slipped the books into my bag. "We'll let you know as soon as we have a date."

She pursed her lips.

"In case you want to come . . ."

She nodded.

I left quickly, feeling like a fraud. I imagined Nan at our wedding, quoting the verse from Proverbs when the preacher asked if anyone had an objection to us marrying.

Clearly she disagreed with what we were doing, but anything she believed was purely speculation—and spot-on intuition. I had no idea how far she might take it.

C H A P T E R

14

The letter came back from Pete's bishop the next week, and I couldn't help but think that his people were as anxious to see him a groom as mine were to see me a bride.

That was confirmed when our district deacon, Stephen Ruff, came to call. He assisted in marriage arrangements, besides seeing to the needy in the district. Dat and Betsy vanished as soon as the man appeared on our porch. I asked him in and offered him a cup of decaf and a slice of Betsy's banana cream pie. He accepted both.

We sat at the kitchen table—me picking at the whipped topping on mine, barely able to concentrate, while he devoured his pie. I quickly offered him a second piece, which he accepted.

He asked all the usual questions, starting with, "So you want to marry Pete Treger."

I nodded, barely.

His face reddened a little. "And you've remained pure during your courtship?"

I swallowed a laugh and simply nodded again.

Then he asked if there was any reason for us to marry so soon besides the need to go to New York.

I shook my head.

"You won't have time to plan a big wedding."

"Jah," I answered. "That's fine with us."

Most Amish weddings took place in the fall, but there were so many in that season that some guests were invited to four or five in one day. It wasn't common, but it wasn't forbidden, either, to have a spring or summer wedding.

"Well, then," he said, "I'm not used to you being so quiet, but nevertheless, I accept all your answers. I'll publish your wedding this Sunday."

"Denki," I managed to say.

"How soon would you like the wedding to be?"

"Two weeks."

"You're that prepared?"

"Jah." We would be, thanks to Betsy.

He took the last bite of his pie, declared it delicious, and stood. "Tell Bob hello. And congratulations."

As I walked him to the door, I felt certain he hoped to have the whole wedding said and done before Pete came to his senses.

A moment later Betsy came through the back door and into the living room, a notepad in her hand. "Is everything *gut*?" She was breathless.

"Jah," I answered.

"Then let's get to work!" She took my hand and pulled me into the kitchen. First she cleared the deacon's plate and my unfinished pie. Then she ordered me to sit.

"So I made a list of people to invite. I kept it to two hundred," she said. "I hope you don't mind."

"Not at all," I said. The fewer people who were there to witness my deception, the better I'd feel.

"I'll ask the chicken cooks and potato cooks tomorrow. It's too late to get chicks to raise for fryers, but I'll order what we need through the grocery." She smiled. "It will save Pete some work." Usually the groom butchered the chickens. "I'm assuming the deacon will arrange for the church wagon, but I'll double-check."

Betsy chattered on and on, jotting down notes as she did. She would make my dress for me—blue to match my eyes. Addie and she would be my attendants—my *Newehockers* or side sitters, as they were also called. Dat would invite everyone in our district at services on Sunday. There were a few others, including Nan, that Pete and I would need to invite in person.

By the time we were done Betsy had filled pages and pages with notes. Thankfully, when it was time for her to marry I could simply redo what she was doing for me.

That was all the more reason for us not to stay in New York for long. I would need to get back to help with Betsy's wedding, however it worked out, as soon as possible.

By the time Dat came into the house, my eyes had glazed over.

"Well, well, well," he said, standing at the head of the table. "We should get started on the planning."

"It's all done," Betsy said. She tore a piece of paper from her tablet. "Here's your list." She handed it to him with a flourish.

Dat took it with a grand gesture. "Mission accomplished," he said.

I groaned.

He wrapped his arm around me. "This is going to be the best thing that's ever happened to you." His beard tickled my neck. "Just wait and see."

The next two weeks were a blur of activity. I tried to stay in my office as much as I could, but even though every aspect of an Amish wedding is prescripted and expected, Betsy kept dragging me into the details of the planning.

I allowed Pete to drive when we took the buggy to Nan's house to invite her. I noted he was still clean-shaven. Usually the groom began growing out his beard in anticipation of the wedding. I couldn't help but wonder if maybe he didn't intend to go through with it at all and asked him as much.

"I gave you my word," he said, turning Thunder into Nan's driveway.

She came out to meet us, and when we announced our wedding she simply said she would be there to support us. I'd expected her to challenge us and breathed a sigh of relief when we left. On the way home, I asked Pete if his family would need to stay at our house, and he simply said no.

I asked how many of them were coming, and he said his mother hadn't gotten back to him yet about his brothers and their families. "I don't imagine they'll come, though, except my oldest brother, maybe. I expect he'll travel with my Mamm and Dat." He kept his eyes on the road.

"And where will they stay?"

"The Zooks said they had room."

"What about your uncle? The one with the publishing business." He was the relative of Pete's I was looking forward to meeting the most.

"Uncle Wes?" He glanced at me quickly.

I nodded.

Pete rubbed his chin. "I doubt he even knows about the wedding."

Perhaps Pete thought the fewer of his folk who met me the better. I kept quiet the rest of the way home, feeling absolutely alone.

Sure, Pete acted cordially toward me. He continued to be a

gentleman. But I couldn't help but miss the banter of our past trips, the talk of books, and the snippets we'd shared about our lives. How would I endure the loss of that for a lifetime?

The day before the service, Betsy mixed up the filling for fifteen apple pies. I peeled and sliced the apples while she made the dough for the crusts. After I had a gallon of slices, she cooked them until they were nearly soft and then thickened it all up, adding butter and vanilla when she was done. Other women would also bring desserts, mostly cookies and cakes.

Oftentimes the groom would stay at the bride's parents' house the night before the wedding, but because his parents would be at the Zooks' place, I didn't think Pete would want to stay at ours. Besides, it would be more comfortable for me not to have him in our home. The less Dat saw Pete and me together before the wedding, the better.

That evening, while we were setting up the benches delivered in the church wagon, Dat asked me where Pete was.

"With his family," I said.

Dat seemed to be fine with that. "Must have been quite a shock to them to have Pete getting married—and so soon," he said. "At least we know Pete's a good person. They have no idea about you."

I knew Dat was joking, but I wasn't in the mood to laugh. I did manage to smile, though.

"I hope you're okay with a smaller wedding," he said.

"Of course." Weddings in Lancaster County were getting so large, more and more often families held them in places like cleaned-out shops to accommodate all the guests. Although we would need two sittings at the meal, we would be able to handle all of the invited guests in the house. And because it was late May, if the weather held, people could spill out onto the lawn and the grounds.

Sadness gripped me as I retreated to my room that night. I walked to the window and looked out over the yard, my eyes falling on the silver maple tree, which was fully leafed out now. Beyond it was the creek. Over the next hill was the cemetery where Mamm was buried.

"I'm sorry," I whispered. How ironic that my getting married was pleasing others but pressed on me like a heavy weight. And the thing was . . . most of them wouldn't have cared if they knew I didn't love Pete and that he didn't love me. They just wanted me married.

But my Mamm would have cared. And Dat would too, if he knew. And Nan cared.

I caught Dat out of the corner of my eye, walking toward the church wagon. When he reached it, he opened the bottom compartment and pulled out a stack of pans. As he turned toward the house, he looked tired . . . or sad. Or maybe both.

"What are you looking at?" Betsy had just stepped into our room.

"Just thinking," I said, turning toward her.

"About?"

"Leaving."

"You'll be back. Dat's talking about building a *Dawdi Haus* for himself."

"He shouldn't," I said. The house was plenty big enough for Pete and me to live with him when we came back.

Betsy put her arm around me. "I didn't expect this to be sad," she said.

In a firm voice, I said, "Don't get sentimental." If she started to cry, I was apt to fall apart.

"You're the best big sister ever," she said.

I leaned my head toward her. "How are you feeling?"

She pulled away. "I still need to hem your dress. Try it on, okay?"

"Betsy . . ."

"I'm not going to talk about any of that now. Tomorrow's your wedding." She marched out into the hall, presumably to her sewing room, and returned with my dress.

"It looks lovely," I said, taking it from her and putting it on.

She pinned the hem quickly, and neither one of us talked, except for her to tell me when to turn. When she'd finished, I took it off and handed it to her. "Want me to keep you company?"

She shook her head, a pin still in the corner of her mouth. "You'll only make me sad. Get some rest."

I could hear the whir of her treadle sewing machine as I tried to sleep. Sometime later she crawled into bed beside me.

"I'll miss you," she whispered.

I nodded, and then finally fell asleep.

We were up by four. Even so, Dat already had the chores done. The three of us sat down to breakfast together. Most families would have already had a houseful, and it seemed a little sad to have our numbers so low.

"Did you invite Pete and his family over for breakfast?" Dat asked.

My voice was meek. "I forgot."

"When are they coming?"

"Pete didn't say," I answered.

Betsy's voice was full of her usual cheer. "They'll be here soon."

"Did he tell you that?" I couldn't help but ask, she sounded so certain.

She shrugged.

I took a bite of oatmeal, but a cold panic gripped me and I barely swallowed it. Finally I pushed my breakfast away. Dat asked if my nerves were getting the best of me.

"I suppose so," I answered.

Between Dat and Betsy, there wasn't much for me to do after I finished up the dishes, so fighting back tears, I went ahead and put my wedding-day clothes on, including my new boots, purchased special for the occasion.

I couldn't help but think how happy I would be if Pete actually loved me. I swallowed hard.

My mind switched to Betsy and her Bobli. A tear slid down my cheek.

I swiped it away.

Determined not to let my emotions get the best of me, I stepped out of the bedroom I'd had my entire life and headed down the stairs.

The service was scheduled to begin at nine. By eight o'clock I began wondering what had happened to Pete and his family. It was customary for the bride and groom to greet guests as they arrived. I had no idea what to do with myself, and finally locked myself in the bathroom.

At eight thirty Dat began knocking on the door.

At eight forty-five I opened it.

"Are you having second thoughts?" His face was pale.

I managed to whisper, "I don't think so."

"Because if you are, we can go talk to Bishop Eicher."

I shook my head, a little too frantically.

"Cate . . ." His voice was as tender as it had ever been. "What's going on with—"

"We already went through this, Dat," I said. "I'm fine."

"There you are!" Betsy came down the hall. "Come out and say hello to your guests."

A look of relief passed over Dat's face. "Pete's arrived?" he asked.

"I think so . . ." Betsy's voice trailed off.

"Have the ushers tell the guests to come on in," I said. "If he's here, let me know for sure." I stepped back into the bathroom and closed the door.

I knew Dat's intentions had been good. I knew he loved me. I knew he'd given me the opportunity to tell him the truth, at least twice now. I knew he thought, at least at the beginning, that his idea was brilliant.

But it was growing more complicated with each passing minute, far more than Dat could have ever anticipated.

At nine o'clock, he knocked on the door again.

I opened it.

"Pete's not here," he said. "Neither is his family."

"What do the Zooks say?"

Dat's face reddened. "His family didn't come."

"What about Pete?"

"He left the Zooks' place early this morning—they thought to come over here." Dat added, "I hope nothing happened to him."

I shook my head. That was highly unlikely. What was more plausible was that he'd changed his mind. I could hardly blame him.

"Bob?" It was Nan's voice coming down the hall. "What's going on?"

"Pete's family didn't come," Dat answered. "And Pete hasn't shown up."

Nan pushed up the sleeves of her blue sweater. "I can't fathom where Pete would be. This isn't like him."

I left the bathroom doorway then and followed Dat and Nan to the sunroom. All of the furniture except the sofa, which was pushed up against the wall, had been cleared out and put in the barn to make room for tables for the dinner. We huddled around in the middle.

"He changed his mind," I said.

"That would be such a shame," Dat moaned.

"No shame but mine," I answered, realizing that what I'd tried to protect my family from was happening anyway, regardless of my intentions.

Dat shook his head. "We're jumping to conclusions. Pete wouldn't just not show up." Dat stepped toward the wall of windows. "He's not that kind of man."

"I can take my car and go look for him," Nan offered.

"I'll go tell the guests to go home." I stepped toward the hallway, nearly bumping into Bishop Eicher.

"There you are. I wanted to have a word with you and Pete, while we're waiting."

I glanced back at Dat, and he stepped forward. "He's been delayed," Dat said.

"I was just going to go get him," Nan added.

A wave of sadness overtook me. Turning away from Dat and Nan, I stepped toward the hall. "He's not coming. I'm going to send everyone home."

C H A P T E R

15

During the walk down our hallway, my sadness turned to humiliation, followed by relief.

I doubted any of our friends and family would actually be surprised that I'd been jilted. Now I could get back to being who I was meant to be—an old maid—although the thought of Dat's pain did hurt.

I figured the bishop might go ahead and give the sermon he'd planned, perhaps a shortened version, and then we could all eat together anyway. Perhaps I could sneak away for a long walk along the creek, with a book for company, to escape the looks of pity and despair.

As I reached the kitchen, Betsy met me.

"It's not going to happen," I said.

"Oh, Cate," she gasped, reaching for my arm.

I stopped. "Pete's not here. Obviously he's not coming."

"Could you wait a few more minutes?" Betsy's eyes filled with tears.

Martin and Mervin, Pete's attendants, had gathered in the archway to the living room with Levi and his little brother, Ben, and by then Dat and Nan had caught up with me, the bishop right behind them.

"If anyone makes an announcement, it will be me," Bishop Eicher said.

I blushed. There I'd gone, overstepping again.

"And I say we wait." He nodded toward Nan. "And that you go see if you can find him. We at least need his answer to all of this."

Nan said she wouldn't be gone long. I turned to head back to the sunroom, but as I did there was a knock on the back door.

"Come in," Dat boomed.

The door eased open, slowly, and Pete's head appeared. Then the rest of him. His straw hat was in his hands, and he wore his everyday clothes, including his blue shirt, although all of it looked freshly laundered and pressed. I glanced down at my dress. It was the norm for both the bride and groom to have new outfits for their wedding day.

"You're here!" Dat stepped toward him.

Nan hurried back from the entryway by the front door. Betsy stood with her hand clasped over her mouth, and Levi looked as if he might sing for joy.

"Back here," Bishop Eicher said to Pete, gesturing toward the hall. Then to Levi, he said, "Tell Preacher Stoltz he can get started with the singing."

Levi nodded and Dat patted Pete on the back. "Do you need a hat? I have an extra." The groom was to give up his straw hat and wear a black one on his wedding day.

"Denki," Pete said, rubbing his still-bare chin as he did. Perhaps he didn't intend to go through with the wedding, after all—maybe he'd simply done the honorable thing by showing up to tell me in person.

Dat led the way down the hall, stopping in his room, while Pete and I followed the bishop into the sunroom. A moment later Dat stepped in, handed Pete a black hat, and then quickly exited.

"Why so late?" Bishop Eicher asked Pete, who twirled the hat on his hand.

He held up his wrist. "My watch stopped. I must have forgotten to wind it." His voice wasn't defensive. Just calm, matter-of-fact, and as polite as ever. "I stopped down by the creek on my way here . . . to pray." He glanced at me. "I'm sorry."

I dropped my gaze, troubled by Pete's tone.

The bishop raised his eyebrows and then asked, "Is your family coming?"

Pete shook his head. "They couldn't make it."

The bishop stepped closer to Pete. "When do you plan to start growing your beard?"

"Today." He glanced at me again, and rubbed his chin for the second time.

As the singing of the first traditional wedding song from the *Ausbund*—one about the church being Christ's bride—began, the bishop leaned even closer to Pete. He didn't flinch.

An Amish wedding was a sacred event. The ceremony, with singing and a sermon, was almost identical to what my parents and grandparents and even great-grandparents had experienced. It wasn't about the bride and groom and their preferences and desires; it was about the commitment they were making to each other and to God.

"Any second thoughts?" the bishop asked Pete as Preacher Stoltz entered the sunroom.

I held my breath.

"No." Pete's face was solemn, the appropriate expression by Amish standards for what was before us.

I exhaled slowly. I wasn't sure what was worse—being jilted or deceiving everyone I knew.

While the congregation sang, the bishops and ministers, often from several different districts, usually asked the couple a series of questions and then offered advice. Perhaps that wasn't going to happen with us. The bishop asked Pete and me to sit on the sofa. We did, on opposite ends. Then the bishop directed Preacher Stoltz out to the hall, followed him out, and shut the door.

When the first song ended, I could hear the murmured voices of the bishop and preacher but couldn't make out what they were saying. The second song, the traditional praise hymn, began. Pete put his head back against the sofa and closed his eyes. I stared out the window. The blue bearded irises, the same color as my dress, were blooming. The epitome of spring.

As the second song neared its end, the bishop and preacher returned. Pete stirred a little. The bishop cleared his throat. Pete sat up and then opened his eyes.

The bishop started to speak but then closed his mouth. On his second try, words came out. "Tell us why you want to marry Cate?" He was looking at Pete again with the same intensity as before.

Pete straightened his back, put Dat's black hat on the sofa between us, and clasped his knee. "I believe it is the Lord's will for me to marry Cate."

The bishop turned toward me. "What is your answer to the question?"

I spoke softly and quickly. "I believe it is the Lord's will for me to marry Pete." My face grew warm, uneasy that I hadn't prayerfully found peace in all of this.

"And both of you have remained pure . . . ?"

We both nodded adamantly.

"And you'll both be committed to your marriage?"

Again we both nodded, but not with as much conviction. "And honor your marriage bed?"

Our heads barely dipped, but the bishop didn't seem to notice.

The second song ended.

"We should get going," Preacher Stoltz said, concluding what was probably the shortest session of premarital counseling in Amish history. Neither Pete nor I moved. The bishop cleared his throat. We both stood, slowly, as the preacher and bishop left the room. Pete and I reached the doorway at the same time, but then he stepped aside and allowed me to go first, his hand brushing my arm as I breezed by into the hallway.

"Listen, Cate . . ."

My face began to grow warm. This was it. The bit about his watch was only an excuse. He was going to back out now.

"About my family—"

Relieved, I blurted out, "I know they didn't come. It's all right."

The singing stopped. A rustling at the end of the hall caught my attention. Betsy was motioning to me frantically.

"Let's go," I said, now ready to get it over with.

Pete crossed his arms and stood his ground. "I probably should have told you this last night, when I found out, but—"

I interrupted him, declaring, "Tell me after the service." Then I grabbed his arm and pulled him down the hall, joining Betsy, Addie, Martin, and Mervin at the back of the living room. We made our way between the men's side and the women's side to the front, where two benches faced each other. I sat between Betsy and Addie on one while Pete and his attendants sat across from us. Out of the corner of my eye, I saw Levi in the third bench on the men's side, his gaze on Betsy.

Preacher Stoltz preached for nearly an hour. Then the bishop preached. All the while, I stared at the hardwood floor of our living room. Betsy must have polished it before we set up the benches. I was amazed at everything she'd accomplished. The one time I did look up, Pete had his head down.

Even though I expected it, I startled as Bishop Eicher said, "Now there are two in one faith, Pete Treger and Cate Miller."

Betsy patted my arm.

The bishop continued. "If there is anyone who knows a reason these two sitting before you should not be married, let yourself be heard now."

I half expected Nan to speak out, but instead there was a long moment of silence, the longest I ever remembered at a wedding. Finally the bishop said, "If it is still your desire to be married, you may in the name of the Lord come forth."

I shifted forward on the bench, looking up to meet Pete's eyes. He kept his head down but stood. I stepped forward, and Pete took my hand. The bishop asked us a series of questions. Although I didn't listen, I simply affirmed each one, only aware of my hand in Pete's. His was cool and calloused. Mine was sweaty and smooth.

The ceremony proceeded until the bishop took both of our hands in his, prayed a blessing over us, and then said, "Go forth in the name of the Lord. You are now man and wife." He let go of our hands, and Pete quickly dropped mine. Then we returned to our seats.

Although Amish wedding services are long, the actual ceremony takes only a few minutes. The bishop continued on with his sermon, then read a passage from the *Christenpflicht* prayer book, including, "'May they also enjoy the benefit of Thy divine comfort in all the affliction, suffering, and forthcoming troubles they meet in their married life.'" I'd hardly heard a word during the entire service, but I heard that. I swallowed hard.

Was that all I had ahead of me? Affliction? Suffering? And troubles?

It would serve me right.

I looked for Pete but couldn't find him. The house had been quickly converted for the meal. The *Eck,* the two tables in an L shape in the corner, were set up. Dat announced it was time for the wedding party to sit.

Someone whispered loudly, "He's missing again."

I stood in the middle of the room, not saying a word, but the looks from a few of the women made my face flush. A few moments later, Levi came through the front door with Pete.

As I followed him to our table, Aunt Laurel whispered, "Poor gentle lamb."

I knew things were bad if even my aunt felt sorry for me.

Her sister Nell clucked her tongue and added, "Poor quiet dove."

Humiliated, I froze. It was one thing for me to pity myself, but to have all the guests view my pain felt nearly unbearable.

But then M&M's Mamm changed the subject, saying that Seth's wife had given birth last night. "A little girl. We stopped and saw them on the way here."

Now it was my turn to feel pity, for the little one, having Seth as her father. Poor thing.

The women drifted away, taking their conversation with them, and the light inside the house shifted when the sun went behind the clouds. As we ate the roasted chicken, potatoes and gravy, sweet-and-sour celery, pickled beets, chow chow, and other pickled dishes, the day—even though it was only noon—grew darker and darker.

"A storm is brewing," Pete said to Mervin. "Must be an omen."

I turned my head toward Addie as I ate, or at least tried to, until Pete pushed his empty plate to the middle of the table and said, "We need to get going."

"Going?" I stammered. "Where?" We had the evening meal to serve and then all the cleanup tomorrow. That was the way it was always done. Then the couple went visiting.

"I tried to tell you this morning, before the service." His gaze was intense. "A driver will be arriving in a few minutes. We're headed to my folks' place."

Betsy scuttled away from the table—to find Dat, I assumed.

"Now?" I stammered. "Why so soon?"

"My Dat is ill . . ."

"I haven't packed," I said.

"Then you should," he answered. "I don't know how long we'll stay."

Dat approached our table. "What is this about you leaving?"

Pete answered, "I got a phone call last night. My father's ill. I—"

"How bad?" It wasn't like Dat to interrupt.

"My oldest brother said I should come as soon as possible."

I sank back against my chair and stole a look at Pete. Maybe it was just another excuse to add to my misery.

"Oh dear," Nan said.

"Is he in the hospital?" I asked.

Pete nodded.

"Is he going to die?"

He didn't flinch at my bluntness. "I'm not sure."

I met his gaze. "You could go on without me."

He sat tall and straight as we locked eyes. "Or not."

"Well, under the circumstances"—Dat turned toward me—"do as your husband requests."

I left the table with Betsy right behind me. When we reached our room, I pulled a suitcase out of our closet. If Pete's father was dying, we did need to go. And the phone call the night before totally explained Pete losing track of time when his watch stopped. I knew I would be stressed if Dat fell ill.

Besides, there was no reason not to look on the bright side. We wouldn't have to fake our lack of love in front of Dat. On the other hand, I'd have to pretend in front of people I'd never met.

Betsy, who'd been uncharacteristically quiet, handed me a new white nightgown. "I made this . . . for tonight."

The bodice was threaded with white ribbon and the fabric was a soft, thin cotton. I took it from her, pained my husband wouldn't be admiring me in it, and stuffed it into the suitcase.

"You should put it on top," she said. "You'll need it first. . . ." Her voice trailed off.

I ignored her and pulled two dresses off the pegs along the far wall. After I packed those, I dug my slippers out from under my bed, grabbed my robe, and opened my top bureau drawer.

Betsy said she best get back downstairs to supervise. I agreed and she slipped away.

I don't know what I expected. Maybe for her to ask my forgiveness. Maybe for her to update me on her life without me having to ask. I glanced at the stack of books on her bedside table. None of them had been moved.

I took the pregnancy book from my stack and put it on top of Betsy's, and then quickly jotted down our doctor's phone number and put that beside the pile.

I gathered up the rest of my books to give to Nan, knowing she would renew the others, if possible, until I got back. After stopping in the bathroom for my toiletries, I headed down the stairs.

Halfway, I stopped. Mervin and Martin were at the bottom, facing me, and Pete was on the first step, facing them. M&M were laughing. Martin slipped something into Pete's hand. In horror I froze, my eyes glued on a white business-size envelope. It couldn't be true.

I shuddered. It was. The envelope contained the money they'd promised Pete—he'd just accepted it.

I stumbled a little, as if I'd forgotten how to use my feet. But then I started moving again, clomping down the stairs in my boots. Martin glanced my way and then ducked his head.

Pete shoved the envelope into the pocket of his coat.

Betsy stood at the bottom of the stairs, off to the side but staring up at me. She'd seen what had transpired too.

"Ready?" Pete asked without turning toward me.

I didn't try to hide the sharpness in my voice. "I need to give these to Nan." I held up the books. When I reached the bottom stair, I dropped my bag at his feet. He grimaced but picked it up as I passed by.

Nan was just around the corner, at the living room window. The trees swayed in the wind and rain began coming down in sheets.

"It's a horrible day to travel," she said. I was sure she was thinking of the accident that had killed her fiancé.

I gave her a half hug and handed her the books. "Betsy still has a few of mine," I said.

She cradled the books in her arms. "I'll renew them."

"Thanks," I said. "I hope there's a bookmobile near Pete's home."

"There isn't," she answered. "Just a library in Randolph."
A car pulled into the driveway and honked.

Nan smiled sadly.

Dat reached for me and gave me a hug. "Write." His voice
was even deeper than usual. "Let me know when you're coming home."

Next he shook Pete's hand. Pete gave him a solemn, silent
look, and opened the door, nodding at me. I pulled my cape
from the peg by the door and looked for Betsy.

She stepped forward and we hugged. Pete cleared his throat.
She didn't apologize. Disappointed, I let her go, and she
stepped back to Levi's side.

I led the way, pulling my hood over my head. When we
reached the car, the lid to the trunk rose and Pete slung my
bag and his pack inside.

Then, already soaked, I climbed into the back seat while
he climbed into the front. I didn't bother to look back at my
house and wave. My humiliation was already complete, or
so I thought.

CHAPTER

16

I seethed in the back seat of the car, replaying the passing of the envelope in my head over and over, wishing I'd told Dat what had happened. It was too late now—even if I found a phone to call him from, he wouldn't listen to his messages until Tuesday.

When we reached Highway 30, the driver pulled over into the parking lot of a convenience store.

"Thank you." Pete opened his door.

The driver pressed a button. Behind me, the trunk opened.

"Come on," Pete said to me.

"What's going on?"

"We're getting out here."

Perhaps there was a bus stop nearby. Traveling that way would be less expensive than hiring a car for the entire trip. And I knew Pete was concerned about money, although he did have the envelope from M&M.

I gasped. In the rush to get out the door, I'd forgotten my purse. I didn't have my ID card or my debit card or any of the cash I'd tucked away for an emergency.

"We need to go back," I said, "and get my purse."

Pete was standing outside the car now, the rain beating

down on Dat's black hat. "We don't have time for that. Besides, we're going to make it on my money—not yours or your father's."

I bristled as I crawled from the car. That was ridiculous. Especially since my father's money was the reason he'd married me.

Pete was already at the trunk, pulling out our bags. He tossed mine to me, catching me off guard. It fell to the ground, landing at my feet. Befuddled, I picked it up, not wanting it to get wet. It wasn't like Pete to act so abruptly.

I rose quickly.

He had both hands up. "Sorry," he said. "I shouldn't have done that."

I held on to the bag as he ambled over to the driver's window and handed him some money.

I remained statue-still.

"Over here," Pete called out, heading toward the highway. He stopped before I reached him and pulled out a cardboard sign. For a horrified moment I thought it was to beg for money. It wasn't. But it was nearly as bad. *Jamestown, NY* was written in bold letters. That was all.

"We're hitchhiking?" I sputtered.

He nodded.

"No," I said, stepping backward.

"I do it all the time."

"I don't."

"You do now." He smiled. "For better or worse."

"I don't think that was in our vows." I couldn't be certain because I hadn't been listening, but I was pretty sure I'd never heard it at any other Amish weddings I'd been to. I thought it was an Englisch thing.

I started to step away, intending to leave a message for Dat, even if he wouldn't get it for a few days, but Pete grabbed my arm. "You wanted a marriage of convenience, right?"

"Jah, but this is far from convenient."

He smirked. "But this is what you chose. We're doing it my way. Bear with me."

Not that word again. "Bear?"

I could only hope his bad behavior was due to stress.

"I told you I'm stubborn. You'll have to learn to live with it." His eyes narrowed. "Wife."

My eyebrows shot upward. "Jah, well, watch me be persistent."

A minivan pulling to the side of the highway interrupted us. Pete stepped forward as the passenger window rolled down.

A middle-aged woman leaned toward him. She looked harmless. "I can take you partway," she called out.

Pete motioned to me. "You sit up front," he said.

The rain had soaked through my wool cape. My feet were damp inside my new boots. And water dripped off my icy hands. Regardless of Pete's wishes, I would leave a message for Dat as soon as I could. But in the meantime, I opened the door of the van, greeting the woman and then glancing toward the back.

"It's just me," she said. "I promise. No serial killers or anything like that."

"We're wet," I said.

"All the more reason to get in quickly," she responded.

Pete took my bag and opened the side door as I climbed into the front seat, easing my hood from my head, noting the smell of wet wool.

"I'm headed to Elmira. My mom's ill and needs some help. You two look safe—I thought you'd be good company."

"Safe, yes," I said. At least I was. "About the good company, I'm not so sure."

The woman laughed out loud, even though I hadn't meant to be funny. In no time we were chatting as she drove, with Pete mostly staying quiet in the back. I simply told her we were going to visit my husband's parents. She didn't notice me cringe when I said the word *husband*. Thankfully she didn't ask how long we'd been married.

I dozed after Harrisburg for a little while and awoke to Pete and the woman talking.

"We should get out here," Pete said. "Before you head east."

It was still raining and I hated to leave the nice woman and her warm van. It was nearing five o'clock, and although the day was still light, it was gray enough out to feel like late evening.

She and Pete decided the best place for us to catch a ride would be on the north side of Williamsport, where the highway split. We would be heading northwest.

After pulling into the parking lot of a grocery store, the woman thanked us for the company and wished us luck. I'd hardly eaten at breakfast or at our wedding dinner and had grown hungry, but Pete didn't suggest going into the store to buy food, so I didn't either.

In a couple of minutes we were back on the side of the highway. Pete had turned his sign around. This time it read *Cattaraugus County, NY*. I couldn't imagine anyone zipping along the highway was headed there.

And I was right, at least for the next three hours. The only blessing was that the rain had stopped and there was a boulder up the road a few yards for me to sit on.

Finally, just after eight, a man in a pickup stopped. He had a gun rack in the rear window and a hound dog in the truck bed. Pete opened the passenger door, indicating for me to crawl in. I shook my head. After a long awkward moment,

Pete took the lead and scooted next to the man, and then I climbed in, pulling the heavy door shut behind me. We both held our bags on our laps.

The man didn't seem very interested in us, nor did he talk about himself except to say he was going as far as Lawrenceville, just over the New York state border. I wondered how much farther Pete's parents' place was from there but didn't bother to ask. I'd find out soon enough.

The day darkened as the sun set, casting a glow through the bank of gray clouds. The engine of the truck was loud, but after a while I dozed again. When I awoke it took me a split second to realize my head was resting against Pete's shoulder. I jerked it up quickly, wiping my mouth.

It was completely dark, and the rain fell again. Soon afterward, the man pulled the pickup to the side of the road.

"Is there somewhere with streetlights, perhaps?" Pete asked, as politely as ever.

The man grunted and pulled back onto the highway. A few minutes later lights appeared and then a gas station.

"How's this?" The man slowed the pickup.

"Perfect."

As the driver stopped, Pete thanked him and we climbed out. My legs were stiff, and I desperately needed to use the restroom. I headed toward the minimart, thankful the facilities were clean. I couldn't help but look in the mirror. My face was as pale as my new white Kapp, and my eyes were rimmed with red, even though I hadn't been crying.

When I came out of the restroom Pete was at the counter buying a bottle of water and a bag of trail mix.

"Want anything?" He held the water in his hand.

"You buying?"

"Yep." His face was matter-of-fact.

I opened the cooler and pulled out another water and then turned toward the rack of candy. Nothing looked appealing. I chose a bag of cashews and put them on the counter while Pete dug into his pocket for more change.

As he paid a second time, he asked the clerk what he thought our chances of finding a ride were.

The man chuckled. "About a hundred to one. Although in those outfits you might get lucky."

I bit my tongue until we stepped outside. "Can't you call someone?"

"And ask them to send a buggy?"

"How about a driver?"

He shook his head.

"You don't know anyone who would come this far at night?"

"That's not it. I don't have the money to pay anyone to come this far at night."

"Use the money in the envelope."

"What are you talking about?"

"I'm not stupid."

He didn't even blush.

I turned on my heels and started marching toward the store.

"What are you doing?"

"Calling home."

"You think your Dat's in his office this late at night?"

"I'm going to call our Englisch neighbors." Why hadn't I called them hours ago? "It's an emergency."

He stepped quickly, planting himself in front of me before I reached the door. "If we don't have a ride in an hour, I'll call a driver."

I glared at him.

"Deal?" He stuck out his hand.

I turned my back to him and marched to the entrance to the store, parking myself under the awning. The storm had picked up again.

My back ached. My head hurt. My eyes burned.

The rain cascaded off Pete's hat as if it were competing with Niagara Falls. Still, he stood there with his thumb in the air. One car slowed but kept on going. Then five others buzzed on by. There was a fifteen-minute lull and then another car sped past.

I checked my watch over and over. After forty-five minutes, I began rehearsing what I would say to our neighbors at midnight. Ten minutes later, just when I thought I had it all down, a sedan pulled over, its lights reflecting off the wet pavement.

The rain had stopped again, and although I couldn't hear what the driver said through the passenger window, I heard Pete say, "Cattaraugus County?" And then, "Great!" He motioned toward me.

I trudged to the car and climbed into the back seat, securing my bag on the floor.

The man was older, probably sixty or so. He wore a baseball cap and a flannel shirt. "Feels like winter, doesn't it?" he said.

"Jah," I answered.

"It's good for the crops, though," he said. At that he and Pete started talking about farming. He grew corn. He'd been to Savona to look at a tractor for sale there and then had dinner with his sister and her husband. "Stayed quite a bit longer than I meant to—got to talking." He was returning to his farm north of Randolph, but he said he'd take us all the way to Pete's parents' farm, because it wasn't too far past his.

"I'm just happy to have company along for the ride," he said.

I stared into the blackness as we drove. The dread that had been building for the last two weeks felt as if it were about to crest. Not only had I just entered a new geographical state, I was also entering a state of both emotional and physical exile. Technically I lived on a farm, but civilization was close by. From the headlights, I could make out field after field after field, some lined with split-rail fences, some not. Very rarely there was a farmhouse and a barn, illuminated by a light fixed atop a telephone pole. I had entered a desolate land.

Pete and the man were talking about local news. It turned out they knew a few of the same people, and the man had heard of his family.

"I know lots of you Amish have big families," the man said. "But fourteen—that has to be a winner."

That many children certainly wasn't unheard of in any Amish community.

The man slapped his knee, and the car drifted a little, the headlights illuminating a herd of cattle, huddled together. I held my breath until the man pointed the car down the middle of the lane again.

"I have to say, children really are a blessing," he said. "We only had two. During their high-school years, that seemed pretty wise. But now, I wish we'd had more. Only have one grandchild—with no more on the horizon. There's a lot that your people do that I envy. If I'm honest." He slapped his knee again as if he'd said something funny.

I couldn't help but smile. He was definitely a likable person.

They were silent for a moment, and then the man looked into the rearview mirror, at me, and said, "You're a quiet one."

Pete chuckled. I blushed.

"Cat got your tongue?" The man shifted his eyes back to the road.

"I suppose so," I answered.

"For the first time ever," Pete muttered.

I bristled, but the man didn't seem to have heard my husband's comment.

"My missus is a quiet one. . . ." The man went on to talk about his wife. It was clear he probably didn't give her a chance to speak, but I was thankful for the man's talkativeness. I could listen to him going on and on and try not to think of what was ahead of me.

We passed through a few small communities and then, just after two o'clock, nearly fourteen hours after we'd left Paradise, Pete told the man to turn off the highway at the next left. "You can let us out," Pete said. "We can walk the rest of the way. It's not far."

"Good idea," the man said. "Otherwise I might wake up your folks."

That seemed like a pretty lame excuse to me, but because I was playing the role of the dutiful wife, I didn't say anything as I climbed out of the car.

Pete thanked the man profusely, and I added my gratitude too. We waited for him to back onto the highway, and then Pete took off down the lane, with me a few steps behind him. On the bright side, it wasn't raining, but it was still pitch-black. And the road was muddy, even though it was graveled. After several precarious steps I managed to land in a pothole—full of water. I squealed as I pulled my foot out. I couldn't see the water dripping out of my boot but could feel it. Pete turned and took my bag, as if that would help me see better.

"Got a flashlight in that pack?" I asked, as sweetly as I could.

"Probably." He unzipped it and dug around a little. "I'm just not sure where. But we're almost there." He might have known the lane like the back of his hand, but I certainly did not. I trudged along, still a few steps behind him. Clearly I wasn't worth the effort—or maybe the battery power.

I stepped in another pothole, soaking my other foot, but didn't miss a beat as I continued my march. I assumed Pete's Mamm expected us and had a meal laid out. The women in their district would have brought food over, with his Dat being in the hospital and all. Then I needed a hot shower. Surely she would be fine with me sleeping in tomorrow, considering it would be just a couple of hours before dawn by the time we got to bed.

Bed. I shivered. Maybe Pete had thought ahead. He probably wouldn't want his parents to know we were sleeping separately. But maybe there were two rooms side by side, on the opposite side of the house from his parents' room.

An acidic whiff of manure stopped my thoughts. In no time it was so strong I had to cover my nose. Pete increased his stride. I stumbled behind him. The clouds parted a little, and I could make out the tip of the crescent moon. It wasn't much light—just enough to see the large dairy off to the left.

"Is that yours?" I asked.

"Nah. The neighbors."

I pinched my nose, appalled. The lane curved a little, thankfully, away from the dairy. The smell grew a little less intense.

"There are a few things I should tell you about my family," Pete said.

I yawned. He'd had every opportunity to tell me anything I needed to know. Why had he waited until now?

"My Mamm can be a bit . . ." He seemed to be at a loss for words.

In my state of exhaustion, I gave way to my frustration. "A bit what?"

He didn't respond.

"What are you trying to tell me?" I already knew she was old. And she was interested in Dat's money. And it seemed, even before her husband took ill, it wasn't a priority for her to make it to her son's wedding.

After another long, silent moment, Pete said, "Actually I don't know what I'm trying to tell you." He gestured toward the dark sky with his free hand. "I've been away for seven months. Maybe she's changed."

I doubted an old woman would change much, but I didn't bother to respond. I needed all the energy I could muster to keep putting one foot in front of the other. I would find out soon enough what Pete's mother was like.

It seemed a near eternity until a house came into view. It was old and fairly small. Probably the Dawdi Haus. My heart lifted. Maybe we wouldn't be staying in the same home as his parents at all. The main house was probably farther down the lane.

Pete angled through the yard to the building. Relieved, I followed him. It wouldn't matter if his Mamm didn't have a meal ready for us. Surely there would be food available, though.

We creaked up the weathered back steps. The rickety door was unlocked, and the hinges groaned as Pete pushed it open. We passed through a mud porch and into the kitchen, which was small with a table in the middle. Pete bee-lined through, but I stopped, my eyes searching the darkness for a refrigerator.

Not able to spot one, I turned around slowly, figuring there was a pantry off the kitchen.

Pete stepped back into the room. "Come on," he said.

"I'm looking for the fridge."

"There isn't one."

"I need some food."

He put his pack on the table and unzipped it, pulling out the trail mix.

"Real food," I insisted.

"The icehouse is out back." He stuffed the bag back into his pack. "Go take a look."

"You're kidding," I stammered, but he was already through the doorway.

I followed. "Pete!"

"Shh." He turned abruptly, and I almost plowed into him. "You'll wake up my Mamm."

"This is where they live?"

"Of course." He headed to the staircase.

There was no way the place could have housed fourteen boys. "This is your home?"

"Was," he muttered.

At the top of the stairs, Pete opened the door to the right and stepped inside. I stopped in the doorway.

A moment later he struck a match and lit the kerosene lamp beside the bed.

"Is this my room?" I asked. There was an old bed—one that a century ago might have been considered large enough for two people but wasn't much bigger than a single—and a little table for the kerosene lamp. That was all.

"It's our room," Pete said.

"I don't think so. . . ." I stopped.

He plopped down on the bed, patting the mattress beside him. "You can have this side."

I shook my head slowly.

He smirked and grabbed the pillow that would have been mine. "Just kidding," he said, springing off the bed and tossing the pillow on the bare floor.

Of course he'd been kidding. What had I been thinking? He didn't want to sleep with me any more than I wanted to sleep with him. My breath caught in my chest.

"You can have the bed." He pulled a mummy bag from his pack and then flung it open, flopping it down beside the pillow.

"How about another room . . ." I pointed toward the hall.

"That might work. The next one over is my Mamm's. Although she might be frightened by you crawling into bed with her." His eyes narrowed as a horrid bearlike noise came from down the hall. "Sounds like Dat's home from the hospital," Pete said. "His room is the last one. They've had separate rooms for years."

For obvious reasons. "Only three bedrooms?" I asked.

He nodded.

"For fourteen boys?"

"By the time I was born, three of my brothers were already gone. . . ."

"Still." That was two rooms for eleven boys. He'd been telling the truth about growing up in poverty. It was no excuse, but maybe it helped explain why he'd been tempted by Mervin and Martin's offer of money—and had succumbed.

I poked my head out into the hall again. "Which one is the bathroom?"

"The one out the window." He jerked his head toward the outer wall.

"I beg your pardon."

"Outhouse," he said. "Ever used one?"

I grimaced. "You're kidding."

Sarcasm filled his voice as he said, "Oh, Poor Cate."

I blushed, remembering the time he'd called me Sweet Cate. How foolish I'd been to think he'd meant it. He was mocking me, even then.

"Take the lamp," he said.

I placed my bag on the end of the bed, then opened it and dug to the bottom for my nightgown, thankful I'd packed my bathrobe and slippers. I wedged my things under my arm and stepped between the bed and Pete, who wormed his way into his sleeping bag.

He didn't say another word as I grabbed the kerosene lamp, the clear liquid sloshing around in the base, and in a moment I was back in the hall and then making my way down the stairs. I'd never bothered to imagine my wedding night, but if I had, never in my wildest dreams would I have come up with such a nightmare.

CHAPTER
17

I awoke out of a deep sleep to a knocking sound. In my half sleep I thought it came from outside, but as I opened my eyes to just a hint of dawn coming through the curtain, I realized it was coming from the closed door, and growing louder. And then I remembered where I was.

"You plan to sleep all day!"

I sat up in bed, squinting toward the floor. In the dim light it was obvious Pete wasn't there. Neither was his sleeping bag. Only bare wood.

The commotion grew louder.

"Just a minute," I said.

The knocking stopped. "Breakfast is almost ready," a woman's gruff voice called out.

I collapsed back onto the bed, remembering I needed to play the part of the dutiful wife, but the next thing I knew someone was knocking again and the room was much lighter. I'd gone back to sleep!

The same voice barked, "We're going to eat without you."

I slipped my feet onto the cold floor, pulled the worn quilt up to the pillow, and grabbed my dress from the peg on the wall, eyeing the door. "I'll be right there," I called out.

I dressed quickly, into one of my everyday dresses, facing the blank wall just in case someone came bursting through the door. After slipping on my Kapp and then my shoes, I left the room. I'd have to figure out where to wash my face and hair later. I cringed, imagining a Saturday night bath in a tub in the kitchen. "Oh, please, no," I muttered under my breath.

An ancient-looking man and an old woman both glanced up at me from the table as I stepped into the kitchen. A fringe of snow-white surrounded the man's head. In contrast, his long white beard was tucked under the table. He was thin and gangly and had tiny gray eyes and a huge nose and ears. I'd read somewhere that a person's facial features kept growing long after the rest of them started shrinking. One look at him convinced me that was true.

The woman, who was turned in her chair so she could get a better look at me, was small and wrinkled like a dried-apple doll. Her hair was remarkably dark, though, with just a few strands of silver. Her Kapp was yellowish and her dress an extra-plain brown.

"I'm Cate." I smiled as best I could. I was their new daughter-in-law, regardless of whether their son loved me or not.

"That's what we figured," the man said. "I'm Walter, and this is Esther."

She looked nothing like an Esther—or at least my ideas of what a woman named Esther would look like, based on the Bible story. I greeted both of them as warmly as I could manage and then said I needed to wash up.

"Basin's in the pantry," the woman said, motioning toward a door across the room.

"I'll be right back." I'd been right about a pantry—just not right about a refrigerator being in it. I eased open the door to a fairly large room. The shelves were lined with colorful jars of canned goods. Two bins stood against the far wall—probably flour and sugar. Perpendicular to them was a table with a basin of water and a towel beside it. The water was grayish. I tested it with my finger. And cold. Next to it was a bar of strong-smelling soap. I picked it up, lathered, and then rinsed my hands quickly. The towel was damp. I wiped my hands on my apron.

As I returned to the table, Esther said, "Sit." And then, "Hope you like oatmeal."

I nodded and pulled out the chair nearest the sink. "Where's Pete?"

"Shoveling manure," his father answered.

"At the neighbors," his mother clarified.

After he finished leading us in a silent prayer, I asked Walter how his health was, wondering what the big emergency was the day before yesterday.

"Can't complain," he answered, gripping his spoon with his leathery hand.

"Why?" Esther leaned back in her chair. "Is Pete still hoping to get a piece of the farm?"

"Oh, no," I said quickly, taken aback by her attitude. "I just wondered how Walter was feeling. Because he'd been in the hospital."

"Oh, that," Esther said. She looked at Walter. "Remember you had that fainting spell. You rode in that ambulance, to the ER."

"Oh, that's right." Walter chuckled.

Had Pete exaggerated his Dat's health condition to force us away from our wedding celebration? Or had he been motivated to take care of his Dat, just like me, only to have the situation not be as dire as he'd been told?

"I'm much better, denki," Walter said.

Esther took a sip of her coffee, and the aroma wafted my way.

"That sure smells good," I said.

"This?" She held the cup toward me.

I nodded.

"Sorry to say there isn't more. I only make a cup a day. It aggravates Walter's prostate."

"Oh." I'd read about prostates, but that didn't mean I wanted to discuss them.

"Pete already ate," his mother said. It looked as if she had too, because she didn't have a bowl in front of her. "He used to be a lazy one too." Her gaze was on me. "Never did like to get up before five."

"Now, Esther," Walter said.

I tried to take another bite, but the cereal was lumpy.

"Pete did the choring before he left," she said. "Now he's off to earn a day's wage."

I nodded. There was no doubt that Pete Treger was a hard worker, whatever the case had been when he was younger.

"Maybe with him back, he can earn enough money to help build us that Dawdi Haus we need." She turned from her husband to me. "Our next-up son, Johnny, runs the farm, but his wife won't move here. Says it's too crowded. So they rent a ways away. Can you imagine? When we have a perfectly good house here—and would love to have the grandchildren nearby."

"How many do they have?"

"None yet."

I nearly choked—even though my mouth was empty. But I managed to ask how many other grandchildren they had.

"Oh, let's see. It's so easy to lose track. Sixty-three, I think." Walter nodded.

"Of course there are great-grandkids too—close to twenty by now. Nine sets of twins in all, between the two generations."

Genetically speaking, twins were attributed to the mother's side, not the father's. But they were more common among the Amish than the general population. Not that any of that would matter for Pete and me.

"My, Christmas around here must be quite the gathering," I said. That was close to a hundred people.

Esther finished her coffee and stood. "Oh, we don't all get together then. Just once a year for a potluck in the summer."

"Everyone will be able to meet you then," Walter said.

"When is it?" I asked.

"A few weeks." Esther looked at Walter. "Or so. We vary it from year to year."

I hoped I'd be long gone before the reunion, whenever that would be.

"You can get started this morning by weeding the garden," Esther said without missing a beat.

"Oh, I'm not very good at gardening. I've been doing office work for the last several years."

Esther didn't hesitate. "We don't have any need for office work around here. Just plain old work."

I tried not to react.

"The hoe is in the tool shed. By the outhouse."

I decided to ignore her first comment. "Speaking of the outhouse," I said, "I need to stop there first. And then get freshened up for the day."

"Basin's in the pantry," she said, pointing to a door across the room. Then she laughed. "Did you forget already?"

I made a conscious effort not to react.

I finished my oatmeal, managing to get it down bite by small bite. Thankfully Esther hadn't served me a large portion. I washed it down with the glass of water at my place. When I was done, I headed to the sink, where I found a hand pump that I hadn't noticed before.

I stared at it for a long moment.

"Just had the pump and sink installed last year," Esther said. "It's made life so much easier."

"I can only imagine," I said, turning toward the cooking stove. Of course it was wood, but thankfully there was a kettle simmering on the back. My eye stopped on the pantry door. "So why have the basin in there? Why not by the sink?"

"So you're a know-it-all too?" She harrumphed.

I shook my head. At least I didn't mean to be. I was only asking a question.

Walter cleared his throat and I turned toward him. "We've always done it that way. Long before the pump and sink were installed."

"Oh," I said, shoving my hand into my apron pocket and balling it into a fist.

"I have quilting to do today." Esther stood with her hands wrapped around the coffee cup, even though it was empty. "Would you get dinner?"

"Beg your pardon?" I tightened my fist.

"Dinner. You know. The noon meal." She laughed. "What's the matter? You don't do much cooking either?"

I turned toward the pump, wanting to say, *Actually I don't*. I began working the handle, wondering if the day could get any worse.

The garden was vast, probably big enough to feed all sixty-three grandchildren. It was certainly far more than Esther and Walter needed to sustain the two of them. I just hoped I would be long gone before it was time to can. The early-morning cold soon gave way to bright sunshine, as different from my stormy wedding day as could be. Weeding the garden and living with Pete's parents would surely be temporary, but I didn't know how I would endure it.

I couldn't wait to get back to Lancaster County.

Betsy would marry and move to Levi's parents' place. Pete and I could sleep upstairs at my father's house. With Dat's bedroom downstairs, he would never have a reason to be on the second floor; he'd never need to know Pete and I had separate rooms. We could go back to our old jobs for the time being, until we figured out a business. Of course we'd have to be able to actually have a conversation before that could happen. But in time we'd be sure to develop some sort of working relationship.

My thoughts twirled around and around as I weeded. After three hours my hands, my arms, and my legs all ached. I longed for my desk, my chair, and my office.

When my watch said it was ten o'clock, I stood back and scanned the plot. There were still lots and lots of weeds. I'd barely made a dent. I stretched my back and glanced over toward the neighbors' dairy, catching a whiff of manure again. I wondered if Pete was shoveling the barns out by hand. I didn't see a tractor or hear one.

After scraping my shoes on the lawn, doing my best to get off as much mud as possible, I headed toward the tool shed, putting the hoe back in its place, and then peeled off the gloves I'd been wearing, putting them away above the potting bench. As I rinsed my hands at the spigot by the garden, I noticed Walter in the door of the barn talking to a man. I presumed it was John, the brother who farmed the place.

I guessed he'd be eating with us—meaning he, along with

everyone else, would expect some sort of meal. I decided to check out the icehouse before heading back to the kitchen. It had to be between the smokehouse and the tool shed. My guess was correct. I eased open the insulated door, stepping onto sawdust. Big blocks of ice lined the walls, insulated with more sawdust. Wedged along the walls were two old refrigerators. Shivering, I opened the one that was entirely surrounded by ice blocks. It was crammed full of white packages of frozen meat. I closed the door quickly, not wanting any cold air to escape. I opened the second refrigerator, which only had ice along the back of it. There were a couple of cartons of eggs. A parcel wrapped in paper. A plastic container of some kind of leftovers—maybe soup. A glass jar of milk.

"Think like Betsy," I coaxed myself, grabbing a carton of eggs. I looked around for some cheese, moving the leftovers, but couldn't find any. I unwrapped the parcel. It was a hunk of cured ham. I took what I had and stopped at the herb garden, pinching off a bunch of chives with my fingernails. Somewhere there had to be a root cellar—or maybe the potatoes and other vegetables were stored in the basement.

I headed up to the house, kicking off my shoes in the mudroom and then entering the kitchen.

I put the food on the table and stepped into the pantry. First I emptied the basin in the kitchen and refilled it—half with cold water and half with the water in the teakettle that was only lukewarm. As I scrubbed my hands I saw a closed cupboard I hadn't noticed earlier. Inside was a loaf of homemade bread, a container of hand-churned butter, a jar of jelly, a glass bottle of maple syrup, and a hunk of cheese. I scanned the shelves again. Tomatoes, green beans, pickled beets, chow chow, pickled eggs, pickles, peaches, pears, cherries . . . I selected pickled beets and pears and headed back to the kitchen.

The fire in the stove had died, so I added a couple of pieces of kindling and some paper and then a couple of minutes later added a big piece of wood.

I found a frying pan in the cupboard and then decided to set the table for five while I was waiting for the stove to heat.

By the time I had the ham cubed, the cheese grated, and the milk and eggs mixed together, the pan was hot. But I decided I'd better put the beets and pears in serving bowls and check with Esther before I started.

The thing was, I had no idea where she was. I walked into the living room and then down a hallway. There were two doors. I knocked on one. No one answered. I knocked on the second.

"Jah?"

"Lunch will be ready in about ten minutes."

"Make it five."

"All right." I hurried back to the kitchen.

Sure enough in exactly five minutes Walter and John, who was shorter than Pete and not nearly as handsome, appeared. "Where's Pete?" I asked.

Walter looked surprised at my question. "He'll eat at the neighbors," John said. That seemed strange, but I didn't ask why. Instead I introduced myself.

"I know who you are," he answered, stepping into the pantry. He didn't seem very friendly, but he didn't seem like the creep Pete had made him out to be either.

A moment later, Esther stepped into the kitchen. "I finally got some quilting done," she said. "It's *gut* to have some help."

I hoped she didn't expect it to be permanent or she would be sorely disappointed.

No one complained about the omelets, which were quite

rubbery. Nor did they compliment them. I'd attempted to toast the bread in the oven, which hadn't really worked because it didn't have a broiler, but no one commented about that either. We ate in complete silence, everyone hunched over his or her plate. The meal didn't last more than five minutes.

When they were all done eating, Esther pushed her chair back and said, "Next time fix a real meal, not breakfast. Or maybe you call this that fancy word. What is it?"

"Brunch?" I ventured.

"That's it. But it's not enough for a grown man to work all afternoon on."

John nodded in agreement.

"Tell me where you keep your food," I snapped, although not nearly as badly as I could have.

"In the icehouse."

"Frozen?"

"Jah." She looked at me as if I were an idiot. "Pick something out to defrost for tomorrow."

Then she told me, because the noon dinner meal had been so sparse, to butcher a chicken for supper. I must have reacted without meaning to, because before Esther had a chance to comment, Walter said he'd help.

"What about your nap?" Esther stood in the doorway, ready to get back to her quilting.

The old man said he'd probably have time to fit that in too. On the way out the door, he pointed out the cooler in the mudroom for me to put the bird in after I'd plucked and gutted it, to cool it down in ice water.

I caught the chicken, but Walter wrung its neck and chopped the head off on the stump behind the chicken coop that had obviously been used many times before.

It wasn't that I'd never done the job before—I just didn't like to do it. Neither did Betsy. Dat did the honors at our house, and I was grateful to Walter for doing the same.

When we got back to the house, I told him he should get his nap, afraid perhaps he'd overdone it. In no time he disappeared, I assumed upstairs to his room.

Lots of Amish women can have a chicken plucked and gutted in ten minutes or so. Not me. By the time I'd filled the cooler with water from the hose, chipped a little ice to add to it, had the chicken submerged, cleaned up the mess inside, and scrubbed the sink, it was nearly time to start dinner. I found potatoes and onions, along with garlic, sweet potatoes, turnips, and carrots in the far corner of the unfinished half basement. I'd use a jar of green beans, and make some biscuits. Once I was back in the kitchen, I glanced at the woodstove, guessing if I burned them in our propane oven back home, I'd probably scorch them here.

As I stoked the fire to cook the chicken, I couldn't imagine how hot the kitchen would be in another month. Some Amish houses had a summer kitchen and living space in the basement or one on a porch, but not here.

I didn't see Pete until supper, and when I glimpsed him through the kitchen window my heart leapt in relief to see someone familiar, someone who knew me. I couldn't help, for a split second as he shuffled across the yard, hoping that he would talk with me.

He came in, smelling like the dairy, in his stocking feet, leaving his rubber boots in the mudroom. I'd just refilled the basin with clean water, and he spent quite a bit of time in the pantry washing up. I expected him to go change his splattered pants and shirt, but he didn't.

His hair was matted from his hat, and his eyes were tired.

I imagined a full day's manual labor was quite a bit more taxing than his time in Dat's showroom.

"Worn out?" I asked.

He shook his head. "Just getting started."

"What do you mean?"

"John didn't finish plowing the north field. I'll have a few hours of daylight left to get that done."

He looked so tired that, for a moment, I felt an inkling of empathy. But then I wondered if he was working overtime to avoid me.

As expected, the biscuits burned on the bottom. The chicken seemed tough, but I was pretty sure it was at least thoroughly cooked and wasn't going to poison anyone. That was my main concern. I'd roasted the root vegetables too—added rosemary from the herb garden and sprinkled them with salt and pepper. Though a little scorched on the bottom, they were edible.

At five o'clock on the dot, Esther came into the kitchen and took her place at the table without saying a word. I finished putting the chicken on a platter, placed a carving knife and fork on each side, and then put the whole thing in front of Walter.

"What's this for?" He eyed it suspiciously.

"For you to carve."

"Oh."

"That might be the way you do things in Lancaster," Esther said, "but not here."

Now it was my turn to say, "Oh."

I picked up the platter and put in on the tiny counter and began cutting. "Actually it might just be something we do at our house. . . ." I couldn't remember what other families did. I just knew Dat always carved the meat.

"Well, that's probably because you have such a small family," Esther said. "That never would have worked when all of us sat down at the table."

I bit my tongue to keep from pointing out there were only four of us tonight. I kept cutting, making a mess out of the whole thing. When I was done, I put it in front of Walter again, keeping it as far from Esther as possible.

After the silent prayer, we all ate—in more silence. No one talked. Neither of his parents asked Pete about our trip. Neither asked how we met. And neither asked what our plans were.

Esther made a show of holding her biscuit and examining the bottom. Walter chewed slowly and methodically. Pete kept his head down, eating quickly. Gone was the lighthearted and confident man I'd first met. My heart hurt for both of us.

Finally Esther, as she held a sweet potato on her fork, said, "These vegetables are awful fancy." She gave me a snide look and then put it in her mouth and chewed slowly. When she was done she said, "You were right about your cooking."

"I'm used to a propane stove," I responded, not that it made much of a difference, but she didn't know that.

She rolled her eyes. "Well, that's not how we do things here."

Biding my time as her daughter-in-law was going to be harder than I thought.

Pete stood first and put his dishes in the sink without saying a word.

Walter let out a big belch. Then he glanced at me. "Do they do that in Lancaster County?" He started to laugh, and I noticed a slight smile on Pete's face before he turned to slip out the door.

"Oh, jah," I said. "The bigger the better." Although I'd never heard one quite as loud as his.

As I cleaned up after supper, on my own, I groaned out loud about how much harder life was here than back home. To think the Englisch thought our lives in Lancaster were inconvenient. My family lived in luxury compared to this.

And without the critical eye of Esther. It wasn't like I hadn't tried to prepare a decent meal. She was as far from the biblical character as I could imagine. She didn't seem to have an ounce of diplomacy or even kindness in her. In fact, Esther was a shrew.

I took the leftovers out to the icehouse, and then scrubbed the dishes, rinsing them in boiling water, determined to get everything as clean as possible. Having to heat the water on the stove added extra time to the task, and by the time I had the dishes put away, the counter and table wiped, and the floor swept, it was growing dark outside.

With nothing else to do, I retreated upstairs. And without a book to read, I was half asleep by the time Pete came into our room. He must have cleaned up downstairs, because he was wearing long underwear and smelled like his Mamm's strong soap. He pulled his sleeping bag from his backpack and flung it open, spreading it down on the floor. I rolled toward the wall, pretending I was asleep. A few minutes later, his breathing changed.

The day had been the longest of my life, I was sure. Longer than even the day before.

I couldn't help but think of Dat and Betsy. They would have spent the day cleaning up, without Pete and my help. Betsy would be sleeping alone in our room for the second time in her life, last night being the first. Or perhaps Levi was tossing pebbles at the window. . . .

I rolled over, not wanting to think anymore about my little Schwester and her beau and the whole mess they'd created.

But I had to take responsibility for the choice I'd made. No one forced me to do it. A sob surprised me, and I clamped my hand over my mouth to muffle it.

After another, I pulled my pillow over my head and tried again to pray. But I couldn't. Instead my mind kept going back to the events of the last two days.

Pete rolled over, and then something cracked against the floor, probably his elbow. I inched over to the side of the bed and peeked out from under the pillow, holding my breath, expecting him to wake up. He'd turned away from me onto his side. The shape of his hip was visible in the little bit of moonlight coming through the worn curtains. His breathing remained steady.

I pulled the pillow back over my eyes, and this time didn't even try to pray.

I was sharing a room with a husband who didn't love me. I swallowed hard, willing myself not to cry, wondering if his parents could tell we weren't a real couple in a real marriage. Or maybe Pete had told them in the morning before I'd gotten up. I wondered if, once again, the joke was on me.

My only hope was that we would soon return to Lancaster County.

C H A P T E R

18

The next morning I awoke, not sure how I would make it through another day, as Pete rolled his sleeping bag.

I sat up, afraid he might disappear before I had a chance to speak.

"Two questions," I said quickly.

He wore long underwear, both top and bottoms. He glanced at me and then quickly away.

I twisted my long, loose hair. "First, how long are we staying?" I asked, tucking my thick strand behind my back.

"I don't know." He dropped his bag in the corner.

"Okay, then—"

"Is this the second question?"

"Actually, it's not." I grabbed my pillow and hugged it, covering the white nightgown Betsy had made for me. "It's a continuation of the first."

He turned toward me and held up his hand. "No. If you ask it, it's definitely the second."

I threw the pillow at him.

He caught it and tossed it in the corner atop his pack. "Denki. I needed more cushioning." He shot me a sarcastic grimace and then started toward the door. He must have left his work clothes in the mudroom.

"Wait." I started to step out of bed and then pulled my leg back, remembering the thinness of my gown.

"Quick," he said, without turning, tugging his long johns up a little at the waist. "The cows are waiting."

"How do I get to the library?"

He held up his thumb. "It's quite a ways."

I shook my head. "I'm serious. How did you get there when you lived here?"

He held his thumb higher.

I wrinkled my nose, not believing him for one minute. "Where do your parents keep their books?" I hadn't seen a single one, not anywhere in the house.

"What books?" He was out the door now.

"Pete!"

He didn't come back.

I was truly in exile. I couldn't live without books.

I crawled out of bed and grabbed my pillow, tossing it back on the bed. Pete's coat was to the side of his pack.

I crossed my arms. "Oh, why not," I muttered, dying to know how much I was worth. I stuffed my hand into the pocket that was visible. It was empty. I reached underneath, into the second one. The envelope was there. I pulled it out, thinking it was either one big bill or not much, because there was no bulge whatsoever to it. I opened it only to find it completely empty. I slipped it back into the pocket, curious to know where he'd moved the money but not enough to paw through his smelly pack.

After breakfast, once Pete had left and Esther had disappeared into her quilting room, I asked Walter about the closest library, hoping a new one had been built since Nan left all those years ago.

"It's not far," he said.

I refrained from declaring Pete a liar. "Exactly how far?"

"In Randolph."

I sighed. So there wasn't a new one. "What about a book-mobile?" Maybe that had changed.

He gave me a sympathetic smile. "Not around here." He seemed softer when Esther wasn't around.

At home I would have simply hired a driver or maybe taken the buggy, even though that was a bit of a distance, but here I had no idea what to do.

And that's what I thought about until late in the afternoon when John and Walter came banging through the back door carrying a tub, which barely fit, and then stumbled their way into the pantry.

It turned out I was right about Saturday-night baths. After dinner, Esther told me I could have the first one. I'd never been so relieved about anything in my whole life. Still I hurried as fast as I could after I spent a half hour filling it with water I heated on the stove in every pot I could find. I set a personal record for washing my hair and soaping down and rinsing. I added more hot water for Esther after I was done and went straight to my room, not wanting to be around to watch her and Walter traipse in and out. I could only imagine how cold the water would be by the time Pete had a turn.

Over an hour later, when he came into the bedroom with his hair still wet and smelling of his Mamm's strong soap, I tried to bring up the subject of getting to the library, but he said he was too tired to talk. I swallowed hard, trying to diminish the ache in my heart. It hurt far worse than just loneliness.

I wondered at his reasons for leaving the farm in the first place. Perhaps it wasn't just because there wasn't any land left for him. Or because he'd been burned by love. Perhaps it was because he had become an indentured servant. Hired out all day and then working on his Dat's farm half the night.

"Pete," I said. "Are you asleep?"

"Jah," he grumbled.

"I was just thinking—"

"You really need to stop doing that."

"It's just it seems to me the sooner we return to Lancaster the better, for both of us. You're working too hard. I need books." No need to bother mentioning how hard I was working; it paled in comparison to him. "I don't see any opportunities for us here."

He didn't answer.

"Pete?" I leaned my head over the edge of the mattress.

He let out a sleepy sigh and then rolled away from me.

One thing was sure, I'd married a hard worker—although a cranky one. I wasn't sure if being exhausted or living with his parents made him so surly. Then again, maybe it was our marriage of convenience, or that he was back where his heart had last been broken.

I was coming to accept that the Pete I'd started to fall in love with in Lancaster County didn't exist. Still, I longed for him.

The next day wasn't a church day for the Tregers' district, so I expected some of their children and grandchildren to stop by—maybe I'd get to meet John's wife—but not one visitor appeared. It was a day of rest, however, except for the choring.

Pete disappeared early in the morning, returned for dinner, and then grabbed his old straw hat and headed toward the back door again.

"Where you off to, son?" Walter asked.

Pete turned back around. "A hike."

"Is your wife going with you?" Walter tugged on his beard.

I took a ragged breath, remembering my two outings with Pete.

His eyes shifted from his Dat to me. "Wife," he said, "would you like to go with me?"

My breath caught in my chest.

Without giving me a chance to answer, he said, "I didn't think so." With that he stepped out of the house.

Esther acted as if nothing had happened and left the room.

"What's got into him?" Walter asked. "He hasn't been himself since he got back."

My face warmed, and it wasn't from the eternal heat of the woodstove or that the day had turned out to be the first scorcher of the season.

"Do you want me to take him behind the woodshed?" Walter was half serious.

"I think it's too late for that."

"I'm sorry," the old man said, reaching for my hand. I knew he never would have been so caring if Esther had been around.

I let him squeeze it and then said, "It's not your fault. It's not even entirely Pete's fault. . . ." He couldn't help it if he didn't love me. And he'd been set up, truly. I should have expected him to resent me. It was only natural. I sighed, pulled my hand away, and stood. "What would a girl have to do to borrow a horse and buggy around here?"

Esther popped back into the kitchen. "Keep up with her chores."

Horrified, I realized she'd been eavesdropping.

"Tomorrow's laundry day. That doesn't leave much time for anything else. And on Tuesday you need to bake—without burning everything." She didn't even stop to catch her breath. "Wednesday is cleaning, and Thursday you need to weed the garden."

"Is that all?" I didn't care that my tone was sarcastic.

It was as if she hadn't heard me. "So you might want to rest up today."

I decided to do just that—not because I was tired but because I needed to escape. After Esther retreated to her quilting room, I asked Walter if there was anything to read in the house, maybe a copy of the *Martyr's Mirror*, the book that recounted centuries of persecution against the Anabaptists, or a prayer book tucked away somewhere. I followed him into the living room, where he opened up the ottoman. Inside there was a hymnal and a couple of other books. He handed me a devotional and a worn King James Bible.

"Denki," I said, clutching them to my bosom.

"The Lord provides, jah?"

I nodded.

Walter smiled and patted my shoulder. "Both were my mother's. Take good care of them."

In the week before the wedding, I'd finished the biographies of Andrew and Eliza Johnson. If I were back home, I'd have been reading about Ulysses S. Grant and his wife, Julia. Perhaps, once I found a way to get to the library, I could start back up.

After I finished the dishes, I headed upstairs. Before I collapsed on the bed, I stood at the window, taking in what I could see of the farm, clutching the books. Beyond the pasture in the far field, a man sat on the top rail of a fence. A woman approached on the other side. She looked young but was partially blocked by the wild roses growing along the fence line.

I stepped closer to the window. I was pretty sure it was

Pete. Maybe the woman was a girl Pete used to court. Perhaps her parents didn't want her to marry him because he was penniless. Perhaps that was why he left with a broken heart. I stood, afraid to move. He jumped down from the fence. They spoke for a moment, and then he took off, following the fence line the opposite direction, toward a freshly plowed field. She stood and watched him go, not leaving until he disappeared into a grove of willows along the creek.

Somehow I managed to conquer Esther's wringer washing machine and get the wash on the line on Monday. Although my work dress was dirtier than it had ever been in Pennsylvania, Pete's clothes were the worst. I scrubbed and scrubbed, and still couldn't get them clean.

The more I observed Esther and Walter, the more I wondered at the life I had ahead of me. They didn't spend any time together, and there were no signs of affection between them. I thought of my Mamm and Dat and how playful they'd been with each other, and how Dat used to steal kisses when she was working in the kitchen. I was sure, had my Mamm lived, that my parents' love would have grown with the years, not soured, as Pete's parents' affection seemed to have. Although, it was probably more Esther than Walter. He was at least respectful of his wife. Their dynamics made me miss home all the more.

That night, in our pitch-dark room, I asked Pete about Esther and Walter's relationship.

"I don't want to talk about it," Pete said.

"They don't seem very happy. I read one time—"

"Look." It sounded as if he turned his head toward me. "Don't go analyzing my parents' marriage." His voice grew softer. "And remember, no one knows what goes on between two people when they're alone."

I winced. That was certainly true in our case. I bit my tongue from saying that was just it—his parents never spent any time alone.

By Tuesday, after I'd completely incinerated one batch of bread and then managed to burn the bottom of the second, I felt sick, both from straight-out loneliness and from the feeling stuck in my chest that was worse than anything I'd ever felt.

Walter scrounged up a pen, paper, and envelope for me, and finally a stamp. After I'd finished the evening dishes, I sat down and wrote a letter. I didn't tell Dat and Betsy how miserable I was, both in my marriage and in my in-laws' house. I did tell them, as nicely as I could, how primitive things were and how much I missed home. I asked specifically how each of them was doing, wishing Betsy would write me privately, hoping perhaps there would be an invitation to her wedding that would pull me home soon. That would be the perfect excuse for me to go, even if Pete wasn't willing to.

When I was done, I addressed it carefully, slipped the pen into my pocket, and started down the lane to the mailbox out on the highway. As I walked, I saw Pete running the team of workhorses quite a ways to the left.

The lane was much more inviting in the daylight. If only I didn't feel so heavyhearted. I looked for a telephone shed as I walked. Walter had assured me they didn't have one, but I knew Esther had talked to Nan on the phone, so I figured someone nearby had one.

It took me five minutes to reach the end of the lane. Much less time, I was sure, than it had taken us to walk up it when we arrived. I found the Treger mailbox out of a half dozen in a row and slipped the letter inside, raising the red flag. Then I scanned up and down the road. About two hundred yards away and across the road was a house. It was even smaller than Pete's parents' home and probably just as old.

The front door opened and a woman stepped outside, her apron loosely tied. I held my hand to my brow, trying to block the lowering sun, squinting to try to see her more clearly. She had something in her hand—a broom. She stopped on the first step and began to sweep, her back toward me. By the time she reached the bottom, I was sure she was the woman who had talked to Pete in the field. Now she walked to the edge of the yard, behind a chest-high hedge, just a few feet from the highway. She was young, probably about my age. She wasn't facing me but was turned toward me as she waved. And waved some more, her hand high above her head. I couldn't see Pete but could clearly imagine what was going on; he must have been encouraging her with his response.

I turned. What had I gotten myself into? Had I married a man who loved someone else? Feeling sick, I swallowed hard and hurried back down the lane, tears stinging my eyes. I'd never felt so sorry for myself in my entire life.

Wednesday morning I tied a kerchief around my head. With all the weeding, gutting chickens, and mucking out the barn, my Kapps would all be ruined before I got back home if I kept wearing them to work in.

I'd been on the Treger farm for almost a week, and in that time no one had gone into town, and no one besides John had stopped by. But that afternoon Esther told me we needed to start preparing for the family reunion.

"When is it?" I asked.

"A week from Sunday."

That made sense. It would be another Sunday off from church.

"I don't know why they want to come here. They all have bigger homes than we do—except for John. But every year they want to come home." She sighed. "Anyway, at least I have you to help me this year."

"Don't they all help?"

She stared at me as if she didn't understand.

"You know. Bring food. Help set up and clean up."

"Oh, sure," she said. "They're *gut* about that."

"What do we need to do?" I asked.

"Clean the house. Tidy up the yard. Make pies. And potato salad. They have their favorites that they expect."

I didn't know what it was like to still have a Mamm as an adult, but I could imagine wanting favorite dishes one had grown up with. I didn't bother telling her to make me a list. I knew she wouldn't. She would just tell me what to do.

I asked Walter a couple of times if he was going into Randolph anytime soon. He said he'd let me know ahead of time when he planned to go. "'Course it could be six months or so. If I'm still kickin'." He grinned.

"Stop teasing," I said.

"What's wrong with the books I gave you?"

"Nothing." I'd read all my favorite Bible stories and had gone through the devotional three times. "But I'll have whole passages memorized soon."

"Sounds like a good idea." His eyes danced the way Pete's had when I'd first met him.

It seemed what was consumed the most in the Treger household was fabric for Esther's quilting. The thin one on the bed

I slept in was completely made of scraps, though. As was the Amish way, when quilting for ourselves.

That evening before supper as we all bowed our heads, I was dumbfounded over what to pray but was convicted that the time had come—I must. I'd always taken prayer seriously—until Seth broke my heart.

Now I realized how much I'd strayed from God in the last two years, and even more so in the last month. I'd gotten myself into this mess by acting willfully and independently, by acting exactly the way God didn't want me to.

All I could manage now was a silent but very sincere, *Help!* as Walter said, "Amen."

That night I read the story of Jonah again. He had been in exile, along with Moses, Joseph, and so many others. I couldn't help but identify. I flipped around, looking for another story I wanted to read that night. Finally, I decided on Esther. It had been years since I'd read the story. As I finished, I realized I identified with her too. I felt her vulnerability. Her need to be patient and bide her time. Her need to be pleasant and submit to others. In earlier readings I'd thought of her as manipulative, but now I saw she was doing what she needed to do to survive, to save her people.

I no longer had any people to save—I'd already tried that. I attempted to be cordial with Pete's mother, as best I could, but I wasn't exactly pleasant. And although I kept cooking, was I really doing my best? Then again, I had to remember who I was dealing with. Surly Pete and his sour mother. I closed the Bible. My mother-in-law was opposite, in every way, of Esther in the Bible.

I kept going with that logic. I'd never wanted to be like Esther in the Bible, which now made me realize I might end up a whole lot like Esther in my all-too-real life. I grimaced.

I'd read somewhere that men often subconsciously chose to marry someone a lot like their mothers. I grimaced again. Was that why Pete, along with the motivation of the bribe from M&M, had been attracted to me in the first place?

I had a quick glimpse of the future me—and it wasn't pretty.

I opened the Bible again, deciding to read the story of Esther a second time. When I finished it, I breathed a prayer, asking God for wisdom. Esther's husband loved her for her beauty, not for who she was. But God absolutely loved her for who she was. And he used her, used who she was, because she was willing to let him. Her willingness was cloaked in wisdom.

My husband didn't love me for who I was either—but God did, regardless of the situation I'd gotten myself into.

I flipped to Proverbs, deciding to find the verse Nan had quoted about the unloved woman. I skimmed through quickly, not finding anything similar until all the way in chapter thirty. "*For three things the earth is disquieted . . .*" I read. Nan had said, " *. . . the earth cannot bear . . .*" but that was a more recent translation, and this was the King James. I skimmed down to verse twenty-three. " *. . . an odious woman when she is married.*"

Odious! Was the woman unloved because she was odious? It was such an . . . *odious* word. It sounded like how the manure from the dairy farm smelled. Repulsive.

Oh, Lord, I prayed, *I don't want to be odious. . . .*

Please help me to be wise, like Esther. You know . . . the one in the Bible—

My prayer was short. Pete entered the room wearing his long underwear.

I'd been wanting to ask him about the other woman for days. I cleared my throat. He ignored me. I cleared my throat again.

He looked up briefly as he unfurled his sleeping bag.

"So what's her name?"

"Whose name?"

"The woman across the street. The one you were waving to in the field."

"She's no one." He blushed.

My heart turned inside out. "She didn't look like 'no one.' She looked like someone who matters to you—a lot."

He stepped toward the bed, standing closer to me than he had in days, but didn't answer.

"Maybe that's why . . ." I stopped, realizing I wasn't sure how to go on. I felt out of sorts with Pete so close.

The smell of smoke and kerosene mingled with the strong odor of lye soap and the manly scent of my husband. Pete's hand fluttered, and for a second I thought he was reaching out to me, but then he turned toward the lamp and turned it off, the flame sputtering as it died out.

He stayed put a moment in the dark but then stepped away.

My heart palpitated as Pete wiggled into his sleeping bag.

Why couldn't he have reassured me that the woman didn't mean anything to him? Sure we'd agreed to a marriage of convenience, but that didn't mean he had a right to pine away for someone besides me.

I turned toward the wall. Why couldn't he love me the way I had started to love him—before I knew the truth?

I stifled a sob.

Because he didn't love me. Because he'd never loved me. Because he would never love me.

His breathing slowed. Pete would have reached out to me tonight if there was any hope.

I knew I couldn't survive this, not on my own. *Lord,* I begged, *I really need your help. I really need your love.*

CHAPTER

19

The next day, as I weeded the garden and prayed again that the Lord would help me, an Englisch woman pulled into the driveway. I stood straight and greeted her warmly, surprised at how happy I, the introvert, was to see a strange face.

She asked for Esther. I started toward the house, but before I reached the back door my mother-in-law appeared. She ignored me as she tottered down the steps, even though I was just a few feet from her. I headed back toward the garden.

"Come back in six weeks or so," she told the woman.

"You said you'd be done by today." Disappointment filled the woman's voice.

"I said I hoped to have it done by today. I've been delayed," Esther said.

I'd reached the garden, stepping carefully to the row of beans I'd been weeding. I couldn't hear any more of their conversation, but a few minutes later the screen on the mud porch slammed, and the Englisch woman walked toward me.

"Excuse me," she said.

I looked up, my hand on my lower back as I straightened.

"Can I ask you a couple of questions?"

I nodded.

"Has Esther been too busy to quilt?"

"I don't think so," I said.

"I was going to give it to my daughter, for her wedding . . ."

"When is that?" I asked.

"Two months."

"She'll have it done." I hoped I was right.

The woman frowned. "She's the best quilter around. But I wonder if she's getting a little old. . . ." The woman shook her head, as if stopping herself. "You must be her new daughter-in-law."

I nodded.

"It's so odd. She told me once you moved in, she'd have more time to quilt."

I shrugged my shoulders. "I don't know anything about her work." I still hadn't been inside her quilting room.

"You're from Lancaster, right?"

"Jah."

For the next ten minutes the woman told me about her trip to "Amish Country" a few years ago, describing the different quilt shops she'd visited. I was familiar with many of them. Finally, as much as I enjoyed listening to her, I said I needed to get back to work. I had to finish weeding before it was time to start dinner.

She sighed. "Well, I'll be back."

I didn't say I'd see her then. I sincerely hoped I wouldn't.

I made tomato soup and grilled cheese sandwiches for lunch, making sure there was plenty for seconds and even thirds. For the first time since I'd been cooking for the family, I didn't burn, scorch, or damage a thing. Of course, no one commented on my accomplishment, but Esther didn't scowl at me either. I was thankful for small blessings.

The days went by, pretty much the same, the only difference

being the chores I did. On Friday a letter arrived from Dat and Betsy, but I found it disappointing. They were happy I was doing well. Betsy said absolutely nothing about how she felt and didn't write a thing about getting married.

On Sunday I went to church with Pete and his parents. It was the first time I'd been in a buggy since I'd arrived. Esther and I rode in the back, while Pete and Walter, who did the driving, rode up front. We plodded along. The horse was one of the workhorses, so I couldn't expect anything more.

I sat by Esther during the service and the meal, and I searched the crowd for a young woman who looked like the one who lived across the highway but didn't see anyone who fit my picture of her.

One of the women sitting at our table asked how I liked living at the Treger farm. I said I liked it fine. What else could I say? Another asked how life there compared to Lancaster. I said there were several things that were the same and several that were different but didn't elaborate. Still the two women exchanged glances. A third asked how I met Pete. I said I met him at the bookmobile.

That made Esther laugh. "He didn't tell me that. He said he worked for your Dat."

"That too," I said.

"Well, there's no one who likes books more than Pete," the third woman said.

Esther made a guttural sound but didn't say anything.

As soon as we were done eating, Esther was ready to go, but Walter was in the middle of a conversation and it seemed she was having a hard time pulling him away. I went outside ahead of them and found Pete waiting in the buggy. Several of the men standing around outside watched me as I walked by, but none of them said anything.

Pete nodded his head toward me, a gesture that seemed intended more for the nearby men than for me. I climbed into the buggy, unassisted, and then we sat silently until his parents arrived. I was pretty sure we were the first family—if you could call us that—to leave.

The next week was spent getting ready for the reunion. On Monday I washed the clothes and then started on the windows. They hadn't been cleaned in several years, or so it seemed. Walter mowed the lawn with the push mower, but after his third rest on the plastic lawn chair under the elm tree in just half an hour, I finished it. Tuesday, Wednesday, and Thursday I cleaned the inside of the house, which I was pretty sure hadn't been done in a long, long time either.

On Friday, my mother-in-law abandoned her quilting and began making pies. She started by bossing me around, telling me to go get the box of apples from the cellar in the basement, then to start peeling the apples. She sat at the table, her hand wrapped around her mug, watching me.

"You're wasting too much of the fruit." She put her coffee down and picked up an apple. "That might be the way you do things in Lancaster, but not here." She reached out her hand, and I extended the knife as I heard a step behind me.

Pete stood in the doorway.

"Why aren't you at work?" Esther asked.

He held up a torn glove. "I have an extra pair upstairs." He'd taken off his boots and was making his way across the kitchen in his stocking feet.

"Well, just as long as you're going back," Esther muttered.

I cocked my head. I couldn't figure the woman out. All Pete did was work. Obviously not anticipating an answer

246

from Pete, she started back in on me. "The idea here is to feed the people—not the chickens or the hogs. They only get the peel, not half the fruit with it." She went on berating me.

I'd been standing but decided to get a bit of a rest while she had my knife, so I sat down.

Pete stepped back into the kitchen, taking his time, as she said, "You do it like this." She peeled the apple deftly and quickly. By the time Pete was back out the door, she had the whole thing done, in one long stretch of peel with just a trace of white fruit on it, hanging from the knife. She dropped the peel on the table.

My face burned and my tongue began to itch, but I literally bit it to keep from responding.

"Watch the waste when you core it too. I know how you young girls are—especially pretty ones from wealthy homes. Around here, though, it's waste not, want not."

She extended the knife back to me, but I had to stand to reach it. As I did, I saw that Pete was still in the mudroom, probably putting on his boots. He looked up, his eyes meeting mine, and smiled warily.

My breath caught, and I turned my attention back to Esther, taking the knife from her and then concentrating on doing it right while she made the piecrust and then rolled it out. An hour later she chided me for taking so long.

"I guess you'll have to finish up these pies," she said. "I'll go ahead and get started on the vinegar ones."

I wrinkled my nose.

"Jah, vinegar. Around here, we're thankful for what the Lord provides, even if it is a bit lowbrow for your tastes," she responded. "We don't have lemons the way you do in Lancaster." She laughed at that, as if she'd made a great joke.

"I could go to town and buy a few," I offered.

"Don't get smart with me." She headed to the pantry.

I hadn't meant to be smart—but she didn't know that. I fixed my eyes on a water spot in the corner of the room up by the ceiling, took a deep breath, and willed myself to stay calm. I'd made a really stupid choice, and now I was living with the consequences. Kicking and screaming wasn't going to make it any better. I knew now what that sort of behavior would lead to when I was old.

That night, I couldn't find the devotional book. I'd finished it the evening before, for the sixth time, and was looking forward to starting it again. I panicked, looking under the bed and then through my things. It was nowhere to be found. I eyed Pete's pile in the corner. Where else could it be? He had a flashlight. Maybe he'd been reading it after I fell asleep. I picked up his pillow and when I did, the book fell to the floor. Relieved, I climbed into bed with it.

When Pete finally came in, I offered it to him.

"Denki," he said. "I've been feeling crazy without anything to read."

"Ach." I sighed. "Me too. How did you survive growing up?"

He didn't answer me.

"Pete?"

"I'd get to the library when I could hitch a ride. The first time I was ten."

I was up on one elbow. "You hitchhiked when you were ten! What did your mother say?"

"A lot. I was grounded from reading for months." He grimaced.

I plopped back down. Esther was worse than I thought. "But you kept going on adventures."

"Jah, now and then. But believe me, I've always felt tremendous guilt for it. I'd stay around mostly, until I couldn't stand it and then take off again. But this last time was the longest."

"What got you through the times when you were home?"

Pete answered immediately. "I started working at the dairy when I was thirteen—of course, all my money went to my folks. It was still worth it, though, because our neighbor has a nice collection of books."

"But he's Amish?"

"Jah," he answered.

"So it's just your parents who don't believe in reading around here?"

"It's not that they're morally opposed—just too frugal to buy books, I think. And they're not interested, so they think it's a waste of time. Plus, Mamm was convinced reading's what made me so headstrong—although I'm pretty sure I was that way before I learned to read."

I bit my tongue from saying he'd gotten his mother's stubborn streak—she just didn't realize it. Instead I told him he could leave the lamp on, adding, "I'll still be able to sleep."

"Denki," he said. "My flashlight battery is getting weak."

I turned over, facing the wall.

"Cate?"

"Jah." I didn't bother to roll back over.

"You were good to my Mamm today. . . . I appreciate it."

"What are you talking about?" I rolled toward him.

"When she was scolding you about peeling the apples."

"Oh, that." I'd put it out of my mind. Maybe I was changing, just a little.

"She doesn't realize she's so harsh."

I found it sweet that he felt protective of her, regardless of the way she'd treated him through the years. "She's wasn't that bad." Not like she'd been in the past, anyway, especially

Pete's past. I told him about the vinegar pie and my comments about the lemons. He actually laughed, although softly, but stopped abruptly at the sound of a knock on the door.

"Put that light out." It was Esther, of course. "You're wasting oil."

I couldn't help the smile that spread across my face.

Sitting in his long underwear, even though the room was hot and stuffy, Pete looked as if he was going to burst into laughter.

"Are you asleep?" she asked as the door flew open. I fumbled to turn the wick down and extinguish the flame.

Her eyes were glued on Pete. "Why are you on the floor?" But then she turned to me. "What kind of woman are you? Not letting your husband sleep in your bed."

With one last turn, I managed to get the light out.

"Shame on you!" She pulled the door shut with a bang. Then her voice, a little shaky, came from the other side of the door. "I thought the two of you'd gone to sleep with the lamp on. That's the only reason I came in."

Neither Pete nor I said a word. A second later the devotional landed on the bed beside me, and I put it on the table by the lamp.

"Good night," I whispered, overcome with regret. My coercing Pete into a marriage of convenience was hurting more than just the two of us.

"Jah," Pete said. "Good night."

I was pretty sure he was lamenting what we'd done as much as I was.

All of Pete's brothers except for John hired a driver to bring them to their parents' house. Besides John, Bert lived the closest at ten miles away. Others lived various places in Chautauqua County. Several of the families lived up to the north. A few lived in Pennsylvania's Big Valley. It seemed the family liked to get around, although none as much as the youngest.

The brothers all greeted Pete warmly, and they seemed happy enough to meet me. The sisters-in-law were polite but not overly so. John was the last to arrive, alone. "Jana's not feeling well," he said.

I already thought it odd that I hadn't yet met the sister-in-law who, by Esther's account, lived the closest. And it seemed as if she would have to be quite ill not to join her husband.

Of course there were grandchildren from nearly thirty years old, older than Pete, to a three-month-old, plus all the great-grandchildren. Livy, Bert's wife, was the biggest help in the kitchen. She was close to fifty and under her bonnet was silvery hair. She was plump and had a warm, friendly smile. For a moment we found ourselves alone, and she asked me how I was managing.

I thought perhaps Esther had told her I was making Pete sleep on the floor, but my face must have been puzzled, because she said, "You know. Living here."

I wrinkled my nose.

"Well, we all think you're a saint."

"Oh?"

"Haven't you wondered why none of us live here? Not even Jana would, even though John will soon have the farm." She frowned. "We all had an advantage, though—we actually had the chance to meet Esther before we married into the family."

"That's true," I answered.

"Well." She patted my shoulder. "Bert and I would like to get to know you better. He's going to talk to Pete about you two coming over soon. Pete's always been like a son to me, since I joined the family before he was born."

I had noticed that Pete was hanging out more with his nephews than his siblings, except for Bert. He seemed closest with his oldest brother. Funny thing was, in all the time we'd lived with his parents, I hadn't seen him interact at all with John. Not once. John often ate dinner with his parents, but Pete was always at the neighbors'. Then John would be gone by suppertime when Pete came home.

"What's John's wife like?" I asked.

Livy's eyes grew wide. "Jana?"

"Jah." I looked at her closely.

"Well . . ." She seemed to be stalling. "She's nice." She smiled.

"Do you know her well?"

"Sure. She's been around for quite a while."

"How long have she and John been married?"

"Oh, less than a year."

"So they courted a long time?"

Livy pursed her lips together as if she wasn't sure what to say. "Something like that," she finally said.

Esther came marching through the door, interrupting us. "Time to put the rest of the food out," she said. "Let's get this over with."

I couldn't help but notice Livy's sad look. And to think I'd seen myself as antisocial my whole life. Compared to Esther, I was top-of-the-chart outgoing.

I carried the pot of baked beans that had been in the oven all morning out to the hot-food table, which was already heaped with dishes.

Pete and his older nephews had a gunnysack race going with the school-aged children, and Esther yelled at them to stop. The kids kept squealing until they saw their grand-mother headed their way. In no time they were on their feet, the sacks wadded in their hands.

I headed to the icehouse and grabbed the first of the two big tubs of potato salad Esther had made the day before. I'd cautioned her about leaving them out too long, saying she didn't want the mayo, homemade, of course, to go bad and poison anyone. She harrumphed and said we didn't need to worry about that. It would all be gobbled up in no time. Then she told me to mind my own business. I answered that safety was everyone's business, but she ignored me.

Now, after delivering them to the food table, I went back for the vinegar pies, which we'd topped with meringue. My arms were still sore from beating the egg whites.

When everyone had gathered around, Walter cleared his throat and said he wanted to say a few words.

"We've been so blessed," he said. "With this farm. And our sons and daughters-in-law and grandchildren and great-grandchildren." His eyes watered. "Haven't we, Esther?"

She stood across the circle and dipped her head.

"God has provided everything we need, day by day." Abruptly he lowered his head and led the silent prayer. I couldn't keep from questioning his words by thinking of all the work that needed to be done on the farm and how their children didn't seem to visit very often. Or how destitute the old couple seemed. I chided myself. It wasn't right to be critical. Clearly God was meeting their needs.

"Amen," Walter called out, and then he and Esther started dishing up their plates. After them, the mothers with the youngest children went through, then Bert and Livy. It seemed there was a prescribed order to the line—and that Pete and I were last.

Just like at a church service, the women sat at different tables than the men, except none of the women seemed very interested in me, except for Livy.

After we were done eating, as the tables were being cleared, Livy asked Pete when he knew I was the right girl for him.

"Oh my," I quickly said, stacking the two completely empty potato salad bowls. "Don't put him on the spot."

"No." Esther stood, her plate in her hand. "Do. I'd like to know."

Bert put his arm around Pete. "We'd all like to."

Pete tugged on his short beard and raised his eyebrows, his expression softening. "Let's see," he said. "I knew Cate was something the first time I met her. Her wit won me over immediately. By the time I asked her to go hiking, I was a goner. And by the time we went kayaking, I was one hundred percent sure she was the girl for me."

He glanced at me again. Instead of the sarcastic smile I expected, his quick expression appeared sincere. "Jah," he said, turning away and back to the others, "I guess you could say I knew that very first day."

"Awww," Livy said.

Esther left the table with a "harrumph." Apparently I wasn't the only one who knew Pete was lying—but I had no idea he'd be so good at it.

Later, as Livy and I were doing dishes in the sweltering kitchen, not wanting the topic to return to Pete and me, I asked her if Jana had come to the reunion the summer before.

"As a matter of fact, she did." Livy added cold water from the pump to the basin of nearly boiling water.

"Where will Esther and Walter live when John takes over the farm for good?" I asked.

"Well," Livy said, "it depends on where you and Pete are living by then."

"Oh, we won't be living here," I said. "John's getting the farm. There's no reason for us to stay."

Livy trailed her fingers through the water, stirring up the bubbles. "You've been a big help to Esther." She leaned toward me. "She said your cooking is getting better."

When I didn't respond, Livy added, "She wants you to stay."

"Oh, no," I blurted out. "We're going back to Lancaster. My sister will be getting married soon. Dat will help us start a business. Being here is just temporary." I could try to emulate Queen Esther for a short while—but certainly not for a lifetime.

Livy scrubbed a plate and plunged it into the rinse water. "Have you talked to Pete? Because that's not what Esther said this morning."

C H A P T E R

20

Talking with Livy made me anxious, but she was still the best thing about the reunion.

It turned out the day of interacting with others had to last me, because it was a few more weeks, other than at services, until I saw anyone else. The dread of Esther thinking she could somehow force us to permanently live in New York weighed heavy, and the days ticked by.

About every third meal I cooked was edible, but I was growing weary of coming up with ideas day after day. I did feel as if my attempt to cook and clean and garden and get along with Esther and with Pete, as much as possible, was changing something in me, though. I wasn't sure what exactly I was learning, but it seemed I was less uptight than I had been. And less prone to react in anger. But that didn't take away my loneliness or the hurt inside.

I was thrilled when Pete finally said we were going to visit Bert and Livy.

"Are we going to hire a driver?"

"I thought we'd take the buggy. On the off Sunday."

I thought of the money he'd spent for us to go hiking and kayaking. But of course he knew if it all worked out, the local bachelors would reimburse him, and more. I admired a frugal person and was one myself, but I worried Pete might end up being a miser like his parents.

We left the farm midmorning on a hot and humid Sunday. The old horse couldn't go fast enough to create a decent breeze, and we sweltered in the heat mile after mile.

Finally I broke the silence, asking, "When will we return to Lancaster?"

"Not sure," was all he said.

I was expecting an invitation to Betsy's wedding. In her last letter she said she'd send one soon. Even Nan, in a recent letter, said she was looking forward to the wedding.

I squirmed on the bench, trying to get comfortable. "We'll go back by the time Betsy gets married, though, right?" She still hadn't told me how she was doing, and I'd given up finding a phone to call her, finally deciding if she needed me, she'd let me know.

"Probably," Pete said. "But I don't know for how long."

I nearly bolted over the front of the buggy. "You mean we'd come back here?"

"Perhaps," he said.

"We've already been—"

"My Mamm likes having you here." His mouth twitched in a near smile.

I took a deep breath and turned my head, pretending to be intent on the farm to my right. The windmill stood statue-still in the heat. A cow switched her tail in the pasture. A Plain boy and girl sat on the porch steps, both barefoot.

Finally Pete asked. "What, no argument?"

"I thought we'd be leaving—"

He didn't allow me to finish. "How about doing what's best for your family?"

"What family?" I crossed my arms.

We rode on in stony silence, finally turning off the main road. By the time a recently whitewashed barn and house appeared I was sticky with sweat. As we approached the porch, an old man who had been sitting in a rocking chair stood. He looked like Walter except heavier and younger.

"Uncle Wes!" Pete called out, setting the brake, jumping from the buggy, and bounding up the steps. I followed him to the porch.

It seemed too good to be true. The uncle who was in the publishing business was visiting Bert and Livy.

The man enveloped Pete in a bear hug and then slapped him on the back, hard, three times.

"And who's this?" Wes stepped back, grinning at me.

"Cate," Pete said.

"You're not from around here, are you?"

I blushed, dreading what was coming next. "I'm from Lancaster County."

"Whereabouts?"

"Near Paradise."

He nodded. "Wonderful place. Great sales around there."

"I can imagine." Although the tourists clogged the roads during the summer months, their spending helped support families all through Lancaster County.

He grinned. "Yep, I got into the business at the right time. Besides the books, I print a map and brochure of authentic Amish sites. It's one of my biggest sellers."

"Uncle Wes is in the publishing business," Pete said.

I nodded. I remembered.

"I'll be right back," Pete said. "I'm going to unhitch the horse. Tell Livy I'll be right in."

"I'll go with you," Wes said to Pete. "I've been wanting

to talk to you for the last year." He laughed. "You've been a little hard to track down."

That was when I noticed the black car on the side of the house. It had to be Wes's.

***

Uncle Wes, Bert, and Pete told one story after another during dinner. I was pretty sure, if it weren't for Esther, that Walter would be like his brother. A kick in the pants and then some. Instead Walter was a man walking on eggshells.

Livy joined in the laughter, clearly amused. I found myself smiling and laughing a few times too.

After dinner, the men went outside to the porch while I helped Livy clean up. We chatted as we worked, of course, mostly about her children and grandchildren, who all lived nearby. Most of them were even in their district. She went down the list, describing each individual. It was clear she was a loving, doting mother and grandmother. After we'd finished, she made us iced coffees. They had a fridge and a freezer, although small, and even vanilla creamer. Their lifestyle wasn't anywhere near as austere as Pete's parents'.

As we sat at the table, I asked her how long they'd lived on their farm.

"Oh, thirty years now," she said. "It belonged to my grandparents. They let us make payments to them. Pete used to come out a lot when he was little."

I cocked my head, encouraging her to say more.

"Esther wasn't well. We'd take him for stretches at a time. Sometimes as long as a couple of months."

I risked asking what had been wrong with Esther. Thankfully Livy didn't appear to mind.

"At the time I didn't know. Looking back, though, I would

say she was depressed." She lowered her voice. "Pete was a big surprise, if you know what I mean. It would be like me having a baby now, almost. And she'd lost a baby a few years before him. A little girl, stillborn. It broke Esther's heart."

I gasped.

Livy continued. "All those boys and finally a girl, only to have her die the day before she was born."

Tears stung my eyes for Esther as I wrapped my warm hands around the ice-cold glass. How tragic.

"She poured herself into John after that. He clearly became her favorite. Not that it mattered to Bert or the older kids, but it was pretty obvious to Pete over the years. Maybe if he'd been a girl, she would have been different. But as it was, she resented him."

Livy took a long drink of her coffee and then said, "Pete had a mind of his own from the beginning. She hated that."

She paused for a moment, but I didn't comment, hoping she'd say more. My waiting paid off. She lowered her voice, "He's never said anything negative about her, though. Never complained. Not even after . . ."

"After what?"

She wadded her hands in her apron. "There I've gone, saying too much." She lifted her head, catching my eye.

I shook my head, wanting her to know I didn't have a clue what she was talking about.

"Pete hasn't told you anything?"

"No." I could say that with assurance.

"He hasn't said anything about Jana?"

I shook my head again as an icy sensation grew in the pit of my stomach.

"She's three years younger than Pete, but they went to

school together." She took a deep breath. "I think I've had too much caffeine today. This is my third cup."

"No," I said, afraid she'd stop talking. "Go on."

"Then they courted," she said. "From the time she was seventeen or so. All of us thought they would marry. Pete worked like crazy at the dairy, but Esther and Walter took every cent he made, even after he turned twenty-one." She drained her coffee. "Then last fall, quite a while after the annual family reunion, we heard John was interested in Jana. The next thing we knew Pete had left—it was well into October—without telling any of us good-bye."

I took a deep breath.

"Although he did tell the bishop—said he wanted to look at other settlements. And then in December, John and Jana got married."

I shook my head, puzzled. "What happened?"

"None of us know, but Esther told me before the wedding it was for the best, that she knew all along Jana was right for John, not Pete. And the thing was, John had always treated Pete badly. He was constantly after him right up until when he stole Jana." Livy's face reddened. "Not that she didn't have a say."

I remembered Pete saying John had always been a bit of a sneak, but it was hard for me to imagine John as mean, because he seemed so complacent, but maybe he'd stopped once he got what he wanted.

"So if Jana and Esther are so close, why don't John and Jana live on the farm?"

"Well, that's just it," Livy said. "Jana and Esther had a falling-out right before the wedding. That's when John rented the house they're in."

"Which is where?"

Livy gave me a confused look. "What do you mean?"

"Where exactly is their home?"

She had a puzzled look on her face. "Across the highway from Jana's grandfather's land . . . which is next to Esther and Walter's place. . . ."

I tried to swallow but instead I choked. The woman talking to Pete along the fence—waving at Pete from her yard—was Jana? She was the woman he had loved? And still did?

"Are you okay?" Livy put her glass on the table.

I shook my head as I tried to say, "Jah." Instead it came out as, "Nah." I took a drink of my coffee, but it went down the wrong pipe, and I started to cough.

Livy patted my back and said, "There, there."

If only that could have really made everything all right.

When Pete and I left late in the afternoon, the humidity was even more oppressive. I stole a glance at Pete. His hat rested back on his head. His bangs curled a tad in the heat, and a trickle of sweat ran down the side of his face. He swiped at it and then wiped his hand on his pants.

But he hummed as he held the reins. Thinking of Livy's story I felt compassion for him. It must have been hard for him to return to the farm. Doubly so with Jana married to John and living across the highway.

Getting away to Bert's and seeing his uncle seemed to have lifted his spirits, though.

"Tell me about Wes," I said, wiggling on the bench to try to get my dress unstuck from my sweaty legs, trying to put the thought of Jana out of my head.

Pete didn't answer immediately. I sighed, certain he was giving me the silent treatment, but then he said, "I was just thinking about him, going over what we talked about."

"Which was?"

"He has a New York City publisher interested in buying his business but keeping him on as the executive editor."

"That's great." I took a deep breath. It sounded as if Uncle Wes had successfully carried out *my* dream. Maybe it was easier as a Mennonite.

"Except he wants to cut back."

"Oh." My brain was twirling.

"He wanted to know if I was interested."

I sat up straight. "In working for him?" In my excitement, I thought, for a split second, that maybe we could be partners in a publishing business, that I could work alongside Pete.

"Jah."

"And with the New York City publisher too?" I couldn't imagine living in New York City.

Pete nodded. "Something like that."

"Oh." I didn't see how that would do us any good. "What kind of books does Wes publish, besides the tourist maps and brochures?"

"School curriculum, devotionals, histories, biographies. Stuff like that for Plain people. But with more Englisch people interested in Plain topics, his distribution and sales are up."

A car honked behind us, and Pete pulled the horse as far over on the shoulder as he could, letting the car pass. "Although the print industry is changing with electronic books, it won't have the same impact when it comes to the Plain market."

That sounded promising. "When did Wes leave the Amish?"

"He never joined. My grandparents became Mennonite about the same time. They were in one of those districts where almost everyone did. Dat and my Mamm had already married by then, though, and were in a new district—she wouldn't consider leaving."

Pete stopped at a crossroads and then turned left. "Mamm always thought I would leave, even after I joined the church. Turns out she was sure I had when I took off like that." He stared straight ahead. "Even though I talked to the bishop before I left."

I swallowed hard. "Livy told me about Jana."

He tipped his hat so I couldn't see his face.

"Pete?"

"I don't want to talk about it."

"I'm sorry," I said. And I was. I, too, knew what it was like to have my heart broken—twice.

A stretch of downhill was in front of us, and the horse began trotting. A thick patch of evergreens rose to the sky on one side of the road and a field of knee-high corn spread wide on the other. The countryside didn't look familiar.

"Did we come this way?"

He shook his head. "I'm taking the scenic route back."

I couldn't help but notice he'd said *back* not *home.*

"Where does Wes live?" I asked.

"In Maryland, not far from Baltimore."

I turned toward the corn. I'd hate to live there too. Maybe even more than on a farm in New York with an outhouse and an icehouse and a tub in the pantry. I remember my grandmother saying, when I'd complain, that *"Things could always be worse."* My new life proved it.

The horse slowed on the upside of the steep hill. I could see a building at the top. As we finally reached the crest, a firehouse, probably the one Pete had mentioned earlier, was ahead of us. Just as we reached it, a siren went off. The horse startled. Pete clucked his tongue and called out, "Giddy up."

I was pretty sure he wanted to get as far down the road as he could before the fire truck went barreling by. But it ended up turning the other way.

We plodded along, silently. I had no idea where we were. About a mile later, we came to the crest of a smaller hill. To the left was a house. It took a split second for me to realize it was Jana and John's home. They were sitting out in the yard in lawn chairs. Jana waved. Pete kept his eyes on the road. I don't know what came over me, but I stuck my head behind Pete's and waved back as we passed, a big smile on my face. Jana's hand froze in midair. And John began to laugh—the first time I'd seen him do so since I'd met him.

Pete stared straight ahead.

Four days later, on Thursday morning, I sat shelling peas in the shade of the willow, a midweek load of laundry flapping on the line a few yards away, thinking about Jana, wondering what she was up to. Why was she so friendly with Pete when she'd obviously chosen his brother? Did she regret her decision? It wasn't like it could be undone.

I grimaced at the irony. Maybe being trapped was something Jana and I had in common.

I chided myself. I was speculating. I didn't know a thing about her. Maybe she was just friendly. Maybe she thought, all along, she and Pete were just friends. Maybe he'd been the one who had blown things out of proportion. Although I doubted it.

A movement from over by the pasture caught my attention. Pete was vaulting the fence, much like he had back in Lancaster when he wiped out in the gravel. This time he landed perfectly and sprinted to the house. I squinted into the hot sun, surprised to see him.

He didn't notice me under the willow, and I didn't say anything. I continued shelling the peas. After a while I could see a figure through the window of the pantry. I was pretty sure it was Pete. Something was up if he was getting all spiffy.

I finished the peas and was tossing the pods into the compost at the edge of the garden when a black car came into view. It was Wes. He parked, and I called out a hello as he got out.

"Is Pete ready to go?"

"I'm not sure." I didn't want to admit I didn't know what was going on. "Come on in. I'll check."

He looped his fingers in his suspenders. "I'll wait out here. Thanks."

I told him to sit in the shade. "It's going to be another scorcher."

He nodded.

When I reached the kitchen, I knocked on the pantry door. "Wes is outside."

"Denki!" Pete's voice was full of cheer.

Then I went to find Walter. He often disappeared during the day, going upstairs to nap, I presumed, but this morning he was in the living room, dozing in his chair.

"Wes is here," I said.

He didn't stir.

"Your brother." I touched his shoulder.

He didn't respond.

"Wes is outside," I said.

Walter smiled slightly, and then his eyes flew open. "What's he doing here?" Walter scooted forward in his chair.

"Seems he and Pete are going somewhere."

Walter struggled to his feet. "Well, I'll be," he said, heading for the back door. I followed, wanting to see the two brothers greet each other.

I stood on the top step as Walter limped across the lawn, his arms outstretched to Wes, who was making his way to his brother. They embraced, clapping each other on the back, and then holding on to each other in a tight embrace, rocking back and forth as one.

Tears filled my eyes. I missed Betsy.

Pete's voice startled me. "I hope they don't knock each other down."

"They're so sweet," I said.

Pete chuckled. "And sour."

"How long since they've seen each other?"

"Ten years? Maybe more."

"Why?"

"I'm not sure. . . . At least not entirely."

The two old men finally stepped away from each other and fell into conversation.

I walked down the steps and looked back up at Pete. He wore his nicest pair of trousers and a clean shirt. His muscles had bulked up even more in the last couple of months, and his beard was filling out nicely. He held Dat's black hat in his hands.

"Look at you, all gussied up," I said.

He pulled the hat onto his head, shading his tanned face. "Want to go with us?"

"Where?"

"To meet with the publisher Wes has been talking with."

I tilted my head. If Pete really wanted me to go, it seemed he would have asked me sooner, but I wasn't going to let that stop me. "Sure," I responded.

"Ready?" Wes called out.

"Jah." Pete hurried down the stairs.

"Missus coming?"

Walter appeared surprised as he turned and looked past me at the house.

Wes laughed. "The new missus, I mean."

Walter chuckled.

Pete nodded his head.

Breathless, I called out, "Give me just a minute." I dashed back into the house, determined to be as fast as I could. The publisher must be staying somewhere nearby. I imagined him at the Chautauqua compound, less than an hour away. I'd read about it over the years and imagined the publisher vacationing there with his family, taking in the lectures and the nearby recreation. Or perhaps he was in Jamestown, which wasn't far either.

I ran up the stairs, pulled off my apron, grabbed a clean one and a fresh Kapp and two pins, slipping them between my lips. I hurried back down the stairs, pulling off my kerchief as I did, nearly knocking Esther down at the bottom, where she stood with her hands on her hips.

"What in the world is going on?"

"I'm going with Pete," I said through the pins, darting past her. "Ask Walter." I skidded through the living room and on into the kitchen, tightening my bun and then pulling my Kapp on my head as I banged through the back door. By the time I reached the car, where Pete was standing in a huddle with his uncle and Dat, I had my Kapp secured.

"Let's go," Wes said, slapping Walter on the back again. "You'll be long asleep—or maybe just getting up—by the time we get back." He took a step back. "It's been really good to see you." The two men hugged again.

I had no idea where we were going, but it sounded as if it was much farther than I'd thought.

C H A P T E R
21

Once we reached the highway, I leaned toward the front seat. "So where are we meeting the publisher?"

Wes gave me an amused look in the rearview mirror and then shot Pete an annoyed look. "You didn't tell her?"

Pete shook his head. "I wanted to wait until you arrived—to be sure it was really going to happen."

"New York," Wes said.

Assuming he meant the city, because we were already in the state, I leaned back against the seat, a smile spreading across my face. I'd always wanted to see the Big Apple but never dreamed I would.

Wes had sandwiches, carrot sticks, and apple slices, which I guessed Livy had packed for us to eat. We only stopped twice, at rest areas. It was midafternoon by the time we arrived in the city. Traffic wasn't bad on the way in, and Wes seemed to know where he was going, right into the heart of Manhattan. I tried my best to take it all in: the tall buildings and the shadows they cast, the streams of people in all sorts of attire rushing along the sidewalks, and the current of cars, trucks, and taxis swept along, this way and that. The billboards captivated me the most. Some were electronic and flashing colors and words. Others were as big as buildings. On one, the height of ten stories, a woman posed in a short, short skirt and gazed over the city. The billboards advertised everything from beer to TVs. Pete's head bobbed up and down too, but Wes seemed unfazed by everything going on around us. He even knew exactly where to park—in a garage crammed with cars.

He led the way to an elevator and then down to the street level. I kept feeling as if I should pinch myself. I'd never dreamed of seeing the city. We walked for a couple of blocks on a crowded sidewalk, past stairs that led down to the subway and then along the front of a department store. Wes stepped into a doorway, and we followed. Another elevator ride took us to the fourteenth floor of the building, and we walked into a waiting area, where Pete and I stood while Wes spoke with the receptionist.

I was beside myself with curiosity but was pretty sure, because Pete hadn't told me about the meeting in the first place, that I shouldn't join them.

"I can wait here," I said.

Pete seemed relieved. "I'm just gathering information. I'm not ready to make a decision."

I nodded.

Wes motioned to us but didn't seem surprised when I sat down in one of the comfy chairs.

As they followed the receptionist down the hall, I picked up a women's magazine and leafed through it for the next thirty minutes. I was surprised when the publisher followed them out to the waiting area.

"I wanted to meet you," he said, extending his hand. He was middle-aged and wore a short-sleeve shirt and slacks. He had a professional look to him with his short blond hair and clean-shaven face but seemed a little frail, at least compared to Pete. "Your husband says you're quite a reader."

"Jah." There was no reason to explain I'd been deprived since I'd arrived in New York.

"I won't ask what you read—Pete says you aren't typical. But what do you think Amish women in general want to read?"

I mentioned pregnancy, first aid, parenting, nutrition, and relationships. I blushed at the word. That was a book I'd never be able to write.

"Bible stories for children," I quickly added. "And recipe books. Most women—probably all except for my sister and a few like her—run out of ideas for dinner at some time or another." I know I did. "But they should be with simple ingredients that one would have on hand. And histories too, and fiction that holds to our values." I wanted to add books on basic sex education, done tastefully, would be a good idea, also, but was too embarrassed to say it.

"Those are all good ideas. And many of them, especially the cookbooks, would cross over to other markets." The man shook my hand again and then turned to Wes and Pete, thanked them for coming. "I'm impressed," he said. "I think all of you have good ideas." He nodded toward Pete. "And I think your uncle's right. I see leadership potential in you. I'll be in touch."

I felt a surge of hope as we left. Pete was a leader. He'd shown that working for Dat.

When we reached the car, Wes said he had another meeting, uptown. He didn't say who it was with, though. "You two could find some food around Central Park."

I was too curious to care if it would be safe. Besides, I'd be with Pete. He'd traveled across the continent and back. He could probably handle Uptown Manhattan.

We bought hot dogs from a street vendor, and as we walked and ate I thought of all the books I'd read through the years set in or around New York. After we finished our dinner and tossed our trash into a garbage can, we turned north toward Central Park, dodging a pigeon pecking along the sidewalk.

Ahead was a carriage, with the base of a skyscraper as its backdrop. I marveled at the contrast and relaxed a little at the familiar clopping of the horse's hooves on the pavement. The carriage stopped, and a man and woman, each with a camera in their hands, disembarked.

We soon caught up to the carriage. I reached out to the horse with my free hand and rubbed the star on his forehead. He lifted his head, looking me in the eye.

"You're a beauty," I whispered.

He dipped his head a little and nudged against me.

"Want a ride?" The driver was climbing back up onto the bench. He wore a top hat.

I shook my head. "Just wanted to say hello to the horse." I feared the driver might be annoyed with me, but he grinned.

"Got one of these back home?" he asked.

I nodded. "A standard-bred. And I really miss him."

A woman with a little boy and girl approached, obviously paying customers, so I backed away, wiping my hands on my apron.

Pete patted the horse's neck and stepped beside me, directing me to walk with him across the street and through the entrance to the park. The benches on each side of the pathway were lined with people—couples, singles, and families—all enjoying the summer breeze.

We followed the cobblestone path, stopping at a kiosk with a map of the park. "Have you been here before?" I asked.

"About six years ago. It was one of my first trips. But just for a day."

"I'd like to see the Alice in Wonderland statue." I stepped closer to the map. "And the castle." I'd checked out a travel book on New York a few years ago. Those were the photos that had stuck in my mind.

We continued walking, side by side. A calm came over me that I hadn't felt since the day of the kayaking trip. It actually felt comfortable to be with Pete.

The pathway grew more crowded. We continued on. I admired the flower beds and the gigantic trees, but mostly I stole glances at the people. Some were obviously tourists with their cameras and travel books. Some were New Yorkers, I was sure. There was a young woman pushing a stroller with a preschooler skipping along beside her.

"I've read about nannies in New York," I whispered to Pete. "I think she's one."

He smiled.

We were past the woman now, and I spoke at a normal volume. "I can't imagine not having room for children to play. . . ." I stopped, the hurt returning. I'd never have to worry about that.

Pete picked up his pace, and I matched him, stride for stride. When we reached the Alice in Wonderland statue, there was a crowd around it. A young woman stood next to Alice, posing, while her beau snapped a photo on his phone. A school-aged boy scampered up the back of the rabbit. A middle-aged couple stood off to the side, their two teenage daughters nearby.

"This way," Pete said, directing me toward a bank of trees and then an expansive lawn. We continued on the path. Soon the crowds of people walking ahead grew thicker.

"There must be an event going on tonight," Pete said.

In no time we were being swept along in a river of people. When we reached an amphitheater, it became clear that was the crowd's destination. They began filing into an entrance.

Pete pointed to the left. "We want to be up there."

I could see the castle on the hill.

He led the way around the crowds, across a lawn where groups picnicked on blankets. Two men threw a Frisbee back and forth. When it went wide, toward us, Pete lunged for it, catching it quickly and then snapping it back to the man it was intended for. Both men waved at him in appreciation.

We neared a small grouping of trees. Two people stood face-to-face under the low branches. The woman wore a long, heavy gown, her dark hair piled on her head, like a crown. The man wore a billowy blouse and funny pants. He was broad shouldered and had a full beard, appearing almost bearlike. They were talking rather loudly, but at first I couldn't make out their words. Then the man practically boomed, "'Why, there's a wench! Come on, and kiss me, Kate.'"

I gasped.

Pete laughed.

I stopped, staring at the couple.

"Let's try it again," the woman said in a normal voice.

They repositioned themselves. I could see the profile of the woman's face.

Her voice was clear and her speech concise. "'But now I see our lances are but straws, our strength as weak, our weakness past compare, that seeming to be most which we indeed least are. . . .'"

I gasped again, not sure what she meant, exactly, but the poetry and power of the words left me breathless.

276

Pete grabbed my arm and pulled me away. "Don't you know it's not polite to stare?"

Just then the man boomed, "'Kiss me, Kate!'" again.

I jerked away from Pete. He laughed again.

"What are they doing?" I whispered. They were kissing now—in public.

"Rehearsing," Pete answered. "They're performing tonight. Didn't you see the sign?"

I shook my head.

"Where all the people were going in."

The costumed couple started down the path, walking hand in hand, away from *us*—the Plain couple that stood, figuratively, a world away. The actress jerked away, wrenching her hand free, and gave the man a nasty glare. Then they both laughed, but only for a moment. She stomped off, swinging her body from side to side like a madwoman, the heels of her boots clicking on the concrete.

"They're getting into character," Pete said. "For a play— *The Taming of the Shrew.*"

"Oh." I'd heard the title, but that was all. "She's the shrew?"

He nodded. "Come on. We need to meet Wes in half an hour."

I didn't want to meet Wes. I didn't want our time to end. I wanted to stay in the park, with Pete, for as long as possible.

We both turned at the same time, stepping toward each other as we did, and our arms collided. A jolt shook me, as if the world had just convulsed. I breathed in deeply. Perhaps it was the heat and all the sights and sounds of the city.

"You okay?" Pete's eyes were bright under his black hat.

"Jah." I exhaled slowly. "I'm fine." I stared at him a moment. His brown eyes danced, the way they used to, as brightly as the sun. He was by far the most handsome man I'd seen all day. And he was his old self, confident and kind.

I inhaled sharply and took off walking again, setting a quick pace, with Pete right behind.

In a few minutes we reached the castle and then the top level. I turned toward the amphitheater. The light was waning and I could barely make out a few figures on the stage. Not the dark-haired woman, I was sure. But maybe a blond woman, also in a long gown.

I wished I could stay leaning against the balcony wall of the castle, looking out over the park, the production far below, but Pete urged me to continue on. I led the way down the steps. Soon we were on the sidewalk between the park and the street. Pete positioned himself between the traffic and me. Horns honked. Another carriage passed by. Pedestrians strolled along.

"What's the play about?" I asked Pete.

"Two awful people . . ." His voice trailed off.

"How does it end?"

"I'm not sure," he said.

But I was pretty sure we both knew. *With a kiss.*

Tears pooled in my throat, catching me off guard for the second time in just a few minutes. I quickly wiped at my eyes.

"What's the matter?" Pete slowed his pace a little.

"Nothing," I answered quickly. "Just the exhaust stinging my eyes." But that wasn't it at all. Something had shifted inside of me.

I stopped, and so did he. "I was just thinking. If you really want to stay in New York, if you really think it's what's best for our . . ." I couldn't say the word *family*. "For us, I'll compromise. Whether it's on the farm. Or in the city." I nearly choked on the last word, recalling my thoughts just an hour before about how horrid it would be to live in Manhattan.

He was laughing. "It wouldn't be here. Not even Wes will work here."

I blushed. "Okay, then. Maryland, where Wes lives. Or whatever. I trust your judgment."

He tilted his head, his brown eyes intent. "Really?"

I nodded. "And I think you'd do well working with Wes, for sure, but I think you'd be successful no matter what you decide to do. Farming. Carpentry. Sales. Anything."

"Denki, Cate." Pete smiled under the shadow of his hat.

Surprised by my own graciousness and unsettled by the emotions welling up inside of me, I took off at a brisk walk again. Through the trees was a small lake with a bridge across it. I increased my pace, and by the time we came to the first intersection beyond the park, I was a few feet ahead of Pete.

A horn honked, then another. A taxi zipped by.

Thinking the way was clear, I stepped from the curb and then startled as Pete yelled, "Cate!" As another taxi careened around the corner, he grabbed my arm and yanked me back onto the sidewalk, the yellow blur of the vehicle just inches from me.

"Denki," I whispered, my heart galloping.

We continued on in complete silence after that, all the way to Wes's car. He was waiting for us, leaning against the car, appearing anxious for us to be on our way.

The men chatted about the appointment with the publisher and then Wes's meeting with his friend, who was an editor, as we left the city.

"He said the deal sounded good," Wes said. "But I'll talk it over with my lawyer and get back to you."

"And then I'll need some time to think and pray about it,"

Pete said. "I've been known to be impulsive. I don't want to make a bad decision."

I placed my hand over my heart as if I'd been stabbed, knowing he meant his decision to marry me.

Around ten, Wes said we'd be back at the farm by three or so.

"Will you stay at Mamm and Dat's?" Pete asked him.

He shook his head. "I don't think your mother would be happy to find me on the couch in the morning. She still hasn't seemed to forgive me for not joining the Amish church. I'll drive to Bert's."

It seemed that Esther had tried to control a wide variety of people for many years. I settled against the seat and closed my eyes, but sleep wouldn't come. I became lost in my thoughts, listening to the hum of the wheels on the road through the window that was open just a crack, letting in the cool night air. I thought about the pending business deal. Of the walk in the park. Of the sassy actress and the burly actor. Of Pete pulling me away from the taxi. I sank farther into the back seat, shifting my weight against the vinyl, my heart contracting. Still, I breathed a prayer of thanks. The day had been an unexpected gift.

Wes commented that Bert seemed to be doing well, and then asked Pete about his other siblings. Pete went down the list one by one.

"And how about John? Any children for him and his new bride?"

I couldn't hear Pete's answer, and I didn't open my eyes to see if he was shaking his head.

"Pardon?" Wes asked.

"No."

"Any on the way?"

I was surprised at how forward Wes was, and not surprised when Pete didn't answer.

"Well, maybe you and Cate will have the next grandchild."

Neither said anything for a long moment. I imagined Pete staring straight ahead out the windshield, not giving anything away with his stoic expression.

"What's her family like?" Wes finally asked.

"Just a sister and their father. Her Dat is a good man, the sort who brings out the best in people."

I held as still as I could.

"Sounds like good stock," Wes said. "And Cate seems like a good match for you. Smart. Adventuresome. Patient."

Pete chuckled.

"Well, she is living on the farm."

"That's true," Pete said. "And she's been amazingly gracious about it."

My heart swelled.

But then the front seat shifted a little, and Pete said to Wes, "What have you been reading lately?"

It was Wes's turn to chuckle. "Don't want to talk about your own life?"

Pete's voice was firm. "I finished *Pilgrim's Progress* a while ago. First time. I'm between books right now, though. I've been too busy."

Wes bit, surely knowing full well the hook had been baited. As much as I wanted to, I couldn't stay awake.

Sometime later I drifted out of sleep to hear Pete say, "I'm sure she reads more than anyone I've ever met. I knew right away she was a smart one. That was what first attracted me."

Inwardly I groaned at him repeating the same made-up spiel he'd pitched to his brothers, sisters-in-law, and parents, not sure why he was saying it again when he didn't have to.

When I awoke again, the car had stopped.

"We're here," Wes announced.

I opened my eyes and Pete stirred. It was clear he'd fallen asleep too.

"Will you be okay driving to Bert's?"

"Sure," Wes said. "It's not much farther. I'll be in touch when I've decided what to do."

I managed to tell him thank you. The moon was nearly full and shone brightly over the yard. I headed straight to the outhouse and then to the back door, aware that Pete was still talking with Wes. I entered the house in a sleepy fog and plodded up the stairs to the bedroom, closing the door firmly behind me.

I'd changed into my nightgown and was climbing into bed by the light of the moon shining in the window, when I saw an envelope on the bedside table. I lit the lamp. It was addressed in Betsy's flowery handwriting to *Mr. and Mrs. Pete Treger*.

I opened it quickly.

She was getting married in four weeks. The first of September, just after she turned eighteen. Earlier than most fall weddings, but not as soon as I thought she might. I'd been gone eight weeks—had she confessed her sins immediately and been under the Bann until now? If she was pregnant and the bishop knew, the wedding day would probably be curtailed. No evening meal, nor as many people attending.

I stuffed the invitation back into the envelope. I'd tell Pete about it tomorrow.

A few minutes later he stepped into the room, wearing a thin T-shirt and his long underwear bottoms. I turned toward the wall as he spread out his sleeping bag, shook out the sheet he'd been using because it was so hot, and lay down.

After a while his breathing slowed, so I rolled back and

peeked over the side of the bed. He slept with his arm under his head, his face turned toward me, the sheet pulled up to his chest. With the full moon there was enough light to make out his features. I draped my hand over the bed, my fingers just inches from his face. My heart contracted again and then did a full flip, radiating an odd warmth through my core, one reminiscent of what I'd felt when Pete put his arm around me when we sat on the log together around the campfire, so long ago.

I jerked my hand back up onto the bed as if I'd touched a fiery coal.

Rolling away from the edge, my head found my pillow again, as I was overcome with actual pain. It was a feeling much worse than being unlovable.

It was the agony of unrequited love—and it *hurt*.

I loved a man who would never love me back. A man who would never love me because, just as I'd always expected, I was unlovable. Because I was a shrew.

I squeezed my eyes against the moonlight, but a single tear still escaped.

Since deciding to marry Pete, I'd assumed a marriage of convenience would be my curse.

Now I knew I'd been wrong. Me loving him, never to have it returned, was much, much worse.

I woke to Esther pounding on the door. Pete was long gone.

As I crawled out of bed, my head throbbed. I felt as if I'd been crying for hours. Perhaps I had—in my sleep.

By the time I managed to get washed up, the oatmeal was cold. Esther and Walter sat at the table, waiting for me. After the silent prayer, I expected them to ask me about New York, but they didn't. And neither asked about the envelope from Lancaster. I yawned several times, but they didn't comment on that either. After I finished eating, Esther took a folded piece of paper from the pocket of her apron.

"Pete asked me to give this to you."

My heart raced as I took it. I turned it over, yearning for some sort of message of endearment, but if that was so, Esther could have easily read it.

I unfolded it. It wasn't so.

Cate,

Would you please take the horse and buggy and go to the library in Randolph? Get everything you can on running a business.

Pete

I read the message again, noting *please*. Granted my husband didn't love me, but at least he was acting like a gentleman again.

I looked up at Esther. "He wants me to go to Randolph."

"So he said."

"Is it all right if I take the horse and buggy?"

Esther pointed to Walter.

He nodded. "It's fine with me."

If we were returning to Lancaster soon there wasn't much point in going to the library, but the thought of taking the horse and buggy anywhere was more than I could pass up.

"Do you need anything from the store?"

"More coffee," Esther said. "And some thread."

I finished the dishes and weeded in the garden for an hour and then hitched up the buggy. I didn't want to arrive in Randolph much earlier than the library opened—just enough to look around and do the little bit of needed shopping. But I did want to get going before it got too hot.

The horse walked slowly up the driveway. I searched the neighbor's field for Pete but didn't see him, but when I reached the highway I heard him holler, "Howdy!"

I strained my neck. He was driving a wagon heaped with hay. I waved back and smiled but then realized he wasn't calling out to me. His boss stood by the barn.

As I turned onto the asphalt, the weight of my emotions came crashing down, as if released by gravity itself. I struggled to compose myself as I passed Jana and John's house. Perhaps if I could actually meet her I would feel better. I stared as I drove by but didn't see anyone in the yard or through the windows. I kept driving. I didn't have the nerve to stop.

The horse kept a steady pace past the firehouse and then down the steep hill. Going up the next incline was another matter. I wondered halfway up if we were going to make it, but we did.

I felt my spirits lift a little at just being in the buggy and on my way to a library. I'd missed my freedom immensely.

The day was clear and bright, hardly muggy at all. Birds chirped in the trees. The wind rustled through fields of corn. A stream gurgled beneath a bridge. It was a beautiful morning, and so peaceful. I was sure there were tourists who visited the Amish communities in New York too, but they hadn't found their way to this back road. No one was driving by gawking. No one was leaning out the window, determined to snap a photo of me. It wasn't like home, at all.

But by the time I reached Randolph, it was hot. The grocery store was on the main road, and I stopped there first, watering and feeding the horse from the bucket and jug I'd brought along.

As I entered, I considered that the store might not carry thread. They did, but then I wondered if it was the right kind. I should have asked Esther for particulars but decided to get it anyway. The coffee was easy—I grabbed a can identical to the big red one Esther pulled out of the cupboard every morning.

I asked the clerk where the library was. It turned out to be just a block off Main Street.

"It's open on Friday mornings," she said. "It's your lucky day."

I'd assumed it would be open every morning. As it turned out, according to the sign, most days it was only open in the afternoon. I walked up the steps of the brick building and entered, appreciating the cool interior but mostly reveling in the sight of all the books, shelf after shelf. I ambled down the first aisle, my hand trailing along the spines of the novels.

"May I help you find something?" The librarian was standing at the beginning of the next aisle.

I stopped, not quite ready to end my walk-through. "Business books. Where would I find those?"

"Last row, middle shelf."

I thanked her and continued touching each book as I passed by, stopping when I reached my destination. There wasn't much of a selection, but I pulled what they had. One on bookkeeping, another on making a business plan, and a third on Internet marketing.

Then I found the biographies, but there wasn't one on Ulysses S. Grant or Julia Grant. I scanned the shelves for quite a while, taking out a book and looking at it, putting it back, then moving on to another. In the end I decided not to check out any more than the business ones. We—or at least I—would be leaving for Betsy's wedding soon enough. After that, I had no idea where we would be.

I was surprised at how trusting the librarian was about giving me a card. She said she knew I would bring the books back. She smiled as she checked out the Internet one but didn't ask any questions.

On the way home, I felt as if I were hanging in the balance between Cattaraugus County and Lancaster County, between New York and Pennsylvania. I needed to talk to Pete about going home for Betsy's wedding. I wanted to find out what Pete's plans were for a business, which I knew depended on Wes's decision. I longed to know where he wanted us to live permanently.

And I needed to know if there would be a chance he would ever love me. . . . That made me think of what he said when I dropped him at the Bergs' for the singing, the line about the two raging fires meeting and then consuming what fed their fury. I wondered what exactly it was that fed my fury. Being bullied? Mocked? Used? Feeling unlovable? Or out of control? And what it was that fed his.

That put my mind back on Jana, and I contemplated stopping to introduce myself. I wondered what Jana did all day with her husband gone. I went cold for a moment. What if Pete went to see her during the day, while John was away?

I shook my head, chastising myself for my suspicions. Pete wouldn't do that—surely not.

I crested the biggest hill and passed the fire station. The horse was going extra slow on the long straight stretch, poor thing, exhausted from the heat and the trip. As the horse conquered the smaller hill and we neared Jana and John's, I bit my lower lip. To stop or not to stop? The horse slowed even more. I checked for traffic. Nothing was in sight, either way. I pulled the reins to the left, across the highway, and into Jana and John's short driveway, parking the buggy under the shade of a gigantic elm.

I smiled on the way to the front door, practicing my congenial look, although I still hadn't decided what I would say. Maybe something like, *I was passing by and haven't had a chance to meet you yet, so I thought I'd stop.*

Something like that.

I just wanted to meet the woman who holds my husband's heart.

No, not that.

I reached the door and knocked lightly. No one answered. I knocked again, a little louder. I heard a voice. I put my ear to the wood, sure I'd heard, "Come in." I heard it again, so I tried the knob. It was unlocked. I eased the door open.

The interior was dark with the drapes pulled, probably to keep the house cooler.

"Who's there?" The voice came from my left.

"It's Cate. Pete's wife." My eyes hadn't adjusted entirely, but I could tell someone was resting on the sofa. "Jana?"

"Jah," she answered.

I stepped closer, starting to say my line, "I haven't had a chance to meet you. I wanted to intro—"

Her legs were flopping back and forth, actually *writhing*, something I hadn't seen before but had read about. And there was something on her stomach.

"Are you all right?" I squinted to try to see better.

"My head hurts." She groaned. "And my back." Her Kapp was off and her blond hair flowed loose on the pillow. She writhed again.

"How long have you felt this way?" I opened the drapes a crack, enough so I could see her better.

"Since morning." Her face was puffy, and so was the hand that was clutching the pillow. I stepped closer. It wasn't a pillow. It was her belly.

"Jana, are you pregnant?"

"Jah."

I grew cold, even in the warm room. "How far along?"

"About seven months."

They'd married last December. It was the end of July. I quickly counted the months. *Seven*. But her mound of belly looked much further along than that.

"When was the last time you saw your doctor?"

"I haven't yet."

"Okay. Are you having contractions?"

She shook her head. "I don't think so."

"Can you sit up?"

She shook her head.

Headache. Swelling. Pain in the side. I thought through the book I'd read on pregnancy. It didn't sound like labor. There was the condition that had to do with hypertension, and I knew, from other medical books I'd read, that a headache could be a symptom of high blood pressure.

I couldn't remember what the condition was called. Toxemia? Preeclampsia? Something like that.

"Should I go get John?"

She shook her head.

"Where does your Mamm live?"

"About five miles away." She started thrashing her legs again.

If her blood pressure was high, it could cause her to start labor. I needed to call 9-1-1.

"Where's the closest phone?"

"The firehouse."

For a second I considered getting Jana out to the buggy and hauling her down to the station, but that wouldn't do—what if her blood pressure was high enough to cause a stroke?

"I'll be right back," I said.

"Don't leave."

"I'm going to get the paramedics." I rushed out the door without waiting for her response, sick to my stomach as I ran to the buggy, trying to figure out why Jana hadn't seen a doctor yet.

There was no way she was only seven months along. I'd been around plenty of women in the days before they delivered. If I was allowed to bet, I'd have wagered the Treger farm that Jana was nine months along, and even if she wasn't actually in labor, she was really close to having her Bobli.

I untied the horse and jumped into the buggy. As I pulled

out onto the highway, my face flushed in the heat but also at my racing thoughts, and I again counted the months backward to December, when Jana and John had wed. Still seven. Chances were she was pregnant before then. Chances were she was pregnant before Pete ever left—

I stopped myself. Right now that wasn't my concern. The well-being of Jana and her Bobli was all that mattered. I urged the horse to go faster and then faster still, leaning forward as I did, but it seemed as if we were going in slow motion.

Heat rose up from the asphalt. I wiped the sweat from my face with my apron, using one hand. The cows in the field stood statue-still. A bird fluttered up out of a poplar tree and then back down, as if moving at all had been a bad idea. Each time I began counting the months again, I forced myself to concentrate on the landscape.

When I finally reached the station, I yelled as I turned into the driveway. "Help!" I called out again as I pulled the horse to a stop.

A man wearing a baseball hat and a blue T-shirt appeared. I quickly told him what was going on and that the house was the first one on the left, up the highway. "I'm going to go get her husband," I said. I knew it was probably a volunteer station and he would need to call for help.

"No," he said. "Go back to the house. I'll send someone to get him. At the Treger farm, right? Just down the way?"

"Jah," I called out, turning the horse around.

John arrived in a pickup truck with an Englisch man just as the paramedics loaded Jana into the ambulance. He left with them, riding up front.

"I'll go tell your parents," I said through the open window.

"Tell Pete first," he answered.

I found Pete in the barn at the dairy, repairing a milking machine. He rode with me back to the farm.

"Oh," was all Esther said when he told her about Jana.

"Do you want to go to the hospital?" I asked.

"Oh, no," she said. "We'll find out soon enough."

"Should we tell Jana's parents?"

"Don't you think they'll get word to them? From the hospital." Esther slipped her hands into the pockets of her apron.

Pete shrugged when I gave him a pleading look. He started for the back door as his mother headed the other way, toward her quilting room.

"Should we go to the hospital?" I asked him.

"How? It's nearly twenty miles away."

"We could hire a driver. Or call your Uncle Wes. John might need some support." Honestly, I thought Jana could use some too. Even though John knew a lot about animal husbandry, he probably didn't know much about human obstetrics or hospitals or what to ask the doctor. "We could go back to the fire station and use the phone there."

Pete rubbed his temple for a moment. "John hasn't been very happy with me."

My heart raced. "Why?"

Pete shrugged.

"But I hate to think of them by themselves. . . ." I searched Pete's face. "They're family," I finally said, truly meaning it, regardless of the circumstances.

He nodded. "But that doesn't mean my brother wants me there." Pain filled Pete's eyes.

"I can tell you want to go," I said, compassion filling my heart. "If John doesn't want us there, we can leave."

Ten minutes later we were at the fire station. The same

man greeted us. When we told him why we needed to use the phone, he said he'd give us a ride. "I was thinking about driving into town to check on the couple, anyhow."

A half hour later we were in a tiny ER room, wedged next to the wall beside John, while the doc explained to Jana, who was on the bed, that she most likely had preeclampsia. "We're waiting for one more test to come back." His expression was very serious. "There's more." He looked from Jana to John. "The reason you're so big is because you're having twins."

John turned beet red, and Jana gasped.

"Our goal is to keep the babies in utero for at least another month, hopefully two."

She really was seven months along! Pete's face remained stoic. It was my turn to blush. Jana gave John a "told-you-so" look without uttering a word. It looked as if I hadn't been the only one harboring a horrible suspicion, but at least I'd only had to live with mine for a couple of hours.

"First we need to get your blood pressure down. Are you particularly stressed right now?" the doctor asked.

Jana glanced at John again. In slow motion, he started to move toward her.

The doctor continued. "Do you need more help around the house? We want you off your feet. You'll have to be on bed rest until your blood pressure drops."

John was at Jana's side now, taking her hand in his. "I'm sorry," he said, oblivious to the doctor.

Jana began to cry. "I only wondered how he was doing. That was all."

I couldn't take my eyes off Jana as she clung to John's hand. She didn't love my husband. She loved hers. I glanced at Pete. But that didn't mean he didn't love her.

The doctor turned toward us. "Do they have the support they need?"

"Yes," Pete answered, his voice firm.

I nodded, except I was leaving for Lancaster as soon as possible.

"There's lots of help," Pete insisted.

The doctor said he'd be back in about a half hour, after the urine test came back.

John and Jana were both crying, but Pete didn't seem to notice. "They can move in with Mamm and Dat," he said.

I must have made a face, because he added, "It will be fine now. John's Mamm's favorite. She'll be thrilled to take care of Jana and the babies. You've given her enough of a rest."

"Are you sure?" I couldn't imagine it. "Where will we live?"

"We're going back to Lancaster."

I gave him a puzzled look. "For good?"

He shrugged. "For now. I saw the invitation, during my dinner break."

"You came home?"

He nodded.

I was about to ask why, when the man who gave us the ride to the hospital poked his head through the curtain and asked if we were ready to leave.

John turned toward us. "Jana has to spend the night. I'll stay with her."

"I'll do your work," Pete said.

"I'll help," I added.

John thanked us, and as we started to leave, Jana's soft voice called out, "It's nice to meet you."

"You too," I said, with as much sincerity as I'd ever felt in my entire life.

For a brief moment as we left the room, I felt Pete's hand on the small of my back, but then, just as quickly, it was gone.

That night Pete came to our bedroom soon after I did. I felt as if I'd had too much coffee that day, although I hadn't had a drop, of course.

"You awake?" He'd just settled into his sleeping bag.

"Uh-huh," I answered.

"Anything you want to ask me?"

I thought for a moment, wondering what to ask first. I'd read enough novels to figure out what John's reaction had been about. He had feared, just as I had, the Bobli was Pete's not his, and that Jana had lied to him about the due date. But now that he knew Jana was having twins and was only seven months along, he knew the babies were his. I didn't need to make Pete tell me that.

What I really wanted to ask him was if there was a chance he would ever love me, but I figured the answer to that was pretty much a lose-lose situation—for me anyway. I didn't need to have it reiterated, again, how unlovable I was.

"Cate?"

I wiggled my leg closest to the wall out from under the quilt, trying to cool down a little. "I'm thinking," I answered.

"I figured."

No, I didn't want to ask him anything that had to do with me. This was about him. So that took me back to Jana. Did Pete still love her? That was probably a lose-lose question too. If he said yes, I'd be mad. If he said no, I wouldn't believe him.

Still . . . Finally I came up with my question.

"Okay . . ." I paused. He didn't answer.

"Pete?" I looked over the side of the bed. His arm was under his head, his eyes closed. "Pete?"

He stirred.

"I thought of a question."

He opened one eye.

"Did you love Jana?"

"Jah. We courted for years," he said, opening his other eye.

"And you thought you would marry."

"Of course."

"What happened?"

He didn't answer for quite a while, but his eyes remained open, and finally he said, "Things became tense between us."

"Why?"

"I didn't have enough money. I didn't have any land. I was full of crazy ideas. She was afraid I couldn't support a family, and honestly, I shared that concern. We went back and forth, trying to work it all out." He fell silent.

"And?"

"One night I overheard Mamm and John at the kitchen table. I was in the living room reading, but they must have thought I'd gone upstairs."

He turned toward me but didn't make eye contact. "Mamm . . ." He tugged on his beard. "She . . ."

I held my breath.

"First you need a little background." He met my eyes, for just a moment. "Jana's grandparents own the land adjacent to this place."

I nodded. "Livy told me."

"Oh." He responded as if he wondered what else Livy had said. "Anyway they'd promised it to Jana when she married. But I never felt like I could make it as a farmer—especially on a small section of land. I'd seen how it had gone for my parents."

That made sense.

He exhaled. "So, that night, Mamm told John *he* should court Jana."

I gasped.

"Jah." Pete slipped his other hand under his head. "John said Jana loved me, and Mamm answered, 'She only thinks she does.'" Pete did a good job imitating his mother and continued. "'She's frustrated with him. Pete's never going to amount to anything, and Jana knows it.'"

"Oh, Pete," I whispered, in horror.

I'd told him something similar that day in the kitchen, back home . . . It came back to me, word for word. *"You will amount to nothing—absolutely nothing—without my Dat's money."* Even when I'd chided him about burning books, I'd implied he'd never amount to anything if he didn't change.

A deep coldness, even in the August heat, chilled me to the core. "I'm sorry," I stuttered.

"Jah, it really hurt. . . ."

I opened my mouth again, wanting to apologize for the things I'd said, but no words came out.

"And then," he continued, "the next thing I knew, John and Jana were courting."

He turned away from me.

I swallowed hard. "I'm sorry," I said. "I . . ."

He rolled farther away, curling into a sleep position. "It's in the past now," he said. "Don't worry. . . ."

"Pete?"

His bicep, the one I could see, bulged against the thin cotton fabric of his T-shirt, and the outline of his hip and leg were obvious under the sheet.

I scooted to the very edge of the mattress, my arm dangling over the edge. I did want to ask if he thought he could ever love me. "I have another question."

"Ach, Cate," he responded, his voice raggedy. "I'm asleep."

I reached out my hand toward him and silently cried. I knew just how Pete felt about Jana. It was exactly how I felt about him.

I poured out my despair to God until I finally fell asleep.

I went through the motions for the next few days, doing the housework, tending the garden, cooking meals, and doing my best to try not to think too far into my bleak future. I fought a growing sadness that, regardless of what Pete had conspired with Mervin and Martin, I had lashed out in anger, wounding him the same way his mother had, reinforcing all his fears.

I asked God to get me through the next fifty years. Or sixty. Or seventy. Amish marriages lasted a long time.

Jana ended up being in the hospital for a whole week. Among the many tests was an ultrasound, which showed the twins were identical girls. That information inspired Esther. She finished the quilt for the Englisch woman's daughter and then started helping around the house more.

Pete quit at the dairy and took full responsibility for the farm so John could be with Jana. Livy, Bert, and their grown sons came to move the couple to the farm, and once that happened we got ready to leave for Lancaster, nearly two weeks after the invitation arrived.

I felt genuine pity for Pete, knowing he still loved a woman who had married another—his brother, to make things worse—and admired how he kept it to himself and strove to serve them, regardless. Jana, now that she needed the help, seemed okay about living with Esther. It turned out her mother still had a houseful of kids and wasn't in a position to do much.

I was thankful to witness the Tregers coming together as a family, but then it dawned on me—regardless of their problems, they'd always been a family, long before I arrived. They just didn't look like my family. Sure, they weren't warm and fuzzy, demonstrative, or even expressive. But they cared for each other, in their own way.

The truth was, if we settled in Lancaster County for good, I'd miss the Treger farm. Life was much different there than back home, but their simpler way of life had its benefits. They were resourceful and wasted nothing. Plus their dependence on the land, and therefore on God, was even stronger than what I saw in Lancaster, where so many families' incomes were boosted by the tourism trade and a larger market for carpentry and other skills.

I could say, without a doubt, that both Esther and Walter depended on the Lord for their needs. And they didn't need me sharing my knowledge, or opinions, with them. They had been doing just fine without them all these years.

It was late afternoon on the day of our departure by the time Pete had readied everything for John. When I carried my bag down the stairs, Jana was in Walter's chair, her feet propped up on a stool, and Esther was draping a cool rag over her forehead.

"There you are," Esther said to me. "I have something for you."

She started toward the hall. I gave Jana a questioning look, and she shrugged. I put down my bag and followed my mother-in-law.

When she reached the door to her quilting room, she opened it wide and let me go in first. It was huge, as big as two bedrooms. I realized that's exactly what it was. The wall between the rooms had been torn down, although there were still two doors off the hallway. Crates filled with remnants of all sorts of fabric had been turned on end to make shelves along the perimeter. A frame stood against the far wall under the windows. The big surprise was the comfy recliner in the middle of the room and the person who sat in it.

Walter grinned.

Next to him was an empty rocking chair.

I wrinkled my nose at my own assumptions. Since my arrival I'd assumed Walter had been escaping to his room to nap when he'd actually been hanging out with Esther in her quilting room.

"I have something for you," she said, picking up a black trash bag. I nearly laughed. Esther's parting gift to me was garbage? Funny, because the family didn't really produce any. Everything was composted or burned. The few plastic containers that came through the home were reused to store dry goods or leftovers.

I stopped myself from laughing. "Well, thank you," I said as pleasantly as I could, holding out my hands.

As soon as she put the bundle in my arms I knew it wasn't garbage. It was a quilt.

"Don't look until you're in Lancaster."

I promised I wouldn't and thanked her, checking my emotions. All those weeks, when she could have been working to make money, she'd been making a quilt for me, with Walter at her side.

She brushed her hands together. "Now I need to get going on the quilts for the babies." She smiled, just a little.

I nodded, happy for her, and a little sad I wouldn't be around to see the newborns.

"You know," Esther said, "I wanted you and Pete to stay, but I should've known better. I always knew Pete wouldn't settle around here—Walter's helped me accept that."

"Oh, I don't know what he's decided for sure," I said. "We may be back."

Esther shot me a condescending look, as if I were just trying to be nice. The truth was, I had no idea what we were doing. As far as I knew, Wes hadn't talked with Pete again. If he had, Pete hadn't told me.

"Pete's always been destined for something different—not better, mind you. Just different. Kind of like Wes, although I'm happy Pete will be staying in the church. Jah?"

"Jah," I answered with conviction.

She seemed relieved and then sighed. "I want you to know I appreciate the work you've done here. I didn't think you had it in you when you first came. You pulled through, though. I needed the rest. And having me doing better has been good for Walter too."

The old man smiled again.

I simply nodded at both of them and stepped toward the door, aware of how I'd misjudged them.

Esther continued. "I think you and Pete can be happy together, if you let him sleep in your bed." She chuckled and then actually winked at me. I didn't know whether to laugh or cry, but obviously Pete hadn't told them about the farce our marriage was. "We all have spats," she said. "Don't we, Walter?" She turned back toward her husband.

"Now, Esther, don't be sharing our business." He gave me another smile and stood, wrapping his arm around his wife and squeezing her tightly. She harrumphed and slapped at his chest.

He winked at me and said, "I'll walk you out."

I was dumbfounded by the two of them. "Denki," was all I could manage to say. "To both of you." And I followed Walter down the hall, telling Jana good-bye when I reached the living room and then picking up my bag with my free hand.

Pete had hired a driver. I wasn't sure if he would take us only as far as a major highway to get a better start at hitch-hiking or all the way home. I figured we'd get there one way or another.

The driver had already arrived in a big old black SUV when Walter and I came out the back door.

"I better go in to Mamm, huh?" Pete said.

Walter shook his head. "No, she's coming."

Pete must have known about the quilt, because he simply took the black garbage bag from me without any questions and put it in the back, along with my bag, as Esther came down the steps.

Pete shook his father's hand and then hugged his mother and held on extra long until she laughed and then chirped.

"Come visit soon," she said.

"Who says we're not coming back for good?" Pete let go of her.

She just shook her head a little and then said, "Get going. You're late as it is."

As we left the farm, I acknowledged to myself that Esther wasn't the bitter old lady I thought she was. Still, I wanted to be a whole lot kinder and gentler and more patient than she when I was old, even if Pete didn't love me.

The driver slowed when we reached the Randolph city limits and then turned on Main Street, parking in front of the library. Pete hustled around to the back of the SUV and retrieved the library books, running them up to the return slot. I sat back against the seat and smiled, impressed that he'd remembered.

An hour later, I was confident the driver was taking us the entire way. As he and Pete chatted, I dozed a little but mostly watched out the window at the passing scenery, thinking about Betsy's wedding. I wondered if Mervin and Martin would stand up with Levi or if Martin would be too hurt with Betsy marrying someone else, although he was surely resigned to it by now. I also wondered if Addie and Mervin were courting—Betsy hadn't said anything in her letters.

M&M's family would surely be at the wedding, though, and Seth too, with his wife and Bobli. I realized I didn't feel as miffed with him as I had for the last two years. Maybe getting away from Lancaster had been good for me.

Pete asked the driver how far he "hauled" Amish.

"New Orleans has been the farthest."

"After Katrina?" Pete asked.

The driver nodded.

"I was down there for a while," Pete said.

"Helping with the cleanup?"

Pete shook his head. "Building houses."

They talked some more. I wondered if that was one of his crazy ideas that had annoyed Jana—but it made me love him even more.

By the time we reached the outskirts of Paradise, it was pitch-dark. Pete directed the driver until we'd turned down our lane. When we reached our place Dat bounded out of the house, hurrying toward us before the driver stopped the SUV.

"Cate!" he called out.

I jumped out the door, and he swept me up into his arms. Tears filled my eyes.

Pete got our bags from the back, and then came around to shake Dat's hand. Dat tried to pay the driver, but Pete said he'd already taken care of it. I couldn't help but wonder if he'd used the money from Martin and Mervin. If so, it had been put to good use.

"Come on," Dat said, taking my bag from Pete. "I have something to show the two of you."

"Where's Betsy?" I asked.

"With Levi," Dat answered. It was late on a Tuesday night, nearly eleven. The morning would be coming soon, which meant chores and work for both of them.

The moon was nothing more than a sliver, but the stars shone brightly enough for us to find our way along the brick path between the house and the vegetable garden and then along the roses. Even in the dark I could see the plate-size blossoms. I breathed in deeply. The sweet scent of the flowers filled the night. It appeared Levi had come through with his promise to teach Betsy how to tend the flowers.

As we rounded the corner, I froze. In the corner of our large backyard was a little house. A Dawdi Haus.

"Dat!"

"Do you like it?" he said, taking my hand. "I built it for me, eventually, but I want you two to stay in it for the next few weeks."

He pulled me along, Pete behind us. It was only one step onto the porch and then another into the house. Dat quickly lit a propane lamp. The living room, dining room, and kitchen were all one room with bookcases lining one wall, a sofa and recliner grouped together, and then a table and four chairs. The kitchen had a tiny fridge and stove and Dat's top-of-the-line cabinets.

"How did you build it so quickly?" I stammered.

"I've been working on the plans for years—and had them finalized a few months ago." He started down a hall, past a bathroom. "It has two bedrooms, in case I want one as an office someday." The first was completely bare but the next one was the master suite, with a built-in closet, a dresser, a bathroom, and a double bed.

Pete placed the black garbage bag at the end of it.

Dat put my bag on the floor and stepped from the room. "It's wonderful to have you back—both of you."

Pete thanked him and told him good night.

I walked Dat to the door. "See you in the morning," I said. "At breakfast."

"Unless you two want to eat here. I stocked the fridge."

I winced at his enthusiasm for us. "We'll eat with you and Betsy." I waved as he stepped onto the porch, and then shut the door securely.

By the time I reached the hall, Pete was already in the empty room, spreading out his sleeping bag. I stopped in the doorway.

He looked up, a pained expression on his face. "What?"

I turned abruptly, hiding my emotions as best I could. "Good night," I managed to say and fled the few steps down the hall, closing the door behind me.

With a heavy heart, I pulled Esther's quilt from the bag. It was a shadow design made from light blue, dark blue, and black fabric. It was beautiful, but still it added to my sadness. That was where I was—in the shadows, still waiting for my life to begin. I folded it neatly and placed it at the end of the bed, stepping back to look at it again, realizing the light blue fabric was the same color as the shirt Pete wore on our wedding day and the darker blue the same as my dress. It was thoughtful of her—but another reminder of my failure.

Regardless, I was thankful for Esther's work on my behalf and for her words that afternoon.

An hour later, I stirred at the sound of Betsy's laughter. For a moment I feared she might come bursting into the Dawdi Haus and find Pete and me in separate rooms, but then her voice faded.

Moments later I heard the clopping of horse's hooves and then the bang of the back door to the big house. I'd see my Schwester in the morning—not tonight in humiliation.

Betsy stood at the stove frying bacon when I stepped into the kitchen with Pete right behind me. She dropped the tongs and rushed toward me, practically knocking me over. I hugged her tightly. She didn't feel any different. She stepped back. She didn't look any different either. She would be four months along, and it seemed she would be showing, at least a little, but I'd read that sometimes women didn't show as soon with their first pregnancy. Maybe she had been able to hide it from everyone, even the bishop.

She grabbed both my hands and held on, pulling me toward herself. "I'm so glad you're finally here. Please don't leave again."

Ignoring her declaration, I asked how she was feeling, searching her face.

"Fine." She squeezed my hands. "You have to tell me everything!"

The grease began to pop, and Pete took over the bacon.

I must have given her a funny look, because she giggled and then said, "Well, not everything."

I ignored her, pulled away, and poured Pete a cup of coffee. Betsy and I would have a talk later, when we were alone. "What still needs to be done?"

"We have all the help arranged. And I'm halfway through the cleaning."

I poured a cup for myself. "What do you want me to do?"

Betsy giggled, seemingly back to her old self. "Your job."

"Pardon?"

"The business." She looked toward the hallway and then whispered. "Dat's been working with an international distributor. Most of the time I have no idea what they're talking about. I hate office work."

"Okay . . ." I took the tongs from Pete, directing him toward the table. "I can take over the cooking too and help with the cleaning."

Betsy's eyes got big. "You're kidding."

I shook my head. "Just let me know . . ."

Dat stepped into the kitchen.

"Let you know what?" he said.

"Cate cooks and cleans," Betsy said. "Or so she says."

"Is it true?" Dat asked Pete.

"Jah," he answered, not looking at me. "She does just fine."

He and Dat started talking business as Betsy and I finished cooking breakfast. I kept an ear on the conversation as Pete told Dat about Wes's work and the possible deal with the New York publisher.

"Let me know when you want to talk about finances," Dat said.

My face burned as I turned back to the stove, aware again of why my husband married me.

The week progressed with me fixing breakfast each day, taking over the office, and preparing dinner. Every time I tried to get Betsy alone, to ask her how she felt and what the doctor said, she evaded me. Clearly she didn't want to share her personal life, and I finally decided to respect that.

The few times I saw Martin and Mervin they smirked at me, as if they knew exactly what was going on, including Pete sleeping in the spare room. I held my head high and didn't respond, parading by as if they were invisible. But inside I still seethed.

On Friday, I left the office early to hitch Thunder to my buggy and head down to the bookmobile. As I was driving past the shop, Pete stepped out the door and waved. I gave him a half nod, realizing my resentment toward him was building again.

"Wait!" he called out.

It turned out he wanted to come along. Perhaps that was better—as much as I wanted to see Nan, I didn't want to say too much to her, not anything I would regret later anyway. And I knew I tottered on the brink of that.

Pete must have sensed my mood, because he didn't speak. As hard as living in New York was, it had been a relief to not be judged by my past and have the added humiliation heaped on me. Once we reached the highway, Thunder took off, happy to be able to trot with me at the reins.

When we reached the bookmobile, Pete jumped down and greeted Nan first. She had a pencil behind her ear, just like always, and gave Pete a hug, telling him she had the books he'd ordered from the library, and handed him a small stack.

He held it up, looking at me as I came around in front of Thunder, patting his neck. "I called Nan a few days ago, asking her to get these. I'm going to put them in the buggy and then head across the street." The roadside coffee hut was still there. "I'll be right back," he said.

After Pete left, Nan embraced me warmly, saying how much she missed me. I followed her into the bookmobile, where she handed me two books. "I've been saving these for you."

It was a biography of Ulysses S. Grant, and one of his wife, Julia. "Thanks." It was as if she'd expected me to come back all along. I squinted out the doorway.

Nan smiled. "Tell me more about New York."

I told her about the trip to the city and about John and Jana and their soon-to-be-born twins. Then I told her about the quilt Esther had made and how much I liked it.

She nodded. "I remember her work well. And how are you and Pete doing?"

I sighed, wondering if I should tell her she had been right. I looked out the door across the street again. Pete stood at the window where the cars were supposed to drive up, laughing with the barista. I turned my attention back to Nan and finally said. "You were right about the verse in Proverbs."

She cocked her head.

"The unloved woman."

It was Nan's turn to look out the doorway and then back at me. "Are you sure?"

I nodded. "And I knew from the beginning—but at the time I didn't love him."

"But now you do?" Nan put her hand on my arm.

"I think so."

"Oh, Cate."

I was determined not to cry.

"Are you sure he doesn't love you?"

"Positive. He doesn't do anything a loving husband does."

"Like?"

I wasn't going to bring up sleeping separately. I couldn't be that open about the intimate details—or lack of—in my life. And I didn't want to tell her about Jana either.

Nan was looking out the doorway again. "Like bring you coffee?"

"Exactly," I said.

She stepped back. Pete was crossing the street, three iced coffees in his hand.

"That doesn't count." I crossed my arms.

"Why not?"

"He couldn't very well get you one and not me."

"Oh, Cate," she said again, taking the pencil out from behind her ear and twirling it between her fingers in a worrisome way I'd never seen her do before. "Maybe you need to give him more time."

I sighed. "All I have is time." Did she think I was going to kick him out of Dat's Dawdi Haus? Or go file for divorce?

"Things will work out. You'll see." She tucked the pencil back behind her ear as Pete reached the bottom of the steps.

On the way home, on edge from my conversation with Nan, as we passed a field of corn stalks rustling in the hot breeze, I asked him what he'd told Mervin and Martin.

"About?" His hand rested on the stack of books between us.

"Us," I answered.

He squirmed a little. "Nothing."

I gave him a wilting look.

"They're not as interested in you as you think."

"Are you saying I'm paranoid?"

"Jah, maybe a little."

"No. They've definitely been giving me weird looks."

"Maybe they like watching you."

I rolled my eyes as I pulled back on the reins to slow Thunder as we neared an intersection.

"Maybe they push your buttons because they know you'll react," he said.

"But I haven't reacted."

"But you are. . . ." He shifted his weight away from me.

We continued along in silence, except for the drumming of Thunder's hooves on the asphalt. I urged him to go faster.

Finally Pete said, "You shouldn't let people's comments define you, Cate—especially not what they said years ago. It probably didn't apply then, and it definitely doesn't apply now."

I stared straight ahead.

"You were teased. I get that," Pete said. "And it sounds as if Seth said something really stupid—and Mervin and Martin too."

I took a deep breath and exhaled slowly.

Pete tipped his hat back a little. "You've grown up. You're a beautiful—"

I couldn't bear his lies. "Stop."

"You don't get it, do you? You are definitely the prettiest Cate in the county. Your eyes are so blue they're almost violet." He was looking at me directly now. "And your hair is so dark it's nearly black—and so thick."

The only time he'd seen it down was on the farm, when we shared a room. Had he stolen glances at me too, just as I had at him?

"Please don't tease," I said.

He threw up his hands. "I'm not."

I shifted my eyes toward him. "So if I'm—" I stopped. I couldn't say *pretty*. I thought for just a moment and then continued—"not homely, then why does everyone like Betsy better?"

"Well . . . she's nice."

I frowned.

"And uncomplicated."

"Yah, I know"—I almost said boys—"men like that."

"Some do . . ."

I was pretty sure Jana was uncomplicated too.

Pete sighed. "Maybe M&M were looking at you because you've changed."

"How's that?" I was desperate for his opinion.

"You're more compassionate. Less prickly."

I kept my eyes on the road.

"Do you want to know why I think you acted the way you used to?" Pete asked.

I nodded but didn't look at him.

"Well, losing your Mamm was big, right? And then you had Betsy to take care of when you were so young. You tried to be successful at that, by controlling all you could. But that didn't work, which made you angry."

Pete sounded like one of the self-help books I'd read.

He went on. "So you became insecure—that's what fed your fury—and you lashed out, which pushed people away. . . ."

I turned my head toward him.

"And then you pushed God away too," he added.

I wrinkled my nose. He was right. But I'd invited God back. That's what had been changing me in New York. God's love.

But I was feeling less confident again now that we were back in Lancaster. Less compassionate. And more prickly. I didn't want to go back to that. Like Queen Esther I needed to keep on trusting God, not my emotions.

I had another thought. If Pete had come to think I was pretty, maybe he could come to love me someday too, or at least appreciate me. I stole a glance at him. He was looking at the first page of one of his books.

My heart skipped a beat.

Then again, chances of that were slim. I'd chosen a marriage of convenience. I was the one who had proposed it. It was my fault far more than his.

I'm sorry, I whispered silently to God.

"Pardon?" Pete looked up from his book.

"I didn't say anything," I said, squaring my shoulders.

He lowered his eyes again. "I must have imagined it, then."

C H A P T E R

24

The next several days were filled with polishing the house from top to bottom and baking pies, cakes, cookies, and rolls. I split my time between the house and the office, where I happened to be Tuesday afternoon when Wes called.

He was as friendly as ever, chatting away with me before asking for Pete. It took me a few minutes to find him in the barn, grooming Thunder. He handed me the comb and took off running. I put it away and followed at a walk.

By the time I reached the office, Pete was saying, "That's great. So we'll need to set up an office, right? And I'll need some training." There was a long pause and then, from Pete's comments, it sounded like Wes would call him back with the final details on Friday.

After Pete hung up, I closed the door to the office and, swallowing my pride, said, "Shall we talk to Dat? About the money."

Pete shook his head. "It turns out I have enough."

I nearly laughed. "Pardon?"

"I thought I was penniless, but my Dat had saved some of the money I'd given him through the years. He gave me the bankbook the night before we left," he said. "But I'll only need to use enough to set up an office. I'll be employed by the publishing house; I won't need to invest anything."

I felt as if the wind had been knocked out of me. "Pete," was all I could manage to sputter.

"Plus I have the money I earned this summer." He grinned. The confident Pete I'd first met had definitely returned. "I won't need your Dat's help at all. In fact, I hope after I've worked with Wes for a while, I can start an additional business on the side. God provides, jah?"

I agreed, marveling at how gracious Pete was acting. I couldn't imagine how upset he must be, inside, now that there was absolutely nothing convenient, for him, about our marriage.

I didn't know what to say, so I kept quiet, for once.

Maybe Dat would let me use the money for my own business. I was going to need something to keep myself busy. It certainly wasn't going to be the love of my husband. Nor a houseful of children. Nor a joint business venture.

Sadness overcame me, and I opened the door, embarrassed by my feelings, ready to refocus on Betsy's wedding to take my mind off my misery.

I stumbled up the path alongside the garden to the back door. I'd told Betsy I'd help her make pies. Busy hands would take my mind off my worries.

Soon we were talking about her side sitters. Because I was married, I couldn't be one. Technically someone who was courting wasn't supposed to be one either, although Betsy had been at mine. Addie was going to be one of Betsy's attendants, though, just like she'd been for my wedding.

"So she and Mervin aren't courting?" I asked as I rolled out pie dough.

"Jah," Betsy said. "It seems Uncle Cap thinks she can do better. He has his eye on the bishop's oldest son."

Poor Mervin.

The day before the wedding, around four that morning, Levi arrived to butcher the chickens. Because there had been enough time to plan ahead, unlike with my wedding, Dat had ordered forty baby fryers seven weeks ago that were now ready to be the wedding dinner. Betsy and I were already up, fixing breakfast. We all ate together and then Dat went out with Pete and Levi to set up the butchering site. The shop, office, and showroom were closed, as they would be on the wedding day, and the day after. After we cleaned up the kitchen, Betsy and I headed out to help pluck the chickens.

Levi worked well with Dat and Pete, taking the lead. It seemed as if, just like his roses, he'd bloomed over the summer, gaining in confidence and stature. It wasn't that he was lacking before—just shy and unsure.

Out of all the young men in the area, Betsy had chosen him, and regardless of the exact reasons, I knew she adored him. That had to have been a huge boost to his esteem. I was seeing, more and more, what Betsy appreciated about him. Besides his skill at gardening, he seemed to be a good listener and eager to help.

Once the chickens were all dressed, the four cooks arrived to take their share of the fowl home to roast. Betsy and I got busy preparing the celery for the sweet-and-sour dish while Dat, Pete, and Levi moved the furniture from the living room into the Dawdi Haus. Then we all geared up to wash windows together.

As I walked to the barn with Dat to fetch a ladder, he said he needed to ask me something. I braced myself, wondering if he'd figured out what was going on. But it turned out that wasn't it at all.

"I've noticed a difference in you, and I've been wondering . . ." He cleared his throat. "I'm not sure how to ask this, but has Pete's love finally tamed you?"

I didn't answer for a moment, afraid I might burst into tears.

"Cate?"

We'd reached the barn door. "Ach, no, Dat," I answered as we stepped inside, into the cool shadows, thinking about my conversation with Pete in the buggy. "But God's love has—at least I hope."

That night, after dark, Dat and Pete took care of a wasps' nest on the far side of the house that we'd noticed when we were cleaning the windows. First they sprayed it with the hose and then knocked it down with a long extension handle. I was in my room, listening to them laugh as they worked.

I stepped to my window. Dat shone a flashlight on the papery nest that had landed on the lawn while Pete approached it with a pitchfork.

"Wait!" Dat shouted. "There's still a lot in there. Let me spray it again."

He aimed the hose and unleashed a powerful force of water. By the beam of the flashlight, I could see wasps flying up and circling around. One took after Pete, and I thought he was going to be stung, but Dat aimed the hose in that direction, soaking Pete and scaring the wasp away at the same time. Their laughter made me smile.

I turned from the window, remembering how waspish I used to be. I knew now it was more from woundedness than meanness and was grateful for Dat's patience with me through the years. I know his parents had been extra harsh on him, which is probably why he'd been so gentle with me—up until proclaiming his edict.

But even then, I was sure, if I had begged to be released from marrying Pete on our wedding day, Dat would have relented. I was sure he'd be hurt even now to know how I'd deceived him.

I think we all fell into bed exhausted, except for Pete, who probably felt as if he were on vacation after how hard he worked in New York. It took me a long time to fall asleep, though, thinking about Betsy's wedding day, wondering what was really going on with her, envious of Levi's love for her and the family they would soon have.

Ach, Cate, I chided myself. Sure, I wasn't Betsy or Jana or all the other pretty young women I knew, but God loved me just the same, just as he'd loved Queen Esther so long ago. Why couldn't I seem to hold on to that?

The next morning we all rose early again and pitched in to get the chores done and finish the last of the preparations. The helpers started to arrive at seven, including Addie, who was already in her attendant's dress, and Aunt Laurel. Betsy headed up to her room to put on her dress, and I followed a few minutes later.

As I entered the room, she stood facing me, bare except for her underwear. I couldn't help but gawk. Her stomach was nearly concave. By my estimation, she should have been a month into her second trimester. Sure, she would be able to hide it with clothes. But without them, she would surely be showing.

Then I realized what happened. "Betsy, why didn't you tell me?" I asked, heartbroken.

"What?" She reached for the new slip she'd made.

"That you lost the baby."

Her face began to redden as she pulled her slip over her head. "Oh, that," she said, wiggling the garment into position. "I didn't lose it." She shrugged. "I was mistaken. . . ."

"What?"

"I was confused. I'd overheard Aunt Laurel, back when she was last pregnant, say that's how she knew, because she was late—so I thought that was the sure sign."

She pointed to the stack of books on her bedside table, the ones Nan had been renewing for so long. "But then I finally read those." Her face was beet red now. "And . . . I had my facts all confused." She giggled. "There wasn't any way I could be pregnant. I think I was just stressed and missed—"

"Betsy!" I fought the old, familiar rage.

"I'm sorry," she said sheepishly. "We did more than Dat—or you—would approve of, but we didn't . . . you know . . ."

I put my hand up for her to stop. "You don't need to say any more."

"I'm sorry," she said sheepishly. "I guess I should have gone to the doctor or at least read the books sooner. Or even told Levi what I was thinking . . ."

"What?" My head began to pound.

"I just told him I wanted to get married. Not why."

"Oh, Betsy." I collapsed onto my old bed.

Her eyes were heavy. "I know I was thinking about myself, about what was best for me. While you were being so unselfish and doing all you could to help. I'm afraid . . ." She heaved a sigh. "I may have . . . hurt you."

She stood in the middle of the room and started to talk a mile a minute. "But I truly think this has all worked out for the best. Don't you? You and Pete make such a good couple.

I was a little worried on your wedding day, when he yanked you away, but I can tell you've grown fond of him. You're going to be really happy. I just know it. And you're such a handsome pair. Your babies—"

"Stop!" I bellowed.

Her face fell. "Cate?"

I stood. I had to get away from her. In one quick motion I grabbed my purple dress, hanging on my side of the room, and fled the bedroom into the bathroom, leaning against the locked door as my anger turned to grief.

A moment later Betsy's voice came through the wood. "Cate? Are you all right? I really am sorry."

"I know," I said through my tears. I was sick that, not only had I altered my life for her, I'd changed Pete's life forever too, on a false pretense.

"Can I come in?" Betsy begged.

I thought for a moment. Of her happiness. Of my misery. I exhaled. "No," I said. "I'll be down in a few minutes."

After I pinned my dress and Kapp, I felt compelled to find Pete.

He was standing in the driveway, talking with two of Addie's brothers who were the Hoestlers for the wedding. Pete was telling them to make sure to feed all the horses at noon. "Give them extra water," he said. "It's going to be hot."

"May I talk with you?" I asked.

He nodded and walked with me to the silver maple tree.

"Betsy's not pregnant," I said quietly. "She was . . . confused."

An odd smile started to spread across his face.

"I'd told her to read about the facts of life. I gave her the books. She didn't—not until it was too late. I honestly thought she was . . ."

He was chuckling now, not loudly or diabolically. Or sarcastically. Perhaps *ironically* best described it.

"I'm so sorry," I said. "It's not how it looks. I didn't intend to rope you into this. . . . And now that you have this business opportunity with your uncle Wes, you don't need me or my father's—"

"Cate!" It was Dat, calling for me.

"We need to talk more," I said to Pete. "About how to fix this. How to make things less complicated . . . for you."

Dat's voice was closer. "Cate!"

Pete wasn't smiling any longer.

"Later," I said. "After the wedding . . ."

Without waiting for his response, I turned and fled.

I'd never heard of an Amish couple getting an annulment—but I'd never heard of anyone in the predicament we were in either. I didn't think I could spend the rest of my life living with someone who didn't love me.

But more than that, I didn't want Pete to live with someone he didn't love. I'd felt trapped on the Tregers' farm at first, but now I knew Pete was the one who was being held hostage. Sure, he hadn't been able to marry Jana, but there was another love out there for him. Someone like her. Someone like Betsy. Someone less complicated than I was. It wouldn't be hard for him to find the right girl.

As for me, I'd learned a lot, including that my suspicions had been proven wrong—twice. There was no doubt Betsy had set me up in a sense, but I'd jumped to conclusions with Jana too. Maybe Pete was right. Maybe I did speculate too much.

In the long run, I was going to bring much more shame to Dat and dishonor to our family than if I'd never married Pete. But I knew, regardless of the pain that was ahead, I needed to set my husband free. Because I loved him.

Dat was standing in the driveway, waiting for me. "Betsy needs you," he said.

I was pretty sure she really didn't need me. She just needed me not to be mad at her. The funny thing was, I wasn't. Sure I was upset about the predicament I was in, but I was relieved she hadn't been as promiscuous as I'd feared.

"And I need to talk to you." Dat's expression was as serious as I'd ever seen it. "I was praying last night, for Betsy and Levi. Then for you and Pete. And God convicted me of my selfishness."

Puzzled, I put my hand flat on top of my Kapp.

"I was wrong," he said. "Besides your commitment to Christ and the church, who you choose to marry is the most important decision of your life. I attempted to control that by coming up with that ridiculous edict, forcing you to choose sooner, perhaps, than God would have had you."

"Dat—"

"Nan helped me see, very gently, of course, that I had no right to do that. My intentions were good. . . ." His brow was furrowed.

"I know," I said.

He relaxed a little. "I'm so relieved it's worked out." Obviously Nan hadn't shared what I'd told her. "I hope you can forgive me."

"I have," I said, my stomach roiling, knowing I needed to tell him the truth.

His face softened. "I thought Betsy was too young to get married, but I've seen some growth in her. And I have to be willing to trust God with her decision and her future, just like I should have trusted him with you."

Dat wasn't a prideful person. I couldn't fathom why I'd been so determined to protect him. Sure, Betsy had labeled it honor and I'd agreed. But he *was* willing to trust God with her decision and her future. Why had I thought he wouldn't have been able to do that if he'd known the truth? Or what I thought was the truth.

I put both my hands over my face.

"Cate?"

"I need to talk to you later," I said through the cracks of my splayed fingers. "After the wedding." I didn't have time to tell him everything now, not before the service.

Betsy's wedding was even more of a blur than my own. A few times I found myself staring at Pete across the aisle from me. Once I glanced up to see his eyes on me. I quickly looked away.

When the bishop clasped Betsy's and Levi's hands together, I teared up and offered a silent blessing, asking God to give them a long and loving marriage, trying my hardest to ignore my situation.

After the service was over, Nan found me in the kitchen and asked what she could do to help. I gave her a quick hug and asked her to make sure my father sat down with the first group. As I was directing the servers, I saw that she and Dat were sitting together at a table with Uncle Cap and Aunt Laurel. I stopped for a moment, staring at them. All four looked like old friends. And Dat and Nan looked so right together. Maybe everyone in my family but me would end up in a happy marriage.

It took three seatings to get everyone fed. I hadn't realized Pete hadn't eaten until I finally had a chance to sit down. He joined me, his plate heaped high, and devoured his meal while I could only pick at mine. When he stood to clear his plate, his arm brushed against mine, spreading goose bumps across my skin.

As I watched him walk away, I spotted Mervin and Martin across the living room. Both wore sunglasses now, even in the house. They looked as forlorn as could be, and a wave of compassion swept over me. I felt their pain. We were three peas in a pod when it came to love, or more accurately, when it came to a lack of love.

Maybe Seth noticed the expression on my face, because he approached me with his Bobli in his arms.

"This is Amanda." He turned the little one toward me.

She looked up at me with big happy eyes.

"I'm sorry we missed your wedding," he said.

"You had a good excuse." I couldn't take my eyes off the Bobli. She was beautiful with her dark hair and round face.

"I'm so happy you found a good man."

I cocked my head, wondering what M&M had told their older brother.

He continued, "You know, I teased you more than I should have, back in school."

I nodded.

His brow furrowed. "And then, that night after the singing, I never should have said what I did."

"Jah . . ." I wasn't going to let him off the hook.

"The thing was, I didn't even mean it. I cared about you, but I didn't know how to show it."

I cringed.

"I know I hurt you," he said. "I can see that, even more now that I'm a Dat. I'm sorry."

I took a deep breath. M&M were walking toward us. "Denki," I said to Seth, "for your words." Then I reached for the Bobli. "May I hold her?"

I stood there for a long minute with the warm weight of the little one pressed against my body—her uncles cooing over her, her Dat as happy as could be.

"I told Cate I was sorry," Seth told his brothers, "for the way I treated her."

"Jah," Mervin said. "Me too. You're not so bad after all."

"Jah," Martin added. "My apologies too."

I gave a curt nod, although I appreciated the gesture, and then addressed Martin and Mervin gently, "Why the glasses, especially inside?"

"We're feeling down," Mervin said quietly.

"About Betsy?" I glanced from Martin to Mervin. "And Addie?"

"Jah," they answered together.

"And you think the glasses will hide your emotions?"

They nodded.

"Please take them off."

For some reason they obeyed, revealing their sad matching hazel eyes. "You'll find the right girls, in time. Someone right for each of you," I said.

"Do you really think so?" Martin asked. Both their faces were as sweet as I'd ever seen them.

"I know so," I answered.

"Ach, Cate . . ." Martin's voice trailed off, and then he smiled too. "I appreciate you caring. And"—he cleared his throat—"I'm sorry about the envelope on your wedding day."

"Jah," Mervin chimed in. "That was really low of us."

I blinked hard, delaying my response for just a moment, feeling the old anger return. . . . But then I swallowed and squeaked out, "I forgive you."

All three brothers nodded in appreciation and then started cooing over the Bobli again. My eyes fell on her too, and when I looked back up, Pete had joined our circle, a look of tenderness on his face. I fumbled the Bobli back into her father's arms, intending to flee to the kitchen. But Betsy came laughing through the front door just then, followed by a befuddled Levi.

In another moment, my public humiliation was complete.

C H A P T E R
25

"We were just down at the Dawdi Haus." Betsy's voice was full of fun. She giggled and pointed at me as she announced to everyone, "They're sleeping in separate rooms."

Silence fell over the room.

"Betsy," I gasped.

She looked around, speaking loudly. "Pete's mummy bag is on the guest room floor." She giggled again and wagged her finger at me. "That's no way to treat your husband."

My hands flew to my face, as if I could cover my shame.

Dat, who had been on the porch, bellowed, "Betsy!"

I couldn't see well through my fingers, so I may or may not have imagined that Pete stepped toward me, but it was Dat who reached me first, firmly taking my elbow.

"Let's walk." He led me through the crowded kitchen and out the back door, past the garden, away from my spoiled Schwester and our curious guests.

"Why didn't you tell me something was wrong?" Dat finally asked as we reached the shade of the barn.

"I'm so sorry." I couldn't stop the tears. "I've embarrassed you again. Shamed you—when that's exactly what I didn't want to happen."

He turned me toward him. "What are you talking about?" He lifted my chin. "You have never brought me shame. You are the one who has always held our family together."

"That's not true," I said, fighting off a new round of tears. "Hear me out." I exhaled. "This is what I would have told you this morning, if I'd had more time." I spilled every detail of the story, including Martin and Mervin paying Pete, right up to Betsy's prewedding revelation.

His face grew paler with each turn of events.

"I'm so sorry for keeping what I thought was Betsy's secret," I said, "and for deceiving you about my relationship with Pete."

He shook his head. "It's all because of that ridiculous edict of mine."

"You already apologized for that. And, in the end, marrying Pete was my choice, mine alone."

In a hoarse voice, he said, "Tell me what I can do."

"Pete and I should probably try to get an annulment. . . ."

"I'll go to the bishop immediately."

"No," I answered. "Wait until I talk things through with Pete."

"Then I'll move you back into the big house tonight," Dat said.

I shook my head. "Pete and I need to figure this out. I'll let you know."

He put both of his hands on my shoulders. "None of this brings me shame. Sure, I wish you'd talked to me, hadn't tried to fix things on your own. . . . But you wanting to do the right thing for your family, now, that's what honors me."

I swallowed hard, determined not to cry again. "Denki," I whispered.

His eyes met mine. "Tell me something I can do to help you, right now."

"Please pray," I said. "For Pete and me."

"Of course," he said, hugging me tightly. "And I'm going to fetch Betsy. She needs to apologize—now."

"Oh, Dat . . ."

"You two need to work this through. Wait here."

He could be a softie, but I knew he wouldn't take no for an answer on this.

As he left, I stumbled through the open barn door and down to Thunder's stall. As I stepped inside, he greeted me with a nudge and then nuzzled my hand. I wrapped my arms around his neck.

A few minutes later, Betsy's steps fell across the concrete floor. "Dat sent me," she said, stopping outside the stall.

"Jah," I answered. "But I'm not so sure I'm ready to talk."

She wrinkled her nose. "Don't be so sensitive. I was only joking."

"At my expense." I felt the old anger rising, but this time I wasn't sure it was a bad thing.

She balled one hand into a fist.

I stepped away from Thunder. "Remember what you said about how I raised you?"

She nodded.

"You were right." I opened the stall gate, passed through, and then leaned against it for support. "I did do a horrible job. "

She thrust her fist into her apron pocket.

I didn't want to rehash all the things I should have done differently. At that moment I just wanted to address what she had done.

My voice was calm but firm. "You had no right to say those things."

A shadow in the open doorway distracted me for half a

second, but thinking it was a bird, I forged ahead. "I don't know if we'll stay here or go back to New York, but I will follow Pete wherever he goes, whatever he decides." Even if that meant getting an annulment, but I wasn't going to share that possibility with Betsy. If that became my reality, she'd find out soon enough.

I continued. "You know nothing about my marriage." My voice rose a notch. "I love Pete." That was true, no matter the outcome of our relationship.

Betsy's eyes widened as a deep voice called out, "Cate?"

Shading my eyes, I made out my husband's silhouette in the doorway of the barn.

I froze for a moment before managing to answer, "Betsy and I were just talking."

As he strode away, he said, in an apologetic tone, "I'll find you later, then."

I started to follow, but Betsy caught my arm. "I'm sorry," she said. "Really, I am. For everything. Dat helped me see how badly I've behaved."

Her eyes brimmed with tears. I reached out and took her in my arms for a quick moment, then squeaked, "I've got to go."

Outside, I placed my hand to my brow against the afternoon sun but didn't see Pete. I hurried around the barn. He was gone.

Near despair and not wanting to face our guests, I snuck behind the shop to the silver maple tree and climbed up onto the bottom branch, my back against the trunk.

"Help!" I said to God again. No matter what happened with Pete, no matter what Betsy had done to me, no matter all the mistakes I'd made, I didn't want to go back to being the shrew I'd been.

That was what mattered most—how I treated God and others.

In that moment, sitting in the tree, I no longer felt the trunk against my back. Instead I felt God's arms embrace me and hold me tight as the breeze played the fluttering leaves like chimes. His comfort finally reached me, deep inside. That unlovable feeling that had haunted my soul for far too long was gone.

God loved me, for sure, whether Pete ever would or not.

That was where Pete found me nearly an hour later.

"Mind if I join you?" He wore a serious expression on his face.

Before I could answer, he pulled himself up quickly, settling onto the branch across from me.

Pete spoke gently, his voice a murmur above the breeze. "When I sat in this tree the very first time," he said, "I knew I wanted to court you."

"Stop." My hand gripped the branch above. "You were paid to pursue me."

"I never took the money."

My heart constricted at his lie. M&M had just apologized to me for paying him. "I don't believe you."

"I was going to, sure. Why not? I figured I might as well let them pay me for what I intended to do anyway. But then I told them no. I said—"

"What about the envelope?"

"It was empty. Their parting joke on our wedding day."

My eyebrows shot up. Martin *had* used the word *envelope* when he apologized, not *money*.

"Honest, Cate. Please believe me."

Both sorrow and relief filled me. Pete *hadn't* betrayed me. Still, I'd ruined everything.

He shifted on the branch, leaning toward me.

"What about Jana?" I asked.

He didn't hesitate. "I quit loving her a long time ago. Before I ever came to Lancaster County."

I thought of him on his journey, his heart breaking . . . and then mending.

"Then going home made it absolutely clear. My Mamm was right—Jana and I weren't good together. I truly forgave all of them then."

Again, both relief and sadness filled me. I took a jagged breath. "What now?" I craned my neck around the trunk, meeting his eyes.

"What are you thinking?"

"Dat said he'd talk to the bishop about an annulment," I blurted out.

Pete shifted back against the trunk. "Is that what you want?"

In the distance, Betsy called my name.

"I—"

She called out again.

"Oh, no!" How could I have lost track of time? "We need to get ready for supper!"

Now Betsy was shouting. "Cate! Where are you?"

"I'm coming," I called back, slipping from the branch and dropping to the ground. "We'll talk afterward," I said to Pete, straightening my apron.

Leaves from the branch above him hid his face, but the tree shook a little.

"All right?"

"Jah," he answered. "We'll talk then."

Torn, I hurried back to the house, running through the list

of what needed to be done. Heat the already-cooked pans of macaroni and cheese. Pull out the slices of cold ham. Arrange the veggies.

I would have rather stayed in the silver maple, but I needed to fulfill my obligation to Dat and our guests, and Betsy too. I'd have the evening meal under control in half an hour. Then I'd be done.

Pete didn't show up to help or even to eat. I noted Dat was missing too. Perhaps my husband hadn't retreated this time, as he had in the past, to escape me. Perhaps, instead, they'd gone to the bishop together.

By the time darkness began to fall, most of the guests had left, except for those closest to us. The women spilled out into the backyard while the men gathered in the kitchen.

Nan was telling us about a Plain woman she'd interviewed who had eighteen children, including four sets of identical twins, when Levi's little brother Ben came bounding down the back steps.

"Levi wants you." He pointed at Betsy. "He's ready to leave." They were spending their first night at the home of her in-laws.

"Well," Betsy answered, her hands on her hips, "I'm not ready to go."

Without responding, Levi's brother turned and clomped back up the steps.

Some of the other women chuckled, but mortified, I stayed quiet. It seemed Betsy's contriteness in the barn had all been show.

Nan finished her story, adding that the first set of twins was born full-term, nine months after the couple's wedding day.

Addie elbowed Betsy. "That could be you!"

Betsy glowed—until the men inside erupted in laughter. Through the window the men slapped Levi on the back. A moment later, Ben started down the steps again.

"I said I wasn't ready." Betsy's hands flew to her hips again.

Ben flashed an impish smile, and then his eyes found mine. "This message isn't for you, Bitsy. It's for Cate—from Pete."

He'd come back.

A couple of the women giggled. My face grew warm. I looked toward Nan. She smiled at me gently.

I stepped forward. "Jah?"

"Pete wants to know if you're ready to"—Ben's volume increased—"go home."

Home? The word reverberated inside my head.

I looked toward the window. There was Pete, staring at me, most likely anxious to report what the bishop had said.

But he'd used the word *home*. That gave me a measure, although tiny, of hope.

My knees grew weak as I followed Ben up the steps and into the kitchen, aware of the women following along behind me. I wasn't willing to think the worst, to even speculate, not when it could be my only chance. I held my head high and looked my husband in the eye.

"I'm ready." I extended my hand. "Please take me home."

His eyes warmed as he stepped toward me. Behind him Martin grinned, and a chorus of sweet murmurs went up from the women. In fact as I glanced around the room, most everyone was smiling—except Levi, who leaned against the counter under the light of the propane lamp staring at Betsy, who stood across the room.

Pete took my hand and pulled me along. As we passed our

new brother-in-law, Pete smiled and said, "God give you a good night."

Several of the men chuckled at that. I turned and found Dat standing next to Nan. Neither of them seemed amused, but both had expressions of relief on their faces.

Out the door we marched and then down the steps in unison. It was as if we were floating, both of us together. But then Pete stopped abruptly in the backyard, dropping my hand and pointing toward the western sky. It was a vivid orange.

"It's fiery again," I said, thinking of the night of the singing when Pete scraped his chin and cut his hand.

"Jah." And then he said the same thing, word for word, he had before, but this time in an even stronger voice. "'Where two raging fires meet together, they do consume the thing that feeds their fury.'"

"What's that from?"

"Shakespeare." He smiled. Not a sarcastic smile. Or an ironic one. This one was pure pleasure.

"Really?"

He nodded. Now he was grinning.

"And we're the two fires? Consuming what feeds our fury?"

"Jah. Us and God." He took my hand again. "Have you read any Shakespeare?" he asked, pulling me along toward the Dawdi Haus.

I shook my head.

"You should. I think you'd like it." He smiled again as he opened the door.

Candles, like a thousand stars and the sun and moon combined, twinkled around the room. He must have found Betsy's stash of tea lights and, I suspected, had Dat's help in lighting them.

Too shocked to speak, I simply followed him inside.

He pulled me down onto the couch beside him. "I never stopped knowing you were the right one for me."

"You stopped acting like it."

"You wouldn't listen."

"I was hurt."

He smiled again. "That's why I used reverse psychology—to win you back."

I wasn't sure if I wanted to kick him or hug him. But in another second I couldn't help but grin back at him. "I've read about that," I said.

"Jah, me too," he answered playfully.

The candles flickered all around, bouncing both light and shadows off the ceiling. "What made you decide to do all this?" I spread my arms wide, gesturing around the room.

"You seeking me out this morning. Listening to those vows again. Overhearing what you said to Betsy in the barn."

"Sure, that was a giveaway."

He agreed. "Jah, but that was when I knew for sure you loved me."

Then he said he wanted us to make a life together—a marriage, a business, a family. A place of our own, full of books. "A *home*, Cate." He squeezed my hand. "We'll live here in Lancaster," he said. "At your Dat's." Pete's eyes shone as brightly as the flames around us. "Unless you want to return to New York."

I quickly shook my head.

He took my other hand and held them both together in the same manner the bishop had on our wedding day. But instead of saying, *"Go forth in the name of the Lord, you are now man and wife,"* he said, "Kiss me, Cate."

"I thought we were being serious," I answered.

"We are."

I leaned toward my husband then, our lips meeting, and then our mouths, our hands still clasped as we kissed. It was tender at first, but then grew in passion as Pete embraced me.

When I finally pulled away, he whispered, "My Sweet Cate." And for once, I was.

We stood then, and he led me down the hall, past the empty room where he'd been sleeping. When we reached the master suite he scooped me into his arms and carried me inside.

With a gentle kick, I shut the door behind us.

Acknowledgments

Many thanks to my husband, Peter, for his endless encouragement of my writing, and to our children, Kaleb, Taylor, Hana, and Thao, for their ongoing support—especially when I'm on deadline.

Thank you also to Laurie Snyder, Tina Bustamante, and Libby Salter for reading the manuscript in its early stages, and to my critique group members, Melanie Dobson, Nicole Miller, Kelly Chang, and Dawn Shipman for your invaluable feedback.

I'm very grateful to the entire crew at Bethany House Publishers, with a special shout-out to David Long and Karen Schurrer. It has been a delight to work with all of you. I'm also grateful to Mindy Starns Clark for all she's taught me about writing and about the Amish, and to Susan May Warren for her help in shaping this story. A special thank you to my agent, Chip MacGregor, for believing in this novel when it was nothing more than a wild idea.

Thank you also to Lynn Ferber and Alan Rosenfeld for providing a much-needed writer's retreat for me in the middle of this project. The timing was perfect.

I gratefully acknowledge the many authors whose books about the Amish I've read, the Mennonite Information Center in Lancaster County, and the Plain people who have shared their stories with me during my research trips and answered my questions since. Any mistakes in this novel are mine alone.

Professor Tony Wolk deserves a special acknowledgment for encouraging me, and so many others, to allow Shakespeare to be a creative inspiration. It was in Tony's class at Portland State University, during my MFA program, that the seeds of this story were planted.

As a preschooler I remember listening with my mother, Leora Houston Egger, to recordings of Shakespeare's plays, and I saw my first performance of *The Taming of the Shrew* as an elementary school student. Although I am by no means a Shakespearean scholar, I've loved his stories for nearly my entire life. The older I get, the more I am amazed by his understanding of human nature and the genius of his writing. I am humbled to have borrowed from his work.

It was also my mother who first shared God's stories of salvation and redemption with me, stories that have shaped my life. I am forever grateful for her influence—and for God's constant direction, inspiration, and blessings.

Leslie Gould is the coauthor, with Mindy Starns Clark, of the #1 CBA bestseller *The Amish Midwife,* a 2012 Christy Award winner, *The Amish Nanny,* and *The Amish Bride.* She is also the author of numerous other novels, including *Garden of Dreams, Beyond the Blue* (winner of the *Romantic Times* Reviewers' Choice for Best Inspirational Novel, 2006), and *Scrap Everything.* She holds an MFA in creative writing from Portland State University and has taught fiction writing at Multnomah University as an adjunct professor. She and her husband and four children live in Portland, Oregon.

Learn more about Leslie at www.lesliegould.com.

More Stories Set in Cloistered Communities
Amish and Mennonite Fiction From Bethany House

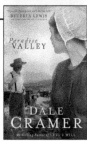
◊ BETHANYHOUSE